THE MAN FROM YESTERDAY

By
HOWARD BROWNE
(originally writing as Lee Francis)

I0541398

ARMCHAIR FICTION
PO Box 4369, Medford, Oregon   97501-0168

*For more information about Armchair Books and products, visit our
website at…*

www.armchairfiction.com

Or email us at…

armchairfiction@yahoo.com

THRUST INTO A CHAOTIC FUTURE...

Avar was a warrior. Not only brave, but curious and fearless. It was his curiosity that had landed him in a world of too many people, and contrivances so foreign that he needed help. Lucky for him the men and women who found him turned out to be scholars. However, not all the population of the 21st century was as learned and open-minded as the few who had mentored this displaced cave man. And not only can men be unforgiving of what they don't understand, they can also fear it. Avar was a man of few words, but his actions made every one of his thoughts explicitly clear.

Love = kiss
Loyalty = protect
Danger = kill!

It was all so simple…

CAST OF CHARACTERS

AVAR (aka Adam Newstone)
A gorgeous man from 20,000 years in the past thrown into the chaos of modern society. Would he be able to survive?

GREGG WHITNEY
It's not often a benevolent millionaire gets a chance to cultivate and befriend a man from the distant past!

LAUREN WHITNEY
Well-mannered, well-groomed, and well-behaved, this young woman was in for some real high-rolling and primal excitement!

JOAN WHITNEY
Being high-spirited and naïve can make for some truly hand-wringing drama, as this young lady found out the hard way.

GENE CAMERON
This guy was said to be quite a charmer and a notorious crook—and gullible rich dames were his game.

SERGEANT KORSHAK
Not one to forgive a misunderstanding, this cop made it his duty to bring the "foreigner" to justice. And by justice he meant "dead."

PERRY SIDDONS
He didn't really care for Avar. He thought of him as an animal, or was that just jealousy talking?

CHAPTER ONE

ALL during that night he pushed his bare, callused feet through the desert sand, sinking ankle-deep with every step. It was a shifting, sucking substance, making each stride a tiring effort, and it seemed to have absorbed and held heat from yesterday's baking sun.

Yet the night air was cold against his almost naked body—not the damp chill of a night in his familiar jungle, but a dry, crackling cold that seemed no less tangible than the hot sand itself.

A full moon swam aloofly in the cloudless sky, its rays cold and cheerless as a mountain wind, bathing in its light an endless vista of dunes and gullies forever changing under the desert's restless air. He could hear the whispering rustle of those minute particles of rock as they shifted and slithered from beneath his feet. Several times he stopped to look back across those endless hollows and heights he had traversed, and always all signs of his passage were already obliterated by the uneasy sands.

He passed his dry tongue across parched lips, feeling again the clawing pain of thirst—a thirst no longer as intense as it had been twelve hours before. It was as though his throat had given up all hope of knowing again the cool wonder of water. Sand gritted between his teeth and he spat angrily to rid himself of it, only to find it still grating against the cracks in his lips.

The mountains that had seemed so near when he first entered this trackless waste were invisible now. For all he knew he might be wandering in a great circle—covering over and over the same territory until complete exhaustion would overwhelm his mighty muscles and pull him down against the sand to move no more— ever. Such stories of the desert's conquest of men rash enough to brave its dangers were occasionally told about the cave fires of his people during the rainy seasons.

On he pushed—on and on and on, fighting back with all his Herculean strength and iron will against the sucking sands. Twice he found he had drawn his flint knife from the folds of panther skin about his loins—gripping it tightly as though ready to give battle to this silently implacable foe.

On he went—on and on and on—until at last the bleak landscape began to waver in the moonlight, to expand and contract before his eyes. Angrily he shook his head to clear his vision, but the phenomenon persisted and finally he ignored it entirely.

At last the moon was gone and later a faint radiance along the distant horizon to his left told of another dawn on its way. By this time however he was blind to all else but the yielding surface over which he moved, his gaze riveted on the sand a few feet in front of him.

Once he stumbled and fell to his hands and knees. The desire to remain there, to rest only a little while, to warm his body with the hot sand, was overpowering. But he beat down the temptation, aware that even momentary surrender meant death.

An hour passed before he lost his footing again; then he fell three times in as many minutes. Little eddies of air whirled the dry particles into his eyes and he was forced to close them tightly to preserve his sight.

Again he fell, this time at full length. Shaking his leonine head like a wounded lion he slowly pushed himself to his hands and knees. But when he tried to resume an upright position his exhausted muscles refused the command, and he sank back again.

Doggedly he pushed ahead on hands and knees, head hanging like a whipped animal's, the thick black strands of his hair hanging before his eyes. An indomitable will power alone was driving him across those sands, operating his tendons and muscles in an insane kind of reflex action like the twitching movements of a body already dead.

ABRUPTLY the crawling man halted, the shock of discovery running through his spent figure like an electric current. His extended hand clenched harshly about the foreign matter it had encountered—clenched and tugged until it had torn the substance from the sand and brought it close to his face.

Those bloodshot eyes open, blinking now in the light of approaching dawn. In the palm of his hand lay a small clump of crushed grass. The desert was behind him.

With an exultant toss of his head he flung back his long hair and lifted his eyes to the scene before him. A low hill lay only a few yards away—a hill covered with greenish yellow grass and dotted with stunted shrubs and bushes. Not far to the left was a shallow gulch where trees were growing and beyond their trunks he caught the glitter of moving water.

At sight of the latter, the almost naked man staggered to his feet and plunged ahead at a half-run, half-stumble, tearing his way through undergrowth and colliding painfully with an occasional tree. Then he was beyond the belt of growing things and kneeling at the bank of a narrow stream, cupping handful after handful of water to his eager lips.

He drank sparingly however, experience cautioning him against flooding his dehydrated system. Without removing his loincloth of panther skin he immersed his body in the cool liquid, and after another half-hour he was ready for food and strong enough to seek it.

Beyond the river rose an impenetrable wall of jungle and forest, familiar surroundings during everyone of his twenty-six years; and beyond that, looming in the near distance, the base of the mountain range he had sighted two days before.

Fording the shallow stream he plunged into the jungle, passing through a narrow belt of bushes before the forest itself. He moved carefully now, keen eyes probing the foliage, ears and nose alert for danger; for his world abounded with lions and panthers and leopards, with huge snakes and their poisonous, but smaller, cousins, with the great apes—even with the most feared enemy of all: men like himself.

There were many sounds: the unceasing hum of the myriad clouds of insects, fluttering strident-voiced birds of brilliant plumage, hordes of racing, scolding, inquisitive monkeys—all as much a part of this untamed world as the trees themselves.

It was into those trees that he went now—vaulting lightly into the lower branches of the first one he reached and moving on through the lower terraces, swinging lightly from bough to bough. Now and then, with the agility and ease of long practice, he sent his body hurtling across a gap between trees, to grasp with unerring accuracy the branch his quick eye had selected. Yet notwithstanding his seemingly reckless pace, his passage was almost soundless; and though the tangled verdure appeared as a solid wall about him, only rarely did his flying figure scrape against the riot of vegetation.

Before long he caught sight of an elephant path below and he altered his course to follow it from above, his movements even more cautious now for he was hunting the one food his body craved: the succulent flesh of deer or zebra.

Not long afterward the game trail came into a small circular clearing, through the center of which a small stream moved sluggishly between reed-covered banks. Even before he had reached the fringe of trees bordering the clearing, his sharp ears caught the satisfied rumblings of a feeding beast, but because he had been downwind at the time he was unable to identify the animal immediately.

From the swaying branches of a jungle giant he looked down at a scene which brought a low growl of disappointment and protest to his lips. Lying across the body of a deer lay a great yellow-maned lion, tearing away and bolting large pieces of his kill, feeding as though many suns had passed since last it had dined.

The man's disgust was not dictated by the lion's table manners. Jungle-wise, he knew that no other wary grass-eater would come here for water until long after the lion had finished feeding and departed. It meant he must seek elsewhere for the fresh meat his belly craved—a galling prospect because the hot blood of the freshly slain deer impinged on his nostrils to set up an uncomfortable gnawing of hunger too intense to be denied. Then, too, there was a matter of pride involved here—pride and prestige. No denizen of all the jungle should be permitted to upset the plans of a warrior of his caliber.

The alternative to looking elsewhere for food was dangerous—dangerous to the point of sheer lunacy when viewed from even a faintly conservative viewpoint. But he was young and very strong and fond of adventure—barren ground for the seeds of conservation…

A BRIEF glance at the surrounding foliage showed him the kind of tree he would need for execution of his plan. Even better the branches of that particular tree extended to a point almost directly above the feeding jungle lord. No longer did the man seek to mask his movements; with almost deliberate carelessness he pushed his way noisily through the arboreal curtains of vines, creepers and leaves until he squatted on a broad branch some twenty feet above the lion.

The tawny-maned beast, aroused by the sound of crackling foliage almost over his head, was standing now and gazing with round, unblinking yellow eyes at the hated man-thing. The great snout, reddened with the blood of a new kill, curled in an angry snarl and a low warning growl rumbled from a cavernous chest.

"Devourer of filth!" the man shouted. "Brother of snakes! Go away or I will come down and tear you to pieces and feed you to the jackals!"

The rumbling growl swelled to a full-throated roar, reverberating through the clearing like the notes of a monster drum. The man, long familiar with the ways of lions, knew he was being warned to keep his distance, that only as long as he remained high in that tree would he be safe. In answer he plucked one of the apple-sized, soft-shelled fruits growing thickly about him, and with a short, hard, sidearm throw, sent it unerringly on its way, to spread in a sticky mess across the cat's upturned face.

Then indeed, did the lion roar. Without warning it rose in an almost vertical spring, the giant body tearing through the leaves and branches. Full across the man's high perch it fell; but he was a full ten feet higher now. For a brief moment the lion hung there, its roar more nearly a scream, and in that moment a second missile caught it squarely against one ear.

When his target dropped back to earth again, the man returned to his former position and began an unceasing bombardment of the enraged beast. It managed to avoid some of those maddening missiles, but they rained down too swiftly for any effective defense.

Again and again the almost hysterical animal leaped for its tormentor, but always he danced mockingly just out of range of those reaching talons.

Twice the lion attempted to settle back to feeding, ignoring the rain of objects from above; but as such a maneuver served only to increase their number and force, it abandoned the effort. An attempt to drag the carcass beneath sheltering bushes lining the clearing was defeated by a hail of broken branches, each of them thrown in the fashion of a spear and drawing blood.

Suddenly the lion turned and bounded toward the wall of jungle bordering the clearing. The instant it disappeared from view, the man dropped lightly to the ground and raced across the carpet of grasses toward the deer's remains. His running steps were completely soundless; his ears, inconceivably sharp, were alert for any indication that the giant cat was returning to trap him here in the open.

Stooping he swung the carcass to one broad shoulder and whirled to retrace his steps, and in that instant the monster cat crashed into view between him and his tree. With a hideous snarl of triumph the animal shot toward him.

The man realized this was no ordinary lion to have trapped him so neatly. All previous lions had doubled back under such circumstances, reappearing almost at the point where they had faded from view. But this one had circled through the jungle just far enough to emerge squarely in his path of retreat.

To escape by flight was impossible, for fleet as he was he could not outdistance over a short stretch a charging lion. Without an instant's hesitation he dropped the deer, swept his flint knife from his belt and sprang forward to meet his ambusher.

The move was so completely foreign to what should have occurred that the lion faltered in its charge, rearing high to strike out at its two-legged enemy. Clearly anticipating the move, the man swerved abruptly, then closed in again, this time from one side. Before the bewildered carnivore could drop back to all fours, the man was on its back, an arm like banded layers of steel encircling that hairy throat and his free hand plunging his flint knife again and again into a vulnerable spot behind the beast's left shoulder.

The lion, voicing a startled shriek that paled into nothingness the sounds of combat, reared high and toppled back full upon this human leech. But the man's steel-thewed legs locked tightly about the animal's loins and his heavy knife continued to sink home.

UTTERING one final choked roar, the great beast staggered to its feet, then collapsed in death. That flint knife had pierced its heart twice in rapid succession before the battle was decided.

Battered and bloody, his nut-brown skin scratched and torn from contact with the earth, the man rose arrow-straight beside his kill. A wave of exultation and quiet pride swept through him as his eyes beheld the evidence of his strength and fighting prowess: no other warrior in all his savage world could boast of having slain Kuo, king of beasts, with only a knife.

The mood passed immediately and he settled down to more serious business. Squatting beside the partially devoured carcass of the deer, he used his knife to hack away a juicy strip from one flank. Quickly he wolfed down a portion of the raw meat, then knelt at the river's banks and drank deeply of the brackish water. A brief dip in those same waters removed the stains of both combat and feeding—and he was ready to take up his interrupted journey.

The mountain range—the goal toward which he had made his way for many sleeps—was very near now, looming dark and forbidding despite the sun's golden rays from overhead. There appeared to be no foothills surrounding those lofty peaks; they seemed to rise almost vertically from the heart of surrounding jungle like the upthrust talons of some fabled monster. Deep, wooded gorges cut into them—ravines filled with tangled foliage and cliffs of sheer granite.

By mid-afternoon the man was passing through the final belt of jungle between him and his goal. Beyond the last line of forest monarchs lay a broad expanse of open prairie, dotted with widely spaced clumps of trees, and which appeared to end at the very base of the mountains themselves.

There were five of those peaks, he saw now—placed side by side in an irregular row, none of them high enough to be snow-capped. The lower two-thirds of each was cloaked with green vegetation interspersed with patches of bare rock, while the remaining third appeared to be crusted with reddish-brown layers of undulating rock that might well have been lava from some ancient eruption.

For a long time he sat there on a broad branch at the jungle's edge, drinking in the lonely scene before him. What mysterious forces lay locked in those towering peaks? What undreamed-of wonders? What fearsome dangers? He recalled vividly old Tycor's words that night about the community fire at the base of the cliff containing the caves of his own people. How deep the hush that had fallen over warriors and women alike as the bent, twisted old man intoned:

"Beasts that defy description lurk among the mountains of that forsaken land. Spirits of evil gods dwell therein, and the breath from their invisible lips poisons the air and kills the trees and grasses. The earth itself opens up to swallow the trespasser. No birds sing above that deadly land; no tiny worm may burrow beneath its surface. No sound comes to the ear, no scent to the nose except the stench of evil. A circle of hot sands too wide for any living creature to cross shuts that horrible place off—placed there by gods friendly to man that he may never approach it. That, then, is the land of Kagoo."

None in all that audience had sought to cast doubt on old Tycor's story, for he was incredibly old and knew many things not given to the ordinary warrior to know. The man in the tree smiled ruefully. Where the rest of his people had shivered in awed fear at the old man's words, he had felt his own heart beat faster with the call to adventure. He must see the wondrous land of Kagoo! Only a few sleeps later he had set out, armed with knife, rope and spear, ostensibly to hunt but in reality to enter that forbidden territory.

The exigencies of jungle travel had cost him spear and rope, but his knife was enough and he had pushed on without taking time to replace them. And now he had succeeded in crossing the hot sands old Tycor had said no living creature could span—and the land of Kagoo lay open before him.

HE SLID lightly from the tree and set off with long swinging strides across the ribbon of open ground, the thigh-length grasses brushing his naked legs. His course was not a straight line toward the mountains, since he was careful to pass near the clumps of trees scattered about the landscape. There was always the chance some savage denizen of this untamed world might charge him, and a tree was always a welcome refuge.

It was late afternoon before he neared a thin border of trees following the base of the five mountain peaks. As he drew nearer he was suddenly conscious of an oppressive stillness which seemed to settle down about him like a tangible substance. Where the foliage of the trees should have been filled with chattering monkeys and the movements of brightly plumaged birds, there was nothing. Even the leaves, creepers and vines seemed to hang motionless in a dead calm.

The man halted, his sharp gray eyes narrowed, his lips pressed into a thin straight line. As of its own accord his right hand closed firmly about the knife of flint sheathed in the folds of his loincloth.

His roving eyes caught a break among the trees to his right and he altered his course toward that point. With a faint shrug of his broad shoulders he entered the trail's mouth and went on, his pace slower now, his eyes, ears and nose alert for an indication of danger nearby.

The wind had been at his back for more than an hour, a condition he did not like as it left his nose, one of his most valuable allies, hardly more than an ornament. There was but little light here under the massive, foliage-laden trees, and he was aware of a spine-tingling certainty that he was moving blindly into the jaws of certain destruction. It was a sensation based solely on the intuition common to creatures of the wild—a sixth sense which he had learned long ago could be depended upon.

He was weighing the advisability of taking to the trees when a glimpse of sunlight ahead told him he was on the point of reaching open ground once more. Despite the ominous silence hemming him in, he felt his tightened nerves relax and he hastened on, his spirits soaring with the thought of reaching open air once more.

And at that moment the undergrowth on either side of the trail was rent apart and five giant warriors, their tanned skins visible in the faint half-light, swarmed out upon him.

But the man from the outer world was in motion even as the first crackle of displaced foliage reached his quick ears. So rapidly did he move that four of the ambushers closed their grasping hands on empty air, and only one of them stood between their quarry and open ground.

It was the fifth man who stood between him and a chance for escape. Before the former could bring his short spear into use it was swept from his hand by a lightning blow and ten fingers were locked on his throat. In a swift maneuver the helpless man found himself serving as an involuntary shield against the spears of his companions; and even as that realization smote him and he cried out in sudden fear, two flint spearheads thudded home in his back.

Lifting the lifeless body above his head as though it was no more than a figure of straw, the intruder hurled it squarely among the remaining four. Three went down beneath that awful impact; but the fourth managed to dodge aside and launch his own spear at the back of the now fleeing man.

True to its mark flew the heavy missile, the saw-toothed blade shearing through two ribs and burying itself in the man's back. He stumbled and fell to his knees, then was up again as the four shouted aloud in satisfaction.

Across the open ground beyond raced the stricken man. So intense was the pain from the spear still buried in his flesh that he felt his senses reel and his stride falter. Behind him he caught the chorus of exultant yells and the thunder of pursuing feet. He knew he could not go on much farther under the awful weight of that spear.

Before him, only a few yards distant, were the shrub-lined walls of a narrow ravine, its floor level with the ground under his feet. Were he but able to gain that point he might yet manage to escape his pursuers.

If only he might stop long enough to remove the heavy spear. He dared not, however; even momentary delay would be fatal. There *was* but one way.

WITHOUT breaking stride he reached his left hand across his opposite shoulder and closed his fingers about the spear shaft, finding it slippery with his own blood. Steeling himself for the wave of agony he knew must follow, he wrenched outward with all possible strength considering the cramped position of his arm. He felt a brief tearing sensation somewhere inside him so painful a black cloud seemed to gather before his eyes, then the wooden spear shaft emerged easily from his torn flesh.

Too easily. In his hand was a short length of cylindrical wood, one end jagged where formerly a flinthead had been attached...a flinthead still buried deep in his body...

The narrow ravine loomed just ahead. Only a few more flying strides and he would be within. But feet were pounding close behind him—so close he knew he must be hauled down short of his sanctuary.

He felt outstretched fingers brush against the naked skin of his back. The contact seemed to close an electric switch, so suddenly did he act. While in mid-stride he twisted aside, leaving one leg extended. He felt the jarring impact of a shinbone against his leg and his pursuer, voicing a startled cry, pitched headlong. Even as the falling man's body crashed to earth, a powerful arm swung a broken spear haft full across his head, staving in the crown like a blown eggshell and reducing the makeshift club to a handful of splinters.

So quickly had the hunted man acted that he had struck and gone on before his remaining enemies were able to gain appreciably on his flying figure. An instant later he was hidden from view within the vegetation cloaked depths of the narrow defile.

He staggered blindly on, his eyes seeing little more than a blurred pattern of light, his breath beginning to labor as flecks of red-tinged foam gathered on his lips. Long experience in such matters told him the others would be slow to follow him blunderingly into a place furnishing a score of excellent spots for ambush.

He moved on slowly now, ears cocked for sounds of pursuit. He could hear nothing—nothing. No hum of insects, no slithering feet of tiny rodents among the shrubs, not even the faintest sough of a mountain zephyr. He might well have been in a world of the dead—in fact, but for the heavy rhythmic pounding of his heart he might have well been dead himself.

After pausing long enough to form a rough poultice of leaves and tie it over his wound by means of cord-like vines encompassing his chest, he pushed on. At first his path was choked with plant life; but as the minutes passed the lane began to thin out, giving way to naked rock as smooth and level as though some giant hand had carved a path through living rock.

Above him the ravine walls began to rise rapidly higher and steeper, the grasses and plants thereon becoming increasingly sparse until at last they disappeared altogether.

Now indeed was he hemmed in by stone. Fully two hundred feet above him lay a thin line of blue marking the sky. On either side, so close his shoulders occasionally brushed simultaneously against both, were the exactly vertical walls of the ravine.

He was aware of the chill trickle of blood along his naked back and there was the taste of the stuff in his mouth and a line of it oozing from a corner of his lips tracing a crooked path to his chin before dripping to his heaving chest.

The awareness that he would probably be dead within an hour or two came to him then, but other than a vague feeling of wonder that this had happened to so mighty a warrior as himself, he was conscious of no special emotion.

A SLOW insidious weakness began to rise within him. His legs faltered and became increasingly heavy; his arms grew weighty and began to round his shoulders with the task of carrying them. Even his head seemed an onerous burden, too heavy by far for the steel tendons of his neck. A film was forming before his eyes and his breathing became increasingly ragged, rasping, labored.

It was this almost overpowering weakness which saved him from plunging blindly over the lip of a crevasse that seemed suddenly to open inches in front of his feet. The opening was not very wide—scarcely six feet across. But its depth was beyond his far better than excellent eyes—straight down into darkness beyond the blackness of Erebus.

A loose stone about the size of his two hands caught his eye and he lifted it and let it fall into the crevice and although he strained his ears for several minutes for a sound of its passage, only silence came up to him from those horrendous depths.

Ordinarily he would have bounded across that six-foot span without thought and gone on. But now, weak as he was from loss of blood, that distance loomed like a gap four times its width. Was he doomed to die here—an abyss before him, an armed and blood-thirsty foe at his back?

For the first time he lifted his eyes and looked into the distance beyond the crevasse—at the continuing stone path ahead. What he saw there both puzzled and exhilarated him.

It seemed the narrow defile ended less than two hundred yards farther on. He could see fading radiance from the setting sun, matted reeds marking a stream, a wall of forest beyond, intersected by tangled undergrowth.

All this he saw—but he saw it wavering, dimming, brightening, swelling, fading. A wall of shimmering air seemed to hang above the opening in the ravine floor immediately in front of him—air distorting his view almost as though he were gazing through water falling in a rippleless curtain before his dazzled eyes.

He tottered there on the brink for an awful moment, then fell back, arms upthrust to shut out so bewildering and frightening a spectacle. It was then he caught a miasmic odor, which seemed to rise from those depths—a noxious stench that set his sensitive nostrils aquiver. The words of old Tycor rose to burn themselves into his brain and the ancient's voice seemed to be droning condemning phrases into his ear.

"...earth...opens...to swallow the trespasser...no bird sings...no sound...no scent except evil..."

His knees buckled, his fingers clawed frantically at the smooth walls of rock and he toppled helplessly forward into the yawning abyss. Blackness poured through his eyes, into his mind. He seemed to fall very slowly, then rise again, only to sink once more, deeper, deeper, down...

CHAPTER TWO

HE OPENED his eyes to the burning brilliance of sunshine everywhere about him. Almost as though one by one his senses came back into use. The ravine was gone, the mountains were no longer there—only an unclouded azure bowl high above him with the sun at its zenith.

Now pain from the spear wound in his back returned to him—rising and ebbing with each breath he took. His hands lay palms down on either side of his body, and beneath them was a short wiry substance he identified as grass.

There were strange odors in the air—only one of which he was able even partially to classify. That one was smoke—not the clean, pungent smell of burning wood, but a nauseous and wholly unfamiliar stink that caused his sensitive nostrils to quiver in open protest.

His ears, keen as any animal's, caught no recognizable sound. As from a great distance he could hear an incredibly faint murmur of what might have been a mixture of many sounds and possibly was no more than the passage of blood through the veins of his head. As that thought came to him, he heard a new sound far distant—the bark of a jackal, he decided, although there was a quality to the sound he had never heard in that animal's voice before.

Bracing his hands, he pushed himself into a sitting position, fighting down a wave of nausea that spun earth and sky like a giant wheel. Slowly his vision cleared and more of his surroundings were visible.

He was seated on one slope of a narrow valley between two low hills covered with a short growth of yellowish brown grass like none he had ever seen before. Only a few feet ahead of him the ground dropped sharply some six feet to a gently curving trail apparently formed of some sort of grayish black rock fully twice as wide as the length of his own body. Beyond the trail was a bank of raw earth similar to the one on his side of it.

Not only was this strange path wider and more level than any he had ever before come upon, but dividing it squarely along its length as far as he could see in either direction was a thin white line evidently set by human hands in its rock-like surface.

For the first time in his twenty-six years he knew fear—not physical fear so much as mental…the paralyzing influx of terror at contact with the Unknown. *Was this Death?* he cried silently, panic rising within him. Had the fall into the abyss taken him out of the world of life?

The pounding of his heart, the movement of his body reassured him. Death was present in a man when his heart no longer pulsed, when the muscles were like dead vines. The memory of men he had slain in combat reassured him he was not as they had been.

I live! his mind exulted. But a new thought came to him immediately and he sobered again. *If I live, why am I not still in that narrow gulch between those mountains? Perhaps this is the land of those evil spirits old Tycor spoke of…*

He staggered to his feet, drawn erect by a superhuman effort of will alone, for so much of his blood had been lost that his strength was nearly gone. *I must go back.*

The motion of his body set the severed ends of his ribs scraping against the flint spearhead buried within him. So terrible was the resulting agony that his senses reeled and an animal cry of pain burst from his lips.

Then anger came—anger formed of fear and hatred and the desire for escape. His mighty fingers curled into claws ready to bury themselves into the throats of whatever evil spirits had brought him here. He was like a lion at bay—ready to charge, to tear, to rend any living thing in his path. Aroused glands poured strength into his torn body; the heavy flint knife came unbidden into his hand and with head erect and shoulders defiantly back he strode across the carpet of grasses.

HE WAS on the point of dropping over the edge of that six-foot embankment bordering the strange path when he caught sight of a square slab of wood fastened to a stake set in the ground nearby. He went to it dropping to one knee the better to examine his find. The wood was of a yellow shade similar to one of the colors used in painting pictures of wild life on the walls of tribal caves. But there were no pictures on this yellow square of wood—only a strange design in black on one side.

FIRE AREA
NO SMOKING
In or Out Of Cars
NO OPEN FIRES
L. A. Fire Dept.
Ord. 77000

As he crouched there, his fingers moving wonderingly across the smooth surface of the odd design, a totally unfamiliar sound came to his ears. It was a low humming note not unlike that of a rising wind and seemed to be steadily increasing in volume. His eyes darted wildly about, seeking to learn the point from which the noise was emanating. Even as he realized it was beyond the rise at one end of the gray-black pathway, he caught sight of what was making the sound, and his scalp crawled with terror.

A black monster was moving swiftly along one side of that trail—rolling on strange circular legs. Two gleaming white eyes were set on either side of a widely distended mouth that was lipless and covered with straight and shining teeth each as long as his own arm. A broad, gently curved shell appeared to cover the rear two-thirds of the monster's length, held above its body by thin sheets of some transparent stone, which reflected the sun's rays.

All this the man on the hill saw in one blinding instant; then his eyes seemed to start from his head in utter amazement. Under that shell, within the body of the monster, were men! Men clad in strange skins and wearing queer objects on their heads.

He stood there, gaping, frozen, as the monster purred toward him. He saw one of the men within suddenly point a hand at him and the others turn their heads. An instant later the monster roared—a high, ringing sound that snapped the spell holding the watcher.

He turned to flee, but all strength seemed to have left his body. His fingers dug frantically into the yellow wood, his body sagged and he fell headforemost into the path of the monster...

"GOOD LORD, Mr. Whitney, look at that!"

The man behind the wheel of the Packard sedan followed the speaker's pointing finger. "Well, for the love— They must be making a new Tarzan picture."

One of the two girls on the rear seat laughed musically. "Give him a beep on the horn, Dad, and see if he moves. He looks more like a statue from Forest Lawn than a human being."

Obediently Gregg Whitney pressed the horn release and a blaring note shattered the silence...

"Hey! Look out! He's going to—"

"Dad! You'll run over—"

Brakes squealed and the heavy car shuddered to a halt, its front wheels only a few feet from the almost naked man in the road. Car doors flashed open on both sides of the Packard and the four passengers gathered about the motionless figure face down on the asphalt.

"He couldn't have hurt himself very badly," Gregg Whitney pointed out as he knelt in the roadway. "It's less than a six foot—" His voice faltered. "This man's been shot or stabbed or something. Look at that hole in his back."

Joan Whitney pushed closer and stared down at the broad expanse of darkly tanned flesh and the gaping red wound, partly hidden by a blood soaked pad of crushed leaves held in place by two vines encircling the giant chest. "What a perfectly *huge* man," she murmured, fascinated. "Can't you *do* something, Dad?"

Lauren Whitney, her lovely, sensitive face even paler than usual, caught her younger sister by an arm and drew her back. "It's nothing for you to see, Joan. Let Father and Perry handle this."

ANGRILY the girl pulled away. "Oh, for Pete's sake. Will you stop treating me like a child. I took first aid in high school and—"

"That'll do, Joany," Gregg Whitney said absently. He was a tall slender man a few years past fifty, with a shock of graying hair under a dark blue Homberg hat and wearing a beautifully tailored lightweight suit of dark gray. His blue eyes were curiously sharp considering the kindly, almost apologetic expression his lean face usually assumed, and his voice seemed deeper and richer than his general appearance suggested. He stood up, sighing. "You'd better give me a hand with him, Perry. We'll get him up to the house and call Blanchard. One of you girls get the car door open. We'll put him on the back seat."

Perry Siddons, his hands oddly gentle considering his powerful build, was carefully turning the unconscious man over on his back preparatory to moving him. At sight of the deeply tanned face he grunted in surprise.

"Good-looking guy, at that," he said. "Hardly the movie pretty-boy type, though. Looks more like an Indian chief."

Whitney passed a hand over the shoulder-length black hair of the half-naked youth. "Young. I'd say only four or five years older than you, Perry. Hair like a girl's. He's no Indian—although there is the suggestion of that in his features. Come on; let's get him into the car."

"It's going to be a job," Siddons observed, locking his arms slightly above the stranger's waist. "I'll bet he's at least six-feet-four and a lot better than two hundred pounds. And if there's any fat on him it must be under his fingernails. He feels like a hunk of concrete."

Between them they managed to ease the giant figure into a sitting position in one corner of the Packard's rear seat. The wounded man moaned a time or two during the maneuver—moans so closely akin to the growls of an animal that Perry Siddons was conscious of a strange prickly feeling along his spine. There was something primitive—prehistoric, even—about this bronzed, half-naked man; an illusion heightened by the crudely tanned animal skin about his middle and the heavy flint knife thrust within its folds. And the body of this man...

Perry Siddons had seen magnificent physiques before this. Three years on the varsity football team at the University of Southern California had brought him in contact with young men as well formed and virile as the modern world could boast. Among them had been amiable young behemoths who probably out-bulked this one; but where those had been lumpy and muscle bound, this man seemed as smoothly supple as a Greek god. Handsome as one, too.

At Gregg Whitney's suggestion Siddons moved into the rear seat beside the stranger, with Lauren Whitney and her sister in front with their father. The powerful motor bore them swiftly on into the hills north of Hollywood, turning finally into a private drive leading to the sprawling residence, part ranch house and part Italian Renaissance castle, of Gregg Whitney.

A wide-eyed gardener and his helper carried the still unconscious barbarian into a first floor guestroom and deposited him on the bed before reluctantly departing. Lauren Whitney left the room to telephone Dr. Blanchard, and after some urging, Joan also withdrew.

At Gregg Whitney's request Perry Siddons closed and locked the guestroom door and joined the older man at the bedside. He was in the act of taking the stranger's pulse, his expression concerned as he timed its beat with the second hand of his watch.

"He's pretty badly used up, I'm afraid," he said finally, letting the tanned arm sink back onto the spread. "I hope we weren't too late to save his life."

"A guy with that kind of constitution takes a lot of killing," the younger man observed. "What d'ya make of him, sir?"

Whitney shook his head briefly. "Impossible to say. Perhaps he's one of these hillside hermits this part of the country's famous for. From the looks of his feet it's obvious he's never worn shoes, and judging from the condition of his skin clothing is equally unknown to him. It seems we have an authentic wild man on our hands, Perry."

Alarm came into Siddons' mild gray eyes. "I sure hope he doesn't turn out to be violent. I always figured I was pretty good in the muscle department, but I don't think I'd have much of a chance against anyone like this."

Whitney said, "We'd better get him out of that loin cloth and into a pair of pajamas. See if you can't dig up a pair of yours, Perry; they'll be too short, of course, but better than none at all. Meanwhile I'll sponge him down with a wash cloth and get him ready for Blanchard."

"Okay, Mr. Whitney."

IN THE hall, the young man encountered Joan Whitney, waiting just outside the door. She grabbed him by one arm. "What's going on in there, Perry? Is he going to be all right? Has he told you who he is and what he's doing in that Tarzan costume?"

Perry Siddons felt the first vague stirrings of alarm. "Hey, what *is this?*" he protested. "You act like you're going overboard for this—this troglodyte!"

"This—*what?*"

"Never mind. Just don't get too interested in him, is all."

She tossed her blonde head impatiently, annoyance evident in every line of her vivid young face. "Oh, stop it. Every time I even look at some man you get excited. Is he really hurt bad?"

"We don't know yet. He's still out like a light. Let go. I got to get him a pair of pajamas."

"Yours? Are you kidding? They'd be much too small."

"So what of it?" Perry demanded, nettled. "I never claimed to be the biggest guy in the world, did I?"

He left her standing there and went to the room set aside for him on the floor above, dug a pair of green-and-white striped pajamas from a dresser drawer and hurried back. In the lower entrance hall Lauren Whitney was just replacing the telephone receiver.

She caught sight of the garment across Perry Siddons' arm. "Think they'll fit him?" she asked, smiling slightly.

He scowled. "How do I know? Everybody makes me sound like a midget."

"How is he?"

"Still unconscious." He stared at the cool, almost aloof beauty of her perfect features and the two ash-blonde braids caught up, without a hair out of place, on top of her head. As always he marveled that two girls so entirely different could have the same parents. Where Joan was vivacious, colorful, inquisitive and generally in a state of excitement over something or other, Lauren seemed to float through life untouched by it—calm, perfectly poised, almost studiously indifferent to the world about her. Secretly Perry Siddons, like most of the young men who moved in the same circle as the Whitney's, regarded Lauren as a cross between an icicle and a goddess from Norse mythology. Not that she lacked for escorts—quite the contrary, in fact; but they were usually intense young men with a Purpose in Life—law, medicine or architecture.

She stirred a little under his fixed gaze. "You can tell Father, Dr. Blanchard promised to come right over. Ten or fifteen minutes, he said."

"Yeah. Sure." He took a few steps, then turned back. "I wish you'd say something to Joan, Lauren," he said earnestly. "She seems mighty interested in this ape man, or whatever you'd call him."

Her smile broadened with quick understanding. Despite the slight difference in their ages she always felt herself to be much older in years and far more mature, mentally and emotionally, than this broad-shouldered young man. "I wouldn't concern myself about it if I were you, Perry. You know how she is. For all her flightiness, though, she thinks you're the greatest guy in the world."

His somber expression brightened. "You really think so? Sometimes I can't help wondering about that."

"You needn't, I'm sure. And certainly there's no point in being jealous of some unwashed neurotic such as we picked up in the hills."

He gave her an awkward, self-conscious salute and said, "Thanks," gruffly and went off down the hall, his shock of curly black hair glinting in the sun light through the open windows.

Joan Whitney was no longer in the hall outside the guestroom. Perry knocked, identified himself through the planking and entered at Gregg Whitney's summons. The stranger lay face down on the bed now, completely naked, a broad band of white skin about his middle marking where the loincloth had been. Whitney, a basin of warm water on the night table beside him, was carefully washing away the traces of dried blood bordering the ragged hole in the man's flesh.

Perry dropped the pajamas onto a chair. "Any change, Mr. Whitney?"

"I don't think so," the older man said, not looking up from his task. "His breathing seems a little less ragged but that's about all. Is Blanchard coming over?"

"Lauren spoke to him. About fifteen minutes, I guess."

GREGG WHITNEY continued to sponge the area of sun-toughened skin about the wound. He was surprised at the almost total lack of hemoptysis, as the right lung had clearly been pierced, and exterior hemorrhaging had evidently ceased of its own accord some time before. He smiled a little as the medical phrases came easily to mind. The combination of almost limitless wealth left him by his father and a wholehearted attempt to ease the pain left him by the death of his wife at the time Joan was born had resulted in his delving into many subjects, both practical and esoteric, using diligent study as a form of anesthesia. As a consequence he had better than a smattering of such unrelated subjects as medicine, stamp collecting, anthropology, card tricks, archaeology, and penology, as well as being able to distinguish between a Cartesian and a Carthusian. Knowledge, he discovered, had done more than bring him an education; it had made him more patient, more understanding, more sympathetic to those about him. It had made him a better parent as well, as he often reminded himself, for now he was not only able to love his two children but to understand them perfectly.

The man on the bed stirred suddenly. A snarl burst from his lips, so completely animal-like that Whitney stepped back involuntarily, and, while still in a prone position, he lashed out abruptly with a clenched fist. Those bare knuckles struck against the heavy wooden nightstand, crushing in its side and sending it and the basin flying across the room.

Perry Siddons, eyes round with astonishment, leaped forward to assist in subduing him. But this proved unnecessary as the injured man quieted instantly, lapsing back into unconsciousness, if indeed he had come out of it at all.

Perry righted the stand shakily, staring unbelievingly at the broken side. "This guy hits like a mule," he muttered. "You realize this stuff is a good half-inch thick?"

"Reflex action, probably. I must have probed the torn flesh a little too hard."

"Reflex action or not, you know what'd happen if he ever hit a *person* like that? Break 'em in two."

"Then we'll have to prevent him from hitting anyone."

"I'd hate to be the one to do the preventing, Mr. Whitney." The young man's voice shook slightly. "There's something wrong about him, sir. Like—like he isn't—well—human..."

"Nonsense. He's as human as either of us. Just stronger and better built, that's all."

"That's plenty. I'm not trying to tell you what to do, Mr. Whitney, but wouldn't it be a good idea to get a couple of police out here? What if this guy turns out to be nuts, or something, when he comes to, and attacks us? He might hurt Joan or Lauren before we could do anything about it."

The older man smiled at the other's troubled expression. "He's far too badly hurt to move around that much. And we can't very well call in the pol—"

A brisk knock at the door interrupted him. "Who is it?"

"Blanchard, Gregg," called a voice from the other side of the planking.

"Come in, Amos."

The door opened and a small, round-bodied man bustled in, carrying a black leather physician's bag. He was completely bald, and whatever dignity of expression his square, heavy-jowled face might have held in repose was lost in the twinkle of his small sparkling eyes and the crooked grin he habitually wore.

"What's going on around here?" he demanded in his peculiar crackling voice. "Lauren said something about you picking some injured vagrant up along Mulholland Drive."

Whitney stepped away from the bed. "There he is, Amos," he said soberly. "I think it's going to take all your considerable skill to save his life."

CHAPTER THREE

AT SIGHT of the long, slender-hipped, wide-shouldered body on the bed, Dr. Blanchard whistled in frank admiration. "If he's a bum he's certainly led a healthy life."

"He's rather a strange chap," Whitney said evasively. Then: "Perry and I had better stand by while you examine him. He seems delirious with pain and he's so incredibly strong he might harm you before he could understand you were attempting to help him."

The doctor bent over the motionless figure and peered long at the jagged hole in the firm flesh of the back. "There's something embedded in the lung," he said finally. "Appears to be a piece of rock. I'd better give him a hypo before I make a more thorough examination."

He took his bag into the bathroom, reappearing shortly with a filled hypodermic needle, several instruments on a small porcelain tray and a supply of gauze, cotton and towels. He put down all except the needle, then, with Siddons and Whitney hovering by ready to act if the patient reacted violently, prepared to make the injection. His long sensitive fingers probed gently at the banded layers of muscle of the forearm, searching for a vein, and his round face betrayed his growing amazement.

"Like a brick wall," he grunted. "Getting a needle into that's going to be a job. ...Here goes."

While Whitney and young Siddons watched tensely, ready to spring into action should the need arise, Dr. Blanchard sank the long needle deep into the tanned forearm. The heavy shoulders moved slightly, sending muscles writhing like snakes under that unclouded skin, then relaxed limply as the physician withdrew the instrument.

A collective sigh of relief rustled in the still room as Blanchard stepped back. "We'll wait for that to take hold," he said. "I gave him a load that would knock out a horse. …Tell me about him, Gregg."

While Whitney recounted what had taken place in the hills half an hour before, the doctor picked up the heavy flint knife belonging to the unconscious man, examining it while he listened. When the gray-haired man had concluded, Blanchard shook his baldhead in surrender.

"Damndest thing I ever heard," he decided. "Looks to me like this man has been living in these hills all his life. Strange nothing about him ever got into the papers."

He held out the flint knife to Whitney. "Look at this. Ten pounds if an ounce. And from the blood on the blade I'd say he's used it recently. Probably goes around killing cows with it, for food."

Whitney took the weapon in his hand. "Beautifully made," he observed absently. "But you'd think he'd have picked up a regular knife from some farm—"

He stopped abruptly in mid-sentence, staring fixedly at the object in his hands. "The Laurel Leaf design," he muttered incredulously.

He looked up into the puzzled face of his two friends and wet his lips. "I'm imagining things," he said. "At least I think I am."

The doctor reached for a pair of rubber gloves. "I think I'm ready to do a bit of exploring. You two had better stand by in case my patient starts acting up…"

A quarter hour later Dr. Blanchard went into the bathroom to wash up, leaving the others to examine the symmetrically formed bit of flint he had removed from the stranger's back. The wound it had left was closed now and covered with bandages. The injured man was sleeping now, on his back, Perry Siddons' pajamas encasing his magnificent frame. The jacket had gone on easily enough, for Perry's torso was well-developed; but the trouser legs came up halfway to the knees and tightened about his thighs like the skin of a sausage, while the belt itself was fully an inch too large around. The white sheet was drawn well up on his chest, leaving the upper line of his broad shoulders exposed.

DR. BLANCHARD came out of the bathroom, bag in hand. "He should sleep for a couple of hours. Keep him in bed. I'll stop by in the morning to change those bandages."

"How long do you think he'll be laid up?" Whitney asked.

"How do I know? If the average man sustained that kind of a wound and lost as much blood you'd probably have to send for an undertaker. But this one may be completely recovered within two weeks. Healthiest flesh I've ever come across and a heartbeat like a bass drum. That's a unique specimen of manhood, Gregg."

"I don't like his looks," Perry said doggedly. "I still say the cops should take him off your hands."

Fingers tapped on the bedroom door. "It's Joan, Dad. What's going on in there?"

Whitney crossed over and opened the door. "Come in. I'm gratified to learn you can bottle up your curiosity this long."

She went quickly to the bed and looked long at the calm face of the sleeping man, her eyes sparkling, alert and intense. "He's awfully handsome, isn't he? Will he be all right, Dr. Blanchard?"

"You bet he will." The doctor's crooked grin broadened. "You planning on adding him to your list of boy friends, Joany?"

She tossed her blonde head, her eyes crinkling as she shot a sidelong glance at the glowering Perry. "Why not? It's not every day a girl could have a pair of arms like *those* around her."

"Joan," Gregg Whitney said reprovingly.

Perry Siddons' pink-skinned young face darkened. "Well, of all the—the asinine things I've ever heard, *that* takes the prize. I never thought I'd see the day you'd start drooling over a damn *animal.*" Sudden color swept into his cheeks. "I'm sorry. I didn't mean to sw—"

"He's *not* an animal," Joan interrupted furiously, her brown eyes snapping. "His face is just as—noble and—and clean-cut as yours. Maybe even nobler. And it certainly is rude of you to talk that way about somebody who's never said or done anything wrong to you, and besides he's hurt and he's our guest and I think you've got a lot of nerve—"

"Well, you don't have to gush—"

"—talking about him that—"

"—over some stranger just because—"

"Are you two at it again?" said a cool voice from the open doorway. "What's all the bickering? They can hear you all over the house."

"Join the party, Lauren," her father said lightly, although the sober lines about his eyes failed to lift. "There seems to be some difference of opinion about the social acceptability of our—ah—guest, as Joan calls him."

Lauren Whitney glanced carelessly at the motionless figure on the bed. "How's he coming along, Dr. Blanchard?"

"Incredibly well. What would almost certainly have been a mortal wound for anybody else turns out to be hardly more than a scratch for him." The doctor took his bag from where he had placed it on the floor. "I've got to be getting on. Keep him quiet and feed him mostly liquids for the time being."

He started for the door, then turned back as a thought struck him and faded his habitual crooked grin. "One thing, Gregg; I'll have to report this case to the police."

"What in Heaven's name for?" demanded Whitney, startled.

"It's a law; you should know that. Any shooting, stabbing and so on must be reported to the authorities by the attending physician."

"But this man isn't a criminal. He's badly hurt; how it happened no one knows. Why he might have fallen on that bit of stone and had it bury itself in his back."

Blanchard's lips twisted in a lopsided smile. "You don't believe that one yourself, Gregg. Look, I'll certify the man is too weak to be moved. The police aren't the way the movies picture them; they'll send out a man or two to question him; and unless he admits some criminal act, you can probably arrange to have him bound over to you, or whatever they call it. I haven't any choice, Gregg," he concluded soberly.

"Of course." Whitney's expression softened. "I'm sure I can work something out. I've taken a great interest in this young man—for reasons so incredible I won't go into them right now."

"Something to do with that flint knife?"

Whitney smiled. "You're pretty sharp. I'll let you know, later."

THE rotund little doctor said his goodbyes and left, refusing Lauren's offer to see him to the door. When he was gone, the three Whitneys and Perry Siddons stood for a moment watching the sleeping man's powerful chest rise and fall under his calm, even breathing.

"You three run along," Gregg Whitney said at last. "I'll sit here and sort of keep an eye on our patient. He's liable to be pretty badly confused when he wakes up and I'll have to warn him to stay quietly in bed."

Perry Siddons shifted uncomfortably. "I'd better kind of stay with you, Mr. Whitney. He might take a pass at you before you could calm him down."

"I'll risk it. He doesn't strike me as being as unmanageable as you try to make out. You shouldn't let your personal dislike of him keep you from being fair-minded in the matter, Perry."

The young man nodded unhappily. "Whatever you say, sir. It's just that I…"

Support for his plea came from an unexpected source. "I think Perry's right, Father," said Lauren Whitney in her calm, cool voice. "It seems perfectly clear he's not at all civilized; and from the size of him I'd say he's probably not very intelligent. I've noticed that most highly developed muscles are controlled by subnormal minds."

"Hey," protested Perry, offended. "How about that? You got me pegged as a moron, too?"

She flashed him an impersonal smile. "Of course not, Perry. But I am trying to take your side of the discussion."

"Yeah. Okay." He subsided, mollified but with the uncomfortable feeling that this lovely, aloof woman had meant that generalization to include him.

"I appreciate all this concern for my safety," Gregg Whitney said, smiling at them, "but I don't believe it's altogether justified. And I do think you'd better leave now—all of you. Our talking may disturb the patient."

Obediently they filed out the door. Joan, on the point of closing it, said, "You'll call us when he wakes up, won't you Dad? I'm *dying* to hear what he has to say."

"If he feels up to talking at all, I'll let you know."

The door closed and they were gone. For several minutes Gregg Whitney stood gazing down at the silent figure. His eyes shifted finally to the saw-toothed bit of flint Blanchard had removed from that giant back and he picked it up once more and fell to examining it carefully.

"That same Laurel Leaf pattern," he muttered. "It's certainly not an Indian flint. Rhyskind will have to go some to explain this."

He drew a chair up beside the bed, sat down and began to examine both the heavy flint knife and the primitive-looking spearhead, as he judged the latter to be.

He had been thus occupied for several minutes when a strangely uncomfortable sensation began to steal over him. Slowly, almost fearfully, he lifted his eyes from the pieces of flint and looked at the face of the man on the bed…and looked full into a pair of narrow orbs which seemed to glow like sunlight on ice—burning with an inner fire that brought a crawling sensation to Whitney's scalp. Instantly he knew these were not the eyes of a human from his world: these were eyes from some terrible world beyond the knowledge and memory of man…

"Hello there," said Gregg Whitney.

FOR a long time he had been aware of an unfamiliar softness beneath him and the sound of another's breathing was in his ears. His nose brought him the Man Smell, very strong; and, faintly, he caught the scent of other men and two separate delicate odors that told him women had been nearby only a short time before. There were other smells and other sounds, none of which he could wholly recognize.

Through the mediums of scent and sound he was able to tell exactly how far away the man was from him and that he was seated on some sort of wooden article. After a long moment he let his eyes open a crack and he took in all details of the scene about him in a single darting glance.

Nothing was familiar to him—nothing. This was another world, frightening in its utter strangeness, yet oddly appealing and soothing in its unearthly beauty. A frail-bodied man wearing the queerly colored skin of some unknown animal over most of his body was sitting on a peculiarly shaped log and looking intently at a stone knife and a spearhead.

The latter reminded him of his wound and he was aware that some foreign substance covered it now and that most of the pain was gone. Evidently this man-thing had removed the spearhead from his back—the act of a friend.

But then doubt came. Was removing the spearhead truly meant as a friendly act? Among his own people that would have been true. But this man was not of his people, perhaps he had taken the spearhead from his back that he might live to be eaten alive by these man-things. Evil spirits often did such things, so old Tycor had warned many times. Perhaps he should spring quickly upon this one and kill him before he could warn others of his kind. If he could do that, then run away, he might be able to get back to his own world.

A new doubt assailed him. Could one slay an evil spirit? Old Tycor had said they were men who had died while running away from their enemies. Good spirits were men who died bravely on the field of battle. It was that simple: a brave man became a good spirit; a coward became a bad spirit. And how could you distinguish between the good and the bad spirits?

He would have to wait awhile, he decided, before doing anything at all. He could not slay a spirit if it was already dead, and he would not want to kill a good one, even if he were able to. He was aware of being very weak and there was a throbbing in his head. He looked hard at the man-thing near him. His face seemed to have nothing of evil about it. In fact it was almost exactly like that of the chief of his own tribe, thinner of course, but with the hair scraped from cheeks, lips and chin as his own people did. The hair on top of his head was cut much shorter than he was accustomed to seeing, and even the head itself appeared smaller.

The man-thing slowly began to lift his head.

Should he close his eyes and pretend to be sleeping? He could not do that forever; sooner or later he would have to face his captors...

An instant later he was gazing unblinkingly into a pair of friendly blue eyes.

A moment passed then the man-thing's lips parted and three strange sounds came from between them, followed by a winning smile.

He was aware of a feeling of sharp disappointment, mixed with wonder. Did spirits, good or bad, change their way of speaking when they became spirits? Those sounds were words, but totally unlike any words he had ever heard before.

A thought came to him. Perhaps spirits could speak in two languages: one for use among themselves, the other for living men. He would tell this man-thing his name and who he was; maybe then the other would talk so he could understand him.

"I am Avar," he said, "—a warrior of the tribe of Kosad. Let me return to my people in peace or they will come here and kill all of you."

ALTHOUGH Gregg Whitney had half expected the strange young giant would be unable to speak a recognizable tongue, he was aware of a sharply let-down feeling upon hearing the stream of wholly unfamiliar syllables issuing from those finely shaped lips. He sensed a threatening tone to the words, however, and sought frantically for some method of reassuring the other of his own friendliness, hitting finally on what he understood was the universal gesture of peace.

He allowed the flint knife and the smaller spearhead to slip to the floor and lifted both hands, palms outward, saying, "I am a friend," several times, speaking slowly and quietly.

The glare seemed to fade from the man's eyes and his body grew more relaxed. Whitney racked his brain for some further means of communication. His name...if they could learn each other's names it would establish at least one bond between them however tenuous.

"Whitney," he said slowly and clearly, touching his chest with one thumb. "Whitney. Whitney."

Those rectangular-shaped eyes seemed to bore into him for a tense moment; then the stranger's lips parted. "Whit-ney," he repeated. The word seemed to fill the room with rich, rolling sound like a note from a mighty organ. "Whit-ney."

"Yes!" cried the older man, trembling with excitement. "Yes. I am Whitney. My name is Whitney. What is yours?"

The glowing eyes remained fixed on him, but the man did not speak again. Once more Whitney indicated himself with a thumb, repeating his name over and over. Then he pointed an unsteady finger at the man on the bed, at the same time lifting his eyebrows in the time-honored gesture of interrogation.

Understanding appeared to cross the wild man's handsome face. "Avar." The word seemed to ring in the air of the room like a muted bell. "*El da* Avar."

Whitney laughed aloud in pure delight. He pointed again at the wounded man and said, "Avar! Avar!" Then he touched his own chest, saying, "Whitney! Whitney!"

Slowly Avar lifted a hand, the biceps of his arm rippling beneath the green and white pajama sleeve, and repeated Whitney's gesture, saying, "Avar," as he pointed to himself, then, "Whitney," as he indicated the older man.

Impulsively Whitney jumped to his feet and thrust out his hand. "An honor to meet you, Avar." He realized at once that the act must mean nothing to his guest, but he remained with hand extended, curious to learn what his reaction would be.

The man's sun-bronzed face wore a faintly puzzled expression. He stared first at the pale, slender hand, then at the eager, smiling face above him, then back at the hand again. Slowly he reached out and took hold of Whitney's hand, almost engulfing it with his own, held it gingerly for a brief moment, then released it, his eyes following the member uncomprehendingly as Whitney drew it slowly away.

Whitney turned and went quickly to the door, opened it and shouted, "Joan! Lauren! Where are you?"

A door slammed nearby and an instant later Joan Whitney came running toward him, her blonde hair flying. "What is it, Dad? What's happened? Is he awake? Can we see—"

"Later," Whitney interrupted, his voice unexpectedly sharp for a man of his temperament. "Tell Martha to prepare a light meal—a tureen of soup, perhaps, and some milk or something—you know, light and liquid but nourishing. She'll know what to do."

She was trying to see past him, into the room. "What's he like, Dad? What's he told you about himself?"

"His name is Avar and he doesn't speak our language," Whitney said with some impatience. "Will you please do as I've asked, Joan? There'll be time enough for questions later."

"Oh, all right. You don't have to bite my head off." She disappeared in the general direction of the kitchen.

LAUREN WHITNEY, descending the wide, sweeping staircase to the lower hall, caught sight of her father and came along the corridor toward him. She was wearing an expensively simple one-piece dress in pale green linen that set off her slenderly rounded figure. Her long, ash-blonde hair was freshly braided and drawn up and around her head in a kind of regal coronet that seemed to add inches to her height.

She smiled at him, and the smile seemed to dispel some of the aura of cool reserve she wore like a garment. "Is everything all right, Father? I thought I heard you call me a moment ago."

"Joan's taking care of it. Our guest is awake and I sent her for some soup for him."

"Has he told you who he is?"

"No. He can't. He...well, he's not like us, Lauren."

Her slim brows lifted faintly. "How do you mean that?"

Gregg Whitney rubbed a palm slowly across the nape of his neck in a gesture that was a mixture of tension and weariness. "It's not easy to explain and I'm probably wrong anyway—but I don't think he's from our—our era."

Her mouth made a small circle of surprise. "What a peculiar thing to say. Just what has he been telling you, anyway?"

"Nothing except his name: Avar. He doesn't speak English—or any tongue that's even faintly familiar to me. Come in and take a look at him, Lauren. Maybe that way you'll get a better idea of what I'm trying to put into words."

She glanced at the dial of her plain gold wristwatch. "If you like. I've only a minute, though. Gene Cameron is taking me out to Brentwood to meet some friends of his."

Her father stiffened slightly and some of the mildness left his eyes. "He's still in the picture, eh? Those newspaper stories haven't changed your mind about him?"

That chill air of reserve about her seemed to form again, but her voice was gentle. "You taught me long ago not to believe everything I read in the papers, Father."

"Those stories were true, Lauren. I took the trouble to investigate them, in a small way, in case you wanted to ask me about them. He's a professional gambler, Lauren, plus a confidence man and a blackmailer of women foolish enough to become involved with them."

"He's excellent company and a wonderful dancer."

"So are a good many honest, decent young men."

"Father, I'm twenty-four and I know my way around. Gene Cameron is nothing I can't handle."

His expression softened. "I know you're age, Lauren. I've spent the last eighteen years trying to be both mother and father to you, and I know I've nothing to fear where your own conduct is concerned. But men like Cameron have a lot of dirty tricks up their sleeves—"

"We'll talk about it later, Father, if you don't mind. He'll be here any minute and if you want me to see this—this wild man of yours…"

"Of course." He bowed his head, masking the pain in his eyes, and she followed him into the room.

At sight of the strange light blazing from the almost rectangular eyes of the man on the bed, she stepped back involuntarily, the back of one hand going to her lips. "Oh… Are you sure he's…safe, Father?" She colored with embarrassment. "I'm sorry. I guess that didn't sound very nice."

Gregg Whitney smiled. "It's all right; he can't understand what you're saying." He drew her nearer the bed, caught Avar's eye and pointed to the girl. "Lau-ren," he said with slow distinctness. "Lau-ren."

Those tanned, finely formed lips parted. "Lau-ren," repeated Avar, and again the sound of his voice seemed to ring like a muffled bell.

"You have now been formally introduced," Whitney said grinning like a boy. "Would you like him to take you for a round of the night clubs?"

She could not seem to tear her gaze from those incredible eyes. "I—I don't think I like him, Father. He's an—an atavism of some kind. You've got to send him away.

Avar understood nothing of what these strange creatures were saying. But his sensitive ears and sharp eyes told him the female both feared and hated him. The realization saddened him for some inexplicable reason. Why should he care what she thought of him? True, she was very beautiful; he could see that despite the strange skin with which she hid her body from view and the ugly way her hair was twisted on top of her head. But then many of the females of his own tribe were very beautiful, yet he had not cared what any of them thought of him. There had been many among them who looked at him with soft eyes and ready smiles and who, he knew, would have been quick to share his cave with him.

Sharp resentment stirred within him. The desire to sweep her into his arms, to crush her against him until she cried out in pain, grew in his mind. He was Avar—the mightiest fighter in all the jungle. Who was this she to look upon him with such scorn?

With the speed of a striking snake his hand lashed out and caught Lauren Whitney by the wrist. Before she was able even to think of resisting he had drawn her across the bed and against his chest, her face inches from his own. Then those strong lips came down and fastened firmly against hers.

Other men had kissed Lauren Whitney—kisses that had occasionally been agreeable, usually uninteresting, and none of them habit-forming. She was totally unprepared, consequently, for the sudden exhilarating *swoooop* of her heart and the electric tingling that raced through her entire body for one breathless second as that savage mouth crushed against her parted lips.

Gregg Whitney uttered a sharp oath and leaped forward; but Lauren, her mind a confused welter of anger, astonishment, embarrassment and wonder, tore her wrist free from Avar's relaxing fingers drew back and with all her might struck him across the mouth with her open hand.

He lay there unmoving, his eyes blazing up at her from an expressionless face as she twisted lithely to her feet and shrank into the circle of her father's arm.

"The—the *beast!*" she cried, so outraged and ashamed she could barely speak. "How *dare* he do that? Are you going to let him get away with it?"

"He doesn't understand our ways," Whitney said hesitantly. He began to wonder at the wisdom of keeping this untamed stranger under the same roof with his two daughters. "You mustn't judge him too harshly, dear. In many ways he is a child."

"There's nothing childish in the way he kisses! He's either completely crazy or a fraud. Father, I won't stay in the same—"

"I beg your pardon, Mr. Whitney."

A middle-aged woman was standing in the doorway, wearing a black-and-white maid's uniform.

"Yes, Anna?"

"Two gentlemen are waiting to see you."

"Gentlemen? Who are they?"

"Only one gave his name. A Sergeant Korshak, sir. From the police, I understand."

CHAPTER FOUR

"AND just in time," said Lauren Whitney decisively. "Show them in here, Anna."

"Yes, Miss Whitney."

She was turning to leave when Gregg Whitney found his voice. "No. I'll see them in the library, Anna."

"Yes, sir."

"Now listen, Lauren," Gregg Whitney said when the maid had gone. "I'm going to ask you to overlook what just happened. It won't occur again, I promise you. I don't want you to make any mention of the incident to these policemen."

She stared at him, her eyes incredulous and faintly troubled. "What's come over you Dad? Why are you so anxious to defend this—this common tramp?"

"Because I don't think he's a common tramp. I think he's…well, never mind that. I want your trust and I want you to respect my wishes in this particular case. Is that too much for a father to expect from one of his children?"

She sighed deeply. "All right. If that's the way you want it. But you can be darned sure I'm going to bolt the door to my room every night until he's out of this house."

He smiled suddenly. "That kiss makes you unique among the world's women, Lauren. That is, if what I suspect turns out to be true."

"What in the world—"

"Skip it. I'll explain when the time comes for the story to be told. "Come, we mustn't keep the police waiting."

As they entered the high-ceilinged library, three of its walls lined with books and the fourth consisting of French doors opening on to a flower-edged terrace of red and gray tiles, two men in plainclothes rose from the depths of leather chairs on either side of the room's large fireplace, and stood waiting, hats in hand.

Whitney went up to them. "I'm Gregg Whitney. This is my daughter, Lauren. You wanted to see me?"

The man on the left said, "Sorry to trouble you, Mr. Whitney," but his tone said he was neither sorry nor glad. "I'm Sergeant Korshak, Hollywood Station. My partner is Officer Gilmer. Mind if we sit down?"

Whitney said, "Not at all," without warmth and the two police officers returned to the leather chairs while their host and his daughter sat together on a leather couch across from them.

Without invitation Sergeant Korshak got out a pack of cigarettes and lit one, dropping the match in the ash-stand between the chairs. He was the taller of the pair and had the air of being its ranking member, as indeed he was. He was wearing a freshly pressed blue serge that fitted him correctly and unobtrusively and his black shoes were newly shined and just a shade too pointed. He was slender, square-shouldered, and his narrow, sharp-planed face contained lusterless black eyes and a thin-lipped humorless mouth. He seemed confident, competent and a trifle bored.

Gilmer, his companion, was different—so different the two of them being teamed together could hardly have been coincidence. He was a big man, paunchy, with a round, freckled face and mild shallow blue eyes. His suit was also blue serge, but shapeless as though a rainstorm or two had come and gone with him in it. His shoes were blunt-toed and unshined and he kept shifting them around on the soft-piled russet carpeting as though they hurt his feet. He breathed audibly through slightly parted lips, and his stubby fingers ceaselessly circled the brim of his battered brown hat.

Korshak gave Lauren Whitney's crossed legs an unmasked stare, then shifted his gaze to the middle-aged man across from him. "A Dr. Blanchard phoned in a report he had treated an injured man in your home, Mr. Whitney. Stab wound, he said. Care to tell me about it?"

"I'll give you what information I have, Sergeant," replied Whitney stiffly. He felt a vague resentment that a more—well—sympathetic officer had not been assigned to make the inquiry. "I'd like to preface my remarks by saying there are some strange aspects to this entire matter which have aroused my deepest interest."

"That's okay," Korshak said. His voice had a flat, metallic quality that Whitney found himself heartily disliking. "Just tell us the story."

BRIEFLY, Whitney recounted what had taken place along that lonely stretch of mountain road, leaving out all details other than exactly what had happened. His callers listened in silence, Korshak's eyes never leaving the speaker's face.

He said, "It doesn't sound like anything I haven't run into before. Man gets taken up in the hills and has a knife stuck in him by some enemy who leaves him there to die. Somebody else comes along and finds him. Where are the 'strange aspects'—as you call 'em?"

Gregg Whitney took a deep breath. "For one thing the man was practically naked. He—"

"They're often found naked, Mr. Whitney. Sometimes because it's robbery; sometimes for reasons not printed in family newspapers. If you know what I mean."

Whitney said, "Suppose you keep quiet until I finish, Sergeant."

Korshak's chin came up an inch but nothing changed in his face. "I'm running this thing, mister. If you've got anything more to tell me, let's have it before I take a look at the guy."

The mildness was gone from Gregg Whitney's eyes by this time. He said, "The injured man was wearing a loincloth fashioned of what I take to be panther skin. I don't mean the American cougar or puma—I mean the kind of panther found primarily in Africa."

Officer Gilmer grunted. "Movie actor, I bet..."

"No," Whitney said maintaining his patience with an effort. "We thought that at first. Later developments proved it was not the case."

He leaned forward, speaking rapidly now, his voice earnest, almost pleading. "He doesn't speak English at all. His body is deeply tanned—more so than in any human I have ever seen before. His hair is straight and black and falls almost to his shoulders. He has the physical strength of a wild elephant, Sergeant Korshak. He was armed with a flint knife that weighs easily ten pounds—a knife made by the most primitive of methods.

"And the wound itself..." He hesitated. "It did not come from a knife. Dr. Blanchard took a spearhead from this man's left lung—a spearhead formed of flint in the same primitive and laborious methods used in making the knife."

Korshak's expression did not change. "I begin to see what you mean by 'strange aspects', Mr. Whitney. My guess is the man you found is a member of some 'back-to-nature' religious cult; I don't have to tell you there's a lot of screwy people in Southern

California. He got in a fight with one of his gang, I suppose, and got cut up. You'd better let me have a talk with him."

"He cannot speak English. I told you that."

"Sure. I heard you tell me. The whole bunch of them probably has some language all their own they claim came from ancient Egypt, or somewhere like that. Against their law to speak anything else. Flash a buzzer on them, though, and they open up."

"A buzzer?"

"An official department shield, Mr. Whitney." He took a blue and gold badge from the side pocket of his coat, displayed it from the center of a long-fingered hand, then dropped it back.

"I see." He knew it was useless to argue the point further. These men were policemen. They fitted everything into neat little pigeonholes formed by their own experiences or by the experiences of others of their kind before them. There was nothing new under the sun: an act of any human had an explanation based solely on the known conduct of criminals. "You know, of course, that the man's injury is such that he cannot be moved."

"So the doc told them at the station. It means leaving a police officer with him until he is capable of being taken in."

Whitney's shoulders jerked sharply. "Are you telling me, Sergeant, that you insist on treating Avar—this man—as though he were a notorious criminal...in spite of your complete lack of proof that he's anything but a thoroughly honest and law-abiding citiz— ah, man?"

"Law-abiding citizens don't make a habit of running around in panther hides, Mr. Whitney."

"Is there a law against it?"

"We could find one... I hope you won't mind my saying so, Mr. Whitney—but I think you're going at this the wrong way. Police don't bother decent people—not even the ones who do screwy things, so long as they don't make nuisances of themselves or become dangerous. But somebody attempted to kill this man—if because he was doing wrong, that's one thing; if the wrong was done him, that's another. But either way it's our business—my business."

WHITNEY was squeezing his hands together until the knuckles shone. "I quite understand that you're trying to do your duty, Sergeant. But this is an unusual case perhaps the most unusual of modern times. I shudder to think what could happen if you turned this man over to a police psychiatrist, or anyone else who, through ignorance or disinterest, might have him—put away."

He had not realized how difficult it was to see into those lusterless black eyes. There was a blankness to them—a metallic opacity as chill and emotionless as two circles of lead. The man behind them said:

"You say you never saw this man before today?"

"No. He was a complete stranger to me."

"He speaks no English at all?"

"None."

"Some other language you *are* familiar with?"

"I'm not a linguist, Sergeant."

"Does that mean no?"

"Exactly."

"Okay. How do you know his name?"

"His— Oh. Of course. He told me."

"How did you manage that?"

"By signs any human of intelligence could understand."

"You said Avar. Is that all the name he gave you?"

"Yes."

"Is that all you found out about him? By signs, of course."

"I don't like your attitude, Korshak."

"That's too bad." His voice said nothing but the words. He turned his head, neither fast nor slow, and looked at Lauren Whitney, who had been following the terse conversation with silent interest. "What's your opinion of the man you found, Miss Whitney?"

Her father's hands twitched suddenly upon themselves. She could ruin ev—

"I doubt that my opinions in the matter are important, Sergeant." Her voice was cool, her manner detached and faintly amused. "However I agree with father that the man is no criminal. Just—impetuous."

"What do you mean—impetuous?"

"Nothing in particular. It was only an observation."

The sergeant's eyes remained steadily on hers for several seconds, then swung back to Gregg Whitney. "I'd like to see him."

Whitney took a deep breath. "Very well. One thing, Sergeant Korshak, this is my home and the man is my guest. I insist that he be treated courteously and sympathetically while he remains under my roof."

He waited a moment for an answer but the sergeant said nothing. He stood up and said, "Come with me, please," and led the way out of the room and along the corridor to the guestroom where he had left Avar.

They went into the room, Lauren being the last to enter. Avar still lay on the bed, his Herculean shoulders propped up by several pillows. A glass-and-walnut bed tray straddled his sheet-covered legs and there was an oval china tureen and a glass on the tray, both of them empty although giving evidence of being recently filled.

Sitting next to the bed and looking up at them with a guileless smile was Joan Whitney, wearing a pastel blue sport dress that displayed her tanned arms and legs, and a ribbon of the same shade as her dress drawn becomingly through her honey blonde hair.

"Joan!" Gregg Whitney's voice was sterner than he intended. "You shouldn't have come in here alone. He might have…"

His voice trailed off and he shot a sidelong glance at Sergeant Korshak. But the officer was staring at the man on the bed, and while he was neither slack-jawed nor wide-eyed, he was visibly impressed by what he saw.

"Don't be silly, Dad," Joan Whitney was saying. "You told me to bring him something to eat, and I couldn't very well stand around and let the stuff get cold, could I? He's perfectly wonderful. We've been sitting here talking and getting along fine. I think he's fascin—"

"Talking?" Whitney exclaimed. "That's impossible, Joan. Are you trying to tell me he spoke to you? In English?"

A TRACE of color darkened the clear-skinned cheeks. "Well—I—I—I guess I did all the talking. But he listened. And he smiled a couple of times when I laughed…you know, just trying to make him feel—at home."

Korshak pulled his eyes from the blazing orbs of the man on the bed—pulled them away with what nearly amounted to a physical effort. They went then to the tray on the bed, and the lids narrowed slightly. Light from the broad open window filtered through the foliage of a pyracantha bush outside and was reflected from the gleaming surface of a soupspoon on the tray its handle wrapped in the undisturbed folds of a damask napkin.

"Excuse me." He reached past the seated girl and scooped up both napkin and spoon. "Did he eat everything you brought him, Miss?"

Joan gave him her "just-who-do-you-think-*you*-are?" glance—a glance that had raised welts on the sensitive skins of young men like Perry Siddons. When she saw it was wasted in this case she said, "I don't think we've met," in a too-sweet voice that made her father's lips twitch faintly, and he hastened to make the introduction.

"This is Sergeant Korshak, from the police, Joan. My daughter, Sergeant."

"Did he, Miss Whitney?" Korshak repeated.

"Eat the soup? Of course. Is it im—"

"What with—*what?*"

"What with?"

"I'm trying to find out what he used for a spoon. Not this one—you can see it's clean and the napkin looks as if it just came from the laundry."

"Oh—that." Her eyes were defiant. "He must have been practically starving, Mr. Korshak. He just picked up the tureen and—and drank out of it."

Lauren Whitney said, "Well. I guess *that* shows he's not like the average person you come across, Sergeant."

Nothing of the officer's thoughts showed in his face. He dropped the spoon and napkin back on the tray and said, "I wonder if you'd let me use that chair, Miss Whitney," to Joan, and sat down beside the bed when the girl rose to her feet and moved over beside her father and sister.

Officer Gilmer, his face attempting to show the same lack of expression as that of Korshak's but succeeding in looking only phlegmatic, approached ponderously and stood alongside his companion. He said rumblingly, "Better watch it, Sarge. This bullneck looks like he don't go for us."

Korshak ignored him. Once more his eyes met the glowing ones of the massive figure on the bed. "What's your name and address, mister?"

Silence. Avar lay completely relaxed, his rectangular-shaped eyes on the man beside the bed, his face as empty of expression as that of his questioner.

"Look, friend." Harshness tinged Korshak's voice. "I'm a policeman and I'm not asking these questions for the fun of it. What's your name and where do you live?"

Silence. A strained silence broken only by the sounds of Officer Gilmer's breathing.

"What were you doing up there on Mulholland Drive?" No answer. No movement. Just those eyes blazing up at him.

"Who cut you up?"

No answer.

Korshak's patience was going fast.

"Think about it this way, mister: you want to be agreeable about this, and cooperate, or do I have to make it tough for you? And my kind of tough is something you won't forget."

Gregg Whitney said, "For Heaven's sake, Sergeant, can't you see you're only wasting your time? This man no more understands what you're saying than a—a mountain lion would."

Korshak appeared not to have heard him. He reached out suddenly and caught Avar roughly by the wrist. "For the last ti—"

There was a blurred impression of motion. Sergeant Korshak rose into the air in one continuous free-flowing movement and sailed headfirst through the open window. There was a ripping sound as the copper screen gave way, followed by the crashing of pyracantha branches and the dull thud of flesh against earth.

Avar was standing beside the bed, the green-and-white coat of his pajamas split up the back by the coiling muscles beneath, his blazing eyes sweeping the room.

"Why you—!" said Officer Gilmer and went for his gun. A mighty hand shot out like the head of a striking snake, tore the weapon from his grasp and flung it aside to shatter against the fire place bricks. Gilmer, freckles standing out against the blanched skin of his face, aimed a blow at the wild man, only to have his fist brushed aside as though it did not exist. Then the room swung before his eyes in a dizzying circle as two enormous arms whirled him aloft; and Avar, dropping to one knee prepared to bring the heavy body down upon that member with all his terrible strength.

LAUREN WHITNEY was first to break the paralysis of horror rooting the onlookers in their tracks. "No!" she cried and threw herself under those upraised arms. "No! Stop it!"

Her face was almost against his own, her hands beat futilely at his arms and chest. "Put him down, you crazy ape! Put him down!"

Avar did not understand why she was attempting to interfere. These men had attacked him and he had the right to kill them. He had sensed from the first that both were strangers to her—why then was she trying to protect them? No, he did not understand; but if she wanted this one alive, she could have him.

With an almost casual motion he flung Gilmer aside and rose to his feet, just as the head and shoulders of Sergeant Korshak, necktie under one ear, a long scratch across one cheek, hair rumpled, appeared outside the open window. There was a blue-steel revolver in his hand and his eyes were completely mad.

He said, "Get out of the way, sister," in what was hardly more than a choked whisper.

Whitney jumped forward, his body blocking the policeman's view of the room. "Put up your gun, Sergeant—we have him under control."

"Like hell you have. That guy's a maniac and I'm going to kill him. Stand aside or I'll give it to you too."

"Get hold of yourself," Whitney pleaded. "If you shoot him now it will be murder. Can't you get it through your head this man isn't inherently vicious—that he not only doesn't know you're a policeman, he doesn't know what a policeman is?"

Some of the crazed light began to die out of Korshak's eyes, leaving a cold hatred no less frightening. He put his hands, the right still clutching the gun, on the windowsill and boosted himself back into the room. Over in one corner; half-buried under books that had fallen when he crashed into a bookcase along the wall, lay Officer Gilmer, unconscious and with a thread of blood tracing a pattern along one fat cheek.

Avar watched him from smoldering eyes, his body crouched slightly, his hands opening and closing with slow menace. Lauren Whitney, the danger postponed if not averted, had drawn away from the wild man, her eyes on the gun in Korshak's hand.

Korshak said, "I'm taking him in, Whitney. If he tries to resist I'll cut him down like the animal he is."

"You have no right to move him from this room, Sergeant. Dr. Blanchard's report—"

"Yeah…" It was more snarl than word. "'Too badly injured to be moved.' That's a laugh! This guy attacked two officers of the law, brother. He gets locked up for that—and if you interfere you get the same thing."

"You're letting anger get in the way of your judgment, Sergeant," Whitney said. "It's of the utmost importance that Avar stays here." His voice dropped soothingly. "Look, I know your pride is hurt at the way this man handled you and your partner. That's only natural. But if you'd been locked in a room with an elephant and come off with as little damage as you've sustained here, your only reaction would be relief at getting off so easily.

"I tell you this man is no more civilized than any elephant in the heart of an African jungle. But he is human—with all the powers of reasoning and intelligence found in any man. Treat him with respect and understanding and he wouldn't hurt a child. Cross him, try to push him around and—well, you saw what happened. He recognizes no authority except that of his own fighting ability."

Korshak looked at him in open wonder. "I don't get this. Everything you say only goes to prove he should be locked up before he really hurts somebody. What do you want, anyway?"

"I want this man left in my custody and care."

"Nothing doing."

"Why not? Because he threw you out that window like you were a handful of straw?"

"That's only part of it. He's a raving maniac and will kill somebody unless he's locked up."

Whitney gestured with a dramatic sweep of one hand. "Would you call a leopard insane for not bowing meekly to a police badge?"

"I'm not going to argue with you, Mr. Whitney. I say this freak goes behind bars or to the morgue. Now stand out of my way."

A HOLLOW groan ended the discussion for the moment. Officer Gilmer sat up his round face stupid with shock and began to brush away the mound of books covering him. He pulled himself shakily to his feet and stood there, reeling slightly, a ham-like hand rubbing his head.

"Snap out of it, Hank," Korshak said shortly, no trace of concern or interest at the other's possible injuries in his voice. "We're taking this character with us."

"Yeah, Sarge…sure." His eyes went blankly around the room. "Muh gun—musta dropped muh gun…"

Joan Whitney, her expression a mixture of awe and dreamy-eyed worship, went over to the fireplace and picked up Gilmer's revolver and handed it to him. "A lot of good it will do you," she said with open contempt.

Gilmer's eyes widened. The cylinder had been torn completely away, the walnut stock was shattered and the hammer knocked awry. He stood there, blinking, his jaw slack.

"Hank," Korshak's voice cracked like a whip. "We haven't got all day."

The shallow, pale blue eyes came up from the gun. There was a spark in each of them now—a spark that suddenly blossomed into rage.

51

"He busted muh gun, Sarge. That damn moose busted muh gun!" And with a sudden sweep of his arm he hurled the battered weapon at Avar.

Avar dodged the missile with a slight motion of his head but made no effort to attack the man who had thrown it. Korshak said, "What's the idea, Hank? You want to start him up again?"

"But he busted muh—"

"All *right*. Forget it. Mr. Whitney, you'd better tell this friend of yours to come along peaceful. Otherwise he's going to get hurt."

Gregg Whitney had been doing some rapid thinking. He said, "I'm going to make a phone call, Sergeant. I'd appreciate it if you and your friend would come with me to the library and hear what's being said."

"Your lawyer can't hold this up, Mr. Whitney," Korshak said coldly.

"I have no intention of calling my attorney. Will both of you come with me, please?"

"And leave this guy alone so he can run away? You ought to know better than that."

"I give you my word he won't escape. I'm asking you to bring Gilmer for his own protection. If he starts up with Avar he'll be killed."

Korshak's eyes narrowed. "On one condition. When you find out nothing's going to prevent me from taking this Avar in, you'll get him to go with us willingly."

Whitney smiled. "I think you give me too much credit, Sergeant. But I promise to do my best to persuade him—if he must go."

"He's going, all right—one way or another. Okay, we'll listen in on your call."

Whitney said, "You won't mind staying here with him, Lauren? Do you think you can—control him?"

"I can try."

"He won't be any trouble, Dad," broke in Joan excitedly. "You just leave him to us."

But Whitney still hesitated, aware that his older daughter had seemed none to sure of how her role of attendant would work out.

He sensed her acute dislike of this incredible stranger and understood her reluctance in remaining with him.

"Let's try to get him back into bed," he suggested. He went up to Avar, smiling, his hands open and raised slightly, and unhesitatingly placed his palms lightly against the man's steel-thewed arms. "Lie down, old man," he said soothingly. "Mustn't start that wound bleeding again."

No one else in the room appeared to be breathing. Those blazing eyes were fixed on the older man's face. And then, understanding the pressure of those gently firm hands, Avar sank down on to the bed and lay back while Whitney drew the sheet up over the god-like figure.

"Whew," Korshak whistled in involuntary tribute, while the others released pent-up breaths.

"I told you he's perfectly harmless as long as he's not aroused," Whitney said. "All right; if you'll come with me, please."

THE three men went down the hall and back into the library. Whitney took a small indexed notebook from a desk drawer, looked up an entry, picked up the phone and dialed the operator.

"Michigan 5211," he said when the girl came on the wire.

He gave his own number and waited. Then: "I'd like to speak to Police Commissioner Abbott, please."

Korshak put a leg across the corner of the heavy walnut desk, his manner indicating the situation was beginning to take on a familiar pattern. He said:

"I can tell you now this isn't going to do you any good, Mr. Whitney. This isn't a traffic ticket you're trying to fix; it's a matter of resisting an officer, assault and battery, disorderly con—"

"Hello, Larry?" Whitney said into the receiver. "This is Gregg Whitney... Fine, how's Mildred...? You know how it is...I've been busy. But we'll make it for dinner some evening... Yes, of course...Listen, Larry, I've run into something of a problem and I need your help... Good...I knew I could count on you."

He glanced at Korshak's thin face, seeing the confident half-smile there as he continued speaking into the receiver. "A few hours ago I picked a strange man up in the hills, along Mulholland

Drive. Huge chap, built like one of these old Greek gods and wearing a loincloth and nothing else. He was badly hurt—had a flint spearhead in one of his lungs...

"No, I'm not kidding you. Listen to me. Anyway, I hauled him out to the house and called in a doctor who removed the spearhead and bandaged him up. The doctor made the usual report to the police department and they sent out a couple of men to check up. But this man doesn't speak English, and in trying to get an explanation from him, one of the officers put a hand on him and got thrown through a window for his trouble. Quite naturally he's sore about it and means to take the man in dead or alive...

"I *know* it's a serious matter. But damn it, Larry, the man just didn't understand. He knows nothing about policemen or laws and... No, he's *not* crazy...

"I'll tell you what I want. I want him left in my care. I'll be responsible for him and I'll see he harms nobody and does no damage. No, he's not a religious crank; he's just out of place... Look, Larry, in all the years I've known you I've never asked a favor before. But this is damned important to me and I think you realize I can be trust— A Sergeant Korshak... Hollywood... Certainly. Whatever you— No... All right, Larry... Yes... Yes... How long...? Thanks, Larry. I won't forget this. Goodbye."

He replaced the receiver gently. Sergeant Korshak, he noticed, was no longer smiling. "I'm going to ask you to wait another few minutes, Sergeant."

"Why?"

"I believe Commissioner Abbott is calling your station. They'll probably get in touch with you immediately."

"Are you telling me he agreed to square this rap?"

"I told you, Sergeant, I didn't want Avar taken from my home. I'm sorry, of course, that you and Gilmer got shaken up a bit, but I honestly believe it was primarily your fault. I'll be glad to pay for the damage to your clothing and for your partner's loss of his gun."

"That's goddam white of you!"

Whitney's jaw developed a hard line. "Keep your sarcasm to yourself, Korshak. I won't stand for it."

Sergeant Korshak looked down unseeingly at his hands to hide the anger and hatred boiling within him. Never before in all his twelve years on the force had he wanted so desperately to make an arrest. If he could only get that freak into one of the station's windowless rooms...

They sat there and waited while the minutes ticked by. Korshak lighted and ground out three cigarettes in rapid succession, his thin sharp-planed face appearing to grow more and more bleak. Gilmer brooded sullenly on one of the leather chairs.

The phone rang sharply. Whitney scooped up the receiver eagerly and said, "Hello... Yes... Yes, he's right here."

He extended the instrument toward Korshak. "For you, Sergeant," he said quietly.

TIGHT-LIPPED, the officer took the receiver. "This is Ed. Hank and I got an investigate order on a knifing case out here in Needle Canyon... I know, Mike, but you haven't heard the whole story. There's a nut of some kind out— Listen, I don't have to take a slap— I don't give a hoot in hell *who* he— Fine thing! A guy tries to do his job and some lousy poli— Yeah...I hear you, I hear you... Okay, but you can bet I'm going to make a full report... I'm not blaming you, Mike, but put yourself in my... So long."

He slapped the receiver back in its cradle with unnecessary force and turned away. Gilmer blinked up at him from the depths of the leather chair.

"Let's go, Hank."

"We takin' the moose?"

"No."

Gilmer lumbered to his feet. "Fix is in, huh?"

Whitney said, "I'll see you to the door, gentlemen."

They went into the central hall and Whitney drew the door open for them. Without a word Korshak and his companion crossed the wide porch and descended the steps, leaving Whitney watching their backs from the threshold.

With Gilmer behind the wheel, the squad car turned on the crushed stone areaway in front of the Whitney home and rolled along the road toward the open gates marking the estate's edge. As they neared that point, a long low-slung blue convertible swung sharply from the highway and roared toward them, the driver waving a casual hand as he passed their car.

Korshak, his voice filled with disbelief, said, "Now what the hell does *that* mean?"

Gilmer blinked at him. "What's chewing you now, Ed?"

"You make the guy in that Packard?"

"I wasn't payin' much attention. Somebody you know?"

"Yeah. I never forget a face, Hank. That was Gene Cameron."

"Who's he?"

"Owns a small gambling club in Westwood. Snookered a few dames out of their money one way and another. One of 'em yelped here six months or so back and it got into the papers. No record far's we know."

"And today he's callin' on the rich Mister Whitney. He sure gets around."

Three miles later Korshak came out of a thin-lipped reverie to say: "I don't forget easy. I have a feeling the knocking around we got at Whitney's is going to be paid for one of these days."

Gilmer rubbed his meaty hands along the smooth wheel. "Don't get yourself hung over on this thing, Ed. Looks like this Whitney packs a lot of weight. What'd Mike say about him?"

"Worth millions and contributes to the right party. Pals with a lot of City brass. It's not him I'm after so much as that piano mover who pushed me out the window."

"I don't see what you can do about it, Ed."

"I don't either—right now. But the time will come." He lit a cigarette with slow care and tossed the match at a passing FIRE AREA sign. "I might even help a little in making it come."

CHAPTER FIVE

GREGG WHITNEY was on his way back to the library when he heard a car in the driveway outside, followed by the sound of feet on the porch. Anna, the maid, was nowhere in sight, so he turned back and was crossing the hall when the door chimes sounded.

A bareheaded man in his early thirties was standing there, his sleekly combed black hair glistening a little, a flashing white smile creasing his slightly puffy cheeks. He was wearing a sport coat and brown gabardine trousers that set off his broad shoulders and narrow hips to their best advantage. He radiated that relaxed self-confidence that most people mistake for charm and his regular features and a small hairline mustache gave him a kind of undistinguished handsomeness.

He said, "You're Mr. Whitney, of course. Lauren has told me so much about you I'd know you anywhere. I'm Gene Cameron."

"How do you do?" Whitney said, a faintly distant note to his tone. "Lauren is expecting you. Please come in and I'll tell her you're here."

He left Cameron on one of the hall chairs and went back to Avar's room. The young man was sleeping quietly and the two girls were seated on opposite sides of the wide bed, Lauren gazing disinterestedly out the window and Joan staring with rapt interest at the calm face of the sleeping giant.

It was Joan who held a quieting finger to her lips and inclined her head toward the sleeping man as her father appeared in the open doorway. Whitney smiled in acknowledgement of the gesture, tiptoed into the room and touched his older daughter on the shoulder. He framed the word "Cameron" with his lips and motioned toward the hall.

After Lauren was gone, Whitney beckoned Joan into the hall where they could talk without disturbing their guest. He said, "I've got some phone calls to make, Blondie," using the nickname she detested most. "You want to keep an eye on him until I get back, or shall I call Luke in?"

"Luke's a gardener, not a nurse, Dad. Avar wouldn't like waking up and finding a stranger watching him. I'll take care of him; he likes me."

"How do you know?" he asked, amused. "He tell you so?"

"A man doesn't have to *tell* a girl when he likes her."

"What's happened to Perry? You're not going to throw him over for Avar, are you?"

The humorous twinkle in her father's eyes piqued her. "Don't be surprised if I do."

His slight smile faded slowly. "Now listen, Joany: don't go making a play for this wild young man. He's not like us and he wouldn't understand. You keep your seductive qualities aimed at the world's Perry Siddonses you hear me?"

"Will you please stop treating me like I was sixteen."

"You're not much past it, Blondie. All right, you keep him under control until I get back. I won't be long."

He was turning away when she caught hold of his arm.

"…Dad."

"Umm?"

"You don't really think he's…you know, insane?"

"Certainly not."

"Well then, who is he? Where did he come from? Why can't he understand English?"

"Those are the things I want to find answers to, Joan. That's why I'm leaving you here while I make some phone calls."

"Who are you going to call?"

"Oh…Professor Rhyskind at Berkeley, Paul Drew Clinton from USC, and Professor Thoretsen, retired, who speaks more languages, probably, than any man in this hemisphere."

She frowned at him. "So you're going to turn Avar into a sideshow."

He was frankly astonished at her vehemence. "Of course not. I want to learn answers to those same questions you asked me only a moment ago. We've got to know who and what he is so that we may understand him and help him."

He grasped her firmly by the forearms and stared deep into her eyes. "Understand me, Joan. I think Avar is a fine, noble man—perhaps the finest in our world today. I do not regard him as a freak or a maniac. But he is different from us; and since he is in our part of the world he must be helped to understand us—for his own peace of mind, if nothing else."

She smiled up at him. "You're my favorite father: no other Joan Whitney can make that statement. Run along and annoy the operator, Pop. I'll keep an eye on your specimen."

SOMEBODY—Lauren wasn't quite sure whether it was the striking gray-haired woman in that Hedda Hopper-ish hat or that little wriggly brunette who had been trying to pump her all afternoon about Gene—at any rate *somebody* shoved another filled-to-the-brim cocktail glass in her hand. It was her fifth, although always before she had stopped with the second, and she was beginning to feel the effects. She quickly gulped down half of it (to prevent it spilling she told herself resolutely) and let her ears go back to picking up the hopelessly tangled conversation rising and falling in the crowded living room like surf on a shore.

"...stole three of his credits before he..."

"...ten percent of *every*thing—and for *what?* I ask you—for *what?*"

"...mink, all right, but a second grade of mink if I ever saw..."

"...and that's only counting the ones she married, the way I hear..."

"Enjoying yourself, darling?"

"...matter of releasing through the right houses. 'Course, United Artists..."

"Lauren. *Lauren!* Are you all right?"

She wheeled quickly, nearly upsetting the rest of her drink. Gene Cameron was standing there, smiling at her, smoke from his cigarette circling his dark head.

"Oh, Gene. Of course, I'm all right. Why do you ask?"

"Well, I wanted to know if you were enjoying yourself and you just stood there like you'd turned to stone."

"I'm sorry, Gene." She put down her glass on a corner of an end table. "I think I'm having a good time. The *woman*-talk I can understand all right; but the men speak a sort of Greek pig Latin— if there is such a thing. Releases and credits and ten-percents...confusing isn't the word."

"Pictures, dearest." He ran his hand lightly along her bare arm. "Cliff is a screen writer and most of the men here fit in at the studio somewhere... Shall we take a powder?"

"A pow— Oh. Why, I guess so—if you like." She squinted at the dial of her wristwatch, laughed. "I think I've had one too many. What time is it, Gene?"

"After six. I thought we'd have dinner somewhere."

"So late? Goodness, how quickly the afternoon passed. Now that you mention it, I'm starving."

"Good. See that side door over there? We'll just sort of drift that way; it lets out on a terrace."

"But our host and hostess, Gene. We just can't disappear without thank—"

"They'll never miss us. Probably don't even know we're here. What's two among seventy or eighty?"

"All right."

In the car, they were silent for a little while as they slipped soundlessly between Brentwood's lovely homes and estates, many of them set back from the streets with high hedges and groves of trees to give complete privacy. They passed a sign that read: WESTWOOD and soon afterward shops began to appear.

The slight dizziness that had come from two cocktails too many was passing and Lauren lighted a cigarette. "Where are we eating, Gene?"

He turned his head momentarily to smile at her. "I thought we'd try my club. I put in a small kitchen last year; so many of the clientele like something to bring back their strength after dropping their bankrolls at roulette or the dice table."

"I'd like that." She laughed a little ashamedly. "You know, Gene, I've never been inside a—a gambling—"

"Mine isn't one of those movie versions of Monte Carlo. It's a small, *intimate* club for a select trade. Reasonably honest and completely safe. I'm sure you'll enjoy it."

Five minutes later the Packard drew up in front of a small white-stucco building of two stories behind a row of thick bushes. There were several cars parked along the curb; but as Lauren accompanied Gene Cameron along the walk to the building's small porch she noticed the venetian blinds were drawn and the only sign of life was a slender man lounging on the porch itself.

He straightened up as the couple came up the three steps. "Evening, Gene." He gave Lauren a flat, disinterested stare.

"This is Miss Whitney, Ralph," Cameron said. "She owns the place."

"Evening, Miss Whitney." His voice was as emotionless as his thin, gray-skinned face.

CAMERON took out a key case, selected one of the contents and unlocked the door, opening it against soft lights and the murmur of voices. They went into a surprisingly large room lined with small square tables covered with white cloth, and along one side of the room, behind frosted glass panels, was a bar.

Half the tables were occupied with diners, couples mostly; but almost every stool along the bar was taken. Lauren was inconspicuous in sport clothes; as at most Southern California gatherings, regardless of the hour, dress is casual.

They had one drink apiece at the bar and Gene introduced her to several people whose names she forgot at once. There was a good deal of that purposeless, lightly amusing small talk that leaves the mind free while the tongue does all the work. Lauren's eyes could find no evidence that this was any different from a thousand other small bistros she had seen, and there was no gambling paraphernalia in sight. No one made any mention of dice, cards or the bouncing ball, and she began to feel let down.

It wasn't until they were seated at a corner table, waiting for their dinners, that she brought up the subject.

"I'm disappointed, Gene."

"I'm sorry," he said, concern evident in his square, good-looking face. "Where have I let you down?"

"Your club. It looks about as unlawful as the YMCA. I expected to find suave croupiers in dress suits; tight-lipped, wasp-waisted men with snapbrim hats and wearing snub-nosed automatics in shoulder holsters; beautiful blondes in skin-tight, low-cut gowns, and who speak in sultry voices and wear their hair over one eye.

"And what do I get? The Brown Derby on a small scale and the same kind of people I've been running into half my life."

He put out a long-fingered, beautifully kept hand and patted one of hers. "You're a refreshing person, Lauren. For all your cool, aloof air and 'nothing surprises me' attitude you are about as innocent and naive as they come. I suppose that's the big reason I've been able to think of nothing else since the day we met."

Her breath snagged a little and for a moment her emotions were a vague tangle of exhilaration and uneasiness. He was much older than any man she had associated with before, and his air of sophistication, his undoubted good looks and these newspaper stories her father had referred to—together they made him fascinating and a little frightening.

But what up to now had been an intriguing but impersonal relationship, was suddenly something else. The touch of his hand on hers, the light shining now in his eyes, the abruptly deep and intense timbre of his voice—these attracted and repelled her simultaneously.

Nothing of all this showed in her lovely face. "You shatter all my illusions, then call me naive. Now I am confused." She freed her hand under the pretext of reaching for a cigarette from the gold-filled case he had placed on the table between them.

"I meant what I said, Lauren," he told her soberly. "I've been able to think of no one else. I've fallen in love with you and now's as good a time as any to tell you so."

He shook his head as she started to speak. "No. I don't want you to say anything, one way or another. I just want you to know how I feel about you—to give you a chance to think it over before I bring up the subject again...

"After dinner I'll take you upstairs and let you try your luck. The tables don't open until eight."

They talked about gambling until the waiter brought their order. Cameron explained the various games in detail, being amusing and entertaining, not once, by word or deed, referring to his love for her.

Shortly after eight o'clock she went with him to the gaming room on the floor above. There were between thirty and forty patrons gathered about the tables—the majority of them playing roulette.

CAMERON and she found places near the wheel. He tore a blank page from a pocket memorandum book, scribbled something on it and passed the slip to the tall, gaunt-faced croupier, who was wearing a dark gray business suit instead of evening clothes as Lauren had pictured. In return for the paper Cameron received three stacks of chips—yellows, blues and reds.

He placed them on the edge of the layout in front of Lauren. "The reds are twenty-five, the blues fifty and the yellows one hundred. Two thousand dollars. Have fun, darling."

The rattle of the pellet against the turning wheel, the muted clatter of chips as the players placed their bets, the calm voice of the croupier—these drowned out her whisper of protest. "I can't take this, Gene. I don't have two thousand dollars."

"Oh, but you do. Right there in front of you."

"But what if I should lose?"

"I'll sue you," he said, smiling. "Please; we're beginning to attract attention. I'll be back in a few minutes."

He gave her an exaggerated wink and slipped away. Her first impulse was to scoop up the chips and go after him, return them to him and walk out of the place. But several of the players were watching her curiously and play seemed momentarily to have stopped.

"Place your bets," intoned the croupier, and while it was clear that he was addressing no one in particular, his eyes were on her.

Seemingly of its own accord her hand closed on the small stack of red chips and she placed four of them on black. Other chips were already dotting the neat squares on the board, and an instant later the pellet began to whirl around the wooden groove.

"Twelve, black," said the attendant emotionlessly, and his stick began to flick about the layout. Four red chips magically joined those she had put down.

An hour later she looked up suddenly to find Gene Cameron, an amused smile creasing his lips, standing beside her. "How're you doing?"

Her eyes were so bright they seemed feverish and there was more color in her cheeks than usual. "Gene. *I'm winning.* I have *no* idea how much."

He gave the stack in front of her an expert glance. There were only a few reds, but the blues had easily doubled and there were three stacks of the yellow chips. "About three thousand to the good, I'd say."

"Seventeen, red," said the croupier and the rake began to flick about the cloth.

"Darn," Lauren said, disappointed. "That's three in a row I've lost."

There was a tall, frosted glass in Cameron's hand and it gave off the tinkle of ice cubes. He said, "Here, you need a drink," and handed it to her.

She drank it avidly, realizing suddenly she was quite thirsty, then went back to playing. After watching her lose four more times in a row, Cameron said, "Your luck has turned. As an old hand at the game, I would suggest cashing in and allowing me to show you the rest of the place."

"Afraid I'll break the bank?" she challenged, laughing.

"You hit it right on the nose. I'm a poor man, lady; have pity on me."

"Quitter." She pushed the chips over to the man assisting the croupier and received a thin packet of bills. "Fifty-one seventy-five," he said casually.

When they were out of the press of people she handed him the bills. "Thanks, Gene. It was a lot of fun."

"Anytime, Miss Whitney." He stripped several bills from the sheaf, slipped them into the inner pocket of his sport coat, then reached out, took the small handbag from under her arm and tucked the rest of the money into it. "Fine thing," he said reproachfully, grinning at her. "Taking over three grand from your deepest admirer."

"Oh, but I *can't*." S he started to draw back the bag's flap, but he put a restraining hand on hers.

"What d'ya mean—*I can't?* If you had lost I'd have charged it up to you."

She stared at him, her eyes troubled. "You're not serious."

"But I am." He pushed the bag under her arm and dropped his hand. "Surely you know my reputation. I ensnare helpless women into my gambling hell and take their money. Only sometimes they take mine."

She hesitated, wavered—and was lost. His reference to the slightly unsavory reports she had heard about him disarmed her completely. Anyone that frank couldn't be actually *bad*.

He took her by the arm. "Now I'd like to show you my combination private office, den, bar and seduction room. No gambling hell can afford to be without one."

THEY crossed the room and he unlocked a door in one of the paneled walls. The room beyond was fairly large, furnished in light wood, with heavy blue drapes at the one window and beige carpeting to the baseboards. There were a pair of blue leather lounging chairs, a modernistic chrome ash-stand or two, a radio combination in a blond cabinet in one corner and large, glass-topped desk in the same wood near the window, a blue leather swivel-chair with a high back behind it. A couch in red leather stood along the opposite wall, with a blond-wood liquor cabinet within easy reach. A black wood cocktail table on a white throw rug had been placed in front of the couch and there were several magazines neatly stacked on its lower shelf.

"It's beautiful, Gene."

"I think so, too." He put her in one of the leather chairs and went over to the liquor cabinet. "We'll drink to that."

"I think I'll pass mine up, if you don't mind." There was an odd twisting feeling in her stomach she had noticed as they were crossing the room outside on their way to his office. "I've had more than my quota already, Gene."

He turned quickly, bottle and glass in his hands. "Are you all right, Lauren?"

"Of course." Her laugh sounded strangely hollow to her own ears. "Just a little tipsy, I guess."

"Can I get you something?"

"No. I'll be all right. Have your drink; I'll watch."

"Right." He mixed a highball briskly, adding ice from a freezer unit built into the cabinet, then came back and took the other lounge chair. "I'll finish this and take you home, if you like."

After a moment she said, "You mentioned something a little while ago that surprised me, Gene."

He blinked at her over the edge of his glass. "I did? What was that?"

"Well…" The queer feeling in her stomach seemed suddenly stronger. "You said something about your reputation—that I must know about it. I sort of…well, it seemed a strange thing for you to say."

He lowered his glass and smiled at her. "The papers gave me quite a bit of attention a few months ago. Didn't you see them?"

"I didn't read the articles themselves. It was before I knew you, so your name really didn't mean…" A sudden sharp pain twisted her stomach and she cried out, clutching her middle.

"Lauren. What's the matter?"

Through a slowly deepening haze she saw him leap from his chair, worry creasing his face, and hurry toward her. She began to bend forward, arms folded across her stomach. "I think—I'm going to be sick. Bathroom."

"Of course. Here; I'll help you."

She managed to get to her feet, his arm steadying her. Then utter blackness opened up in front of her and she pitched headlong into it…

"HERE…drink this, Lauren."

The rim of a glass touched her teeth lightly and she swallowed some cool liquid that seemed to have no taste. The pain was gone from her stomach but her head was throbbing heavily. She opened her eyes.

She was back in the blue leather chair, in Cameron's office. He was bending over her, glass in hand, concern in his expression.

"I'm all right now." She tried to smile but it was pretty much a failure she knew.

He said, "Wow," in such utter relief that she *did* smile. "You scared the pants off me, darling. You realize you've been completely out for over an hour?"

"Honestly?" She managed to sit erect with his help. "I'm sorry I made such a fool of myself, Gene. I guess I just can't drink past the two mark."

"So I see. From now on I'm feeding you nothing but ginger beer. The place for you, young lady, is home in bed. Feel up to getting down to the car? Or would you rather sit here for a while?"

"I'm fine," she said. "Take me home, Gene."

"Why, sure. Here, let me help you up."

The room pitched a little, but only for a moment. He said, "We'll take the back stairs so no one will see you. You look a little used up, honey."

THEY went through a door in one of the paneled walls—a door she hadn't realized was there, so cleverly was its outlines made to appear a part of the wall itself—through a bedroom, very masculine and simple in its furnishings, and through another door that opened onto a flight of carpeted steps. The door below let them out into the night at one side of the building and he helped her along a flagstone path to the front of the building and the car at the curb.

The movement of cool air against her face banished her headache and by the time they entered the hills north of Hollywood she was almost completely herself again. Cameron talked amusingly about nothing in particular, evidently trying to relieve her of any embarrassment at the turn the evening had taken.

He drew the Packard to a stop in the wide circle of crushed stone in front of her home. The air was cool and rich with the odors of flowers. From the direction of the stables a horse whinnied and a dog barked briefly. Lauren noticed light streaming from the window of the guestroom where Avar had been placed.

"Feeling better, Lauren?" Cameron asked.

"Uh-huh." She smiled at him in the half-light from the distant porch fixture. "I'm sorry I made such a pig of myself."

"Think nothing of it." He twisted around and ran an arm lightly about her shoulders. "You're one of those lucky women who aren't cut out to be drinkers."

"I'd better go in." She was acutely conscious of the arm resting against her. "Good night, Gene, and thanks for showing me your club." Her last words reminded her of something. "Won't you please take back all that money? I haven't any right to it; you know that."

"We've been through all that." His arm tightened a little. "I'm thinking of something else, darling. I'm thinking of what I said to you earlier."

She said, "I don't know." It was all she could think of to say.

. "I want you to think a great deal about it, Lauren. I'm not the greatest guy in the world and a lot of nice people would tell you you'd be crazy to give me a second thought. But I love you. I'd do anything in the world for you."

"You're sweet, Gene. I'm—very fond of you."

His face was near to her now and she could see his faint smile. "That will do—for a starter. May I kiss you goodnight, Lauren?"

She did not draw away, and very gently he put his lips down against hers. She was aware of the smoothness of his skin the faint scent of shaving lotion and a prickly feeling in her toes and fingers.

And then suddenly and with complete unexpectedness Avar's face seemed to rise before her, bringing the sharp memory of what *his* lips had done to her.

Before she realized fully what she was doing she brought up her hands and pushed Cameron away, pushed him more forcibly than she had intended.

He drew back, his expression puzzled and tinged with anger. "I'm sorry," he said stiffly.

"Don't be." She bit her lip, realizing the words, and the way she had said them, might be misconstrued. "It's just that I…oh, I don't *know*, Gene. I suppose I'm still too mixed up after what those drinks did to me. I'd better go in."

"Of course." He got out on his side of the convertible and went around to open the car door. "I'll see you to the door."

They went up on the porch and she fished the key from her bag. "…Good night again, Gene, and thanks for everything. I had a very good time at your party."

"See you tomorrow?"

"Tomorrow? Let's see… I have to be at the dressmaker's in Beverly Hills in the morning. And the Mason's are having a lawn party in the afternoon. Mildred said I should bring a man."

"I'm a man."

She laughed. "So you are. Three o'clock would be about right."

"It's a date." He gave her a mock salute and went down the steps to the car. She watched him turn the Packard about, waved to him and he was gone in a cloud of blue exhaust smoke.

SHE went into the deserted hall, blinking a little in the light. The murmur of muted voices reached her from down the corridor; voices coming from behind the closed door to Avar's room. Men's voices, she decided, wondering who they belonged to. There were lights in the library and the door was open; she crossed over and glanced in, finding the book-lined room deserted. Three hats lay side by side on the desk's glass top—the kind of hats worn by conservative men of middle age.

She shrugged, returned to the hall and started slowly up the stairs on the way to her room.

Halfway up, she heard the sound of a key in the front door and turned to see who was coming in. It was Joan, wearing a light coat over a black party dress, her golden blonde hair shining in the light. Despite the distance, Lauren could see anger riding her sister's lovely face.

Behind Joan came a glum-faced Perry Siddons, his shoulders bulking competently in a tuxedo coat, the front of his dress shirt gleaming. He closed the door with exaggerated gentleness that told of an inner desire to slam the thing.

Joan wasn't waiting. She started to cross the hall, her heels clicking angrily against the parqueted surface. Perry said, "Don't be like that Joan."

She stopped but did not turn around. Perry sighed and went over and prodded her lightly in the back with one of his fingers. "Gosh, I'm sorry, Joan," he said gruffly. "But I don't see why you have to get all worked up just because I said a few things that were on my mind."

She whirled on him. "Just a few things, my foot! You were insolent and—and *crude*. Next thing, you'll be telling me how to *breathe.*"

Lauren had no desire to eavesdrop on the quarrel. "Hello, you two."

They glanced up at her, their expressions suddenly casual. Joan said, "You're home early."

"So are you. And both of you looking so partyish. Anything wrong?"

"Of course not." The way she said it proved to the contrary. Over her shoulder she said, "Good night, Perry," her tone cold, then went lightly up the steps to join Lauren.

Perry said, "Good night," making it sound like an oath, and stalked off toward the library.

While they were walking along the upper hall, Lauren said, "Perry's an awfully nice boy, Joan."

The younger girl curled a corner of her lips. "Boy? He's past twenty-one. But he acts about twelve. He gets hateful and pouty and—and impossible. He had the gall to tell me I mustn't be 'too interested' in this man we found today. Avar."

They stopped in front of Joan's room. Lauren said, "He loves you, Joan. He's jealous and he's young enough not to be able to cover it up. But surely this—this muscle ad doesn't really interest you."

Joan shrugged impatiently. "How do I know? He's the handsomest thing I've ever seen in my life and he's built like a dream and nobody else in the world has eyes like those. But he may have a wife and five kids for all I know—all of them wearing animal skins. What burns me up is Perry's assumption that I simply melt at the sight of a set of sinews."

"A tongue twister if I ever heard one," Lauren said, laughing. She sobered quickly. "Far be it from me, Joan, to try living your life for you. But I don't think this Avar, for all his good looks and splendid body, is a very—well, a very desirable person. Our kind of folks don't run around in panther hides, carrying flint knives and with flint arrowheads in their backs." The sudden memory of Avar's unexpected kiss made her flush. "Some of his actions are pretty much uninhibited too, I'm afraid."

"What does that mean?"

"I'd rather not say." She yawned delicately, covering her lips with the backs of two fingers. "I'm going to bed, Blondie. I had a couple of drinks too many and my head's killing me."

Joan looked down at her own dress. "And I thought tonight was going to be fun. That darn Perry; why couldn't he have waited until it was decently late before picking a fight."

Lauren smiled and patted her arm. "There'll be other nights. Be nice to him, Joan. He's something pretty special."

She went on down the hall to her own room.

CHAPTER SIX

THEY had arrived around nine o'clock, within minutes of one another, and Gregg Whitney put them in the library and shoved a highball glass into each right hand. The talk was general and had nothing to do with the urgent and unexplained summons each had received earlier from their host. The unvoiced attitude of each of the three was that Gregg Whitney had been overly mysterious over the telephone and he was the one who would have to bring up the apparently earth-shaking matter that had brought them together.

As soon as the inevitable lull occurred in the conversation, Whitney rose to his feet and said, "Gentlemen. I'm going to make a speech."

Professor Myles Rhyskind (he of the shaggy white hair, bushy brows and stooped, frail body) said, "Speeches. Up to here." He indicated the upper section of his thin wrinkled neck with a bony finger. "I'm filled with other people's speeches. Tonight I had hoped for two mild drinks and some pleasant talk with mine friend Gregg Whitney."

Whitney smiled. "You shall have two drinks Myles—and a conversation...discussion...is a better word—that will mark tonight as the high point in your career as one of the world's leading anthropologists and biologists."

His keen blue eyes swung to the self-effacing little man perched stiffly on the edge of a leather lounge chair—Professor Paul Austin Cabot, who looked the part of an underpaid bookkeeper and whose clothing was always shabby, and who was one of the foremost archaeologists in America. "And you, Paul—tonight should excite you out of that shell of yours."

The third guest stretched his long legs and winked at the others over his highball glass. "Sounds like you've dug up another Rosetta Stone, Gregg. Where do I fit in—as translator of hieroglyphics?" He was Emil Thoretsen, once holder of a professorate in languages at the University of Southern California until his retirement two years before. He was in his late sixties—a tall, extremely thin man with a knife-blade face, piercing black eyes, almost completely bald—and he spoke fluently more languages and dialects than most people realized existed.

Whitney took a deep breath. He was tremendously excited, although the only sign of his state of mind was the light blazing in his sharp eyes and a faint unsteadiness to his hands.

"You'll see, Emil," he said in reply to the linguist's question. "But first my speech... Shortly after noon today, I was driving home through the hills north of Hollywood, accompanied by my two daughters and one of their friends."

He went on from there, speaking slowly and distinctly, and while his voice quivered a little from time to time, none of his listeners noticed, so rapt was their attention to his story.

When he had concluded he remained standing, waiting for his guests' reactions. Rhyskind was pawing absently at his white hair, giving it an unkempt appearance beyond its never very orderly condition; Cabot looked like a bookkeeper who had just received an unexpected increase in salary; while Thoretsen's face seemed bleaker and sharper than ever.

Surprisingly, it was Cabot who spoke first, his voice as colorless as his personality. "The spearhead Dr. Blanchard removed from this man's back, Gregg. I'd like very much to examine that spearhead."

Whitney said, "Exactly. More than anything else, I think, it was that bit of flint which caused me to call you gentlemen here." He bent and drew open the desk's middle drawer, took out a bit of dark stone and handed it to Cabot.

At the archaeologist's clearly audible gasp, the others crowded around him. One glance was all Rhyskind needed before he rudely plucked the flint from Cabot's fingers, whipped a pair of thick-rimmed glasses from his breast pocket, and peered myopically at the object.

A MUSCLE was twitching in one of Cabot's cheeks. He said thickly, "My word, Rhyskind, this is incredible. That spearhead is Solutrean if I ever saw one."

Rhyskind seemed not to have heard him. "A Laurel Leaf Point yet. *Gros Gott.* Like it was made yesterday. How can this be?"

"No," Cabot said sharply. He snatched at the stone, but Rhyskind jerked it aside, scowling. "No," Cabot repeated. "It can't be a true Paleolithic specimen, Myles. The flint is freshly flaked; we both can see as much. This man must be a member of some lost tribe in the mountains—Indian, probably—a tribe which makes its own weapons and which has hit on the Stone Age technique."

"Bah!" For a second it appeared that Rhyskind was about to strike his colleague. "You haff the impudence to call yourself an archaeologist? *Schlimeil.* In your head are holes. This spear was born in Europe twenty thousand years ago; on that I stake my reputa—"

"But Osborn says in his—"

"Pfui! Osborn! Don't quote Osborn to me, you hear? Read sometime the Abbe Breuil, who has forgotten more about Aurignacian culture than you and I put lengthwise. I myself, in my personal collection, haff an obsidian knife that came from the Dordogne region—a knife that could haff taken shape under the same hand responsible for this."

"But its newness—its freshness... I tell you, Rhyskind—"

"Gentlemen. Gentlemen." Whitney began to pound his hand against one side of the desk to make himself heard over the heated discussion, particularly that part of it supplied by Rhyskind's booming voice. Thoretsen, an amused smile playing about his thin lips, leaned back in his chair and began to stuff tobacco into a short-stemmed briar. Rhyskind, the spearhead still clutched tightly in one hand, pulled away from Cabot, looked blankly at Whitney still attempting to restore order, then dashed over to Thoretsen and thrust the bit of flint under his nose.

"Emil," he shouted, "you are a man of science! Look once at this. Name for this *dumkopf* the period it belongs to."

His explosive words blew out the match with which Thoretsen was lighting his pipe. The linguist's smile became a grin. "You know me better than that, Rhyskind. I deal in languages, not stones. As far as I'm concerned this hunk of rock could have come from either Paleozoic or Holocene periods."

The white-haired anthropologist thrust both fists ceiling-ward in almost physical agony. *"Lieber Gott.* Am I with fools surrounded."

Cabot, no longer resembling a bookkeeper, gave a sudden cry of triumph. "It is Mayan! It must be. I was in Chichen Itza five years ago and I saw—"

The manner in which Rhyskind's arms fell limply to his sides, the "Lord, give me strength" expression on his flushed face, were a panegyric in reverse. Twice his lips opened and closed without a sound passing between them as he sought for adequate words with which to blast this heretic into oblivion.

The abrupt silence gave Gregg Whitney an opportunity. He said, "Have you gentlemen forgotten that this spearhead was found in a man's back. A man whose bones have not been dust for twenty millennia—a man who is alive and in full possession of his faculties—a man who is within thirty seconds' walking distance of us right now?"

They stared at him. Rhyskind said, "What does it matter? From what you haff told us I would think he is some sun worshiper from the hills maybe. What could he know about an artifact from the Post-Glacial Quaternary?"

"Why not ask him?"

"*Herr Gott,* how can I ask him? You say he does not speak English. Is he German then?"

"I doubt it. The words he spoke belonged to no language I have ever heard before. Have you forgotten our good friend Thoretsen is present?"

Understanding dawned in the faces of Whitney's three guests. Rhyskind's heavy white brows came together to form a divot above his lumpy nose. "Just what, my friend, do you expect to learn from this man you found? The secret of making perfect Laurel Leaf spearheads, *nicht wahr?"*

Whitney did not smile. "Who could teach us better than a man from that period?"

Cabot was frowning. "What are you trying to tell us, Gregg?"

WHITNEY looked down at his hands, pressed palms down on the desk's glass surface, and took a deep breath. "Not yet, Paul," he said quietly. "I have a theory...no, it's more than that—I am as sure as I'm standing here... My friends, I want you to meet Avar."

They were impressed; anyone with half an eye could see that. They stared at Whitney and then at each other before Thoretsen pulled his long, loose-jointed body from the depths of his chair and said, "Lead the way, Gregg. I confess, I'm quite curious about this wild man of yours."

"Excellent." Whitney came around from behind the desk and took the glasses from the hands of his guests. "He's in one of the guestrooms down the hall. You can leave your hats here."

They followed him along the corridor and Whitney touched his knuckles lightly against one of the closed doors. A moment later it swung silently back, revealing in the faint light from a table lamp beside the bed a broad-shouldered man of middle age, his face and hands wrinkled and weather-beaten from many hours out of doors.

Whispering, Whitney said, "How is he, Luke?"

"Sound asleep, sir. Has been, ever since I came in."

"Good. You go ahead; if I need you I'll send word."

The gardener said, "Yes, sir," and went off down the hall. Whitney stepped silently into the room and beckoned the others to join him.

Rhyskind, the last one to enter, stared at the long, beautifully symmetrical lines of the figure under the sheet, at the leonine head with the wealth of black hair falling almost to the wide shoulders, at the darkly tanned and majestic features...and his jaw seemed to come unhinged.

"*Himmel!*" he shouted. "Can I believe what I see? This is fantastic."

Instantly those closed eyes opened and turned their blazing light on the four men. There was a sudden hush in the room while a strange uneasiness crept into the faces of the three scientists. Thoretsen said, "You've awakened him with that bull voice of yours, Rhyskind." Absently he put his pipe between his lips and struck a match.

Cabot's eyes were round with wonder. "A disharmonic," he muttered. "The rectangular eye sockets. The pentagonal shape of the cranium as a result of prominent parietals. Yet the head is long and narrow."

"*Ja! Ja!*" growled Rhyskind. "I have eyes. *Herr* Cabot. But what you are thinking—what *both* of us are thinking—that is impossible. This man can be no more than an atavism—in spite of bringing with him a Solutrean spearhead."

The archaeologist was not listening. He said, awe in his voice, "He's staring at your pipe, Thoretsen. Tobacco must be something outside his experience."

Rhyskind glared at him. "By you that proves something? There are many men in the world who know nothing of tobacco."

"In Southern California?"

Whitney cleared his throat. "I'm a little disappointed in you, Rhyskind. Instead of trying to prove Avar out of existence, why don't you listen to your experience and training? Forgetting there are such words as 'impossible', from what race of mankind would you say this—this 'atavism' has sprung?"

Rhyskind shrugged. "You want it games we should play? Very well. If I were walking across the Iberian peninsula some twenty thousand years ago and came upon this man, I would know him. I would say, "Aha! A Cro-Magnard. Then a tree I would climb. *Schnell.*"

The others smiled. Whitney said, "What about you, Paul? How would you classify this man?"

Cabot shrugged faintly. "I need not go strolling back twenty thousand years into Time. I say the man on yonder bed is a true member of the Cro-Magnon race."

"Foolishness," snorted Rhyskind. "Are you a scholar, *Herr* Cabot, or a Sunday-supplement scientist? Cro-Magnon man has been extinct for ten thousand years."

Whitney stepped into the rapidly widening breach. "I suggest we examine our—er—specimen a little more closely before arriving at a definite opinion. Perhaps his language will give us a clue to his real identity. Emil, talk to him, will you?"

"I'm afraid my study of the Cro-Magnon tongue has been sadly neglected," Thoretsen admitted wryly. "However I shall be pleased to give it a try."

HE TURNED one of the straight-backed chairs about, pushed it closer to the bed and straddled the seat with his long legs, resting his arms across its back. The remaining three men stood behind him, their faces solemn, and the sounds of their breathing was suddenly audible in the complete silence.

For a long moment Thoretsen stared deep into those glowing, rectangular shaped eyes...

Rhyskind prodded the linguist with an impatient thumb. "Talk to him already. Has the sight of him tied your tongue?"

Thoretsen glanced up at him, his expression thoughtful. "Once," he said soberly, "I looked into a lion's eyes. This was in a zoo and there were bars between me and the lion. What I saw in those eyes made me wonder if man did not belong behind bars for lions to look at. In the eyes of that lion were a majesty and a dignity beyond expression—a calm contempt for mankind and its works. I stood there, a product of civilization, and compared myself and the rest of my species with this product of the jungle. I and my kind came off second best."

He laughed shortly—a laugh without humor. "I'm wondering again, gentlemen… This man whom Whitney calls Avar does not compare with the men of our world. If he comes from a world of the past, then we have slipped from a once high estate; if he is from the future, then our race has something to look forward to."

"A remarkable observation," Rhyskind said sourly. "Next week I shall find myself a flint knife and a loincloth of panther skin and go to Africa to live. But now—tonight—I am interested in learning if this lion-man has a language we degenerate creatures of a moribund civilization can understand."

"I apologize," Thoretsen said, smiling slightly. "Let's see what, say Latin will do."

Latin did nothing. Avar lay unmoving, eyes studying the movements of the strange god's lips while he listened to the totally unfamiliar words. He sensed these elderly gods (or were they spirits?) were attempting to convey a message to him, but he knew it was senseless for him to speak in return.

Thoretsen passed from Latin to Greek, then into several of the modern languages, without eliciting a glimmer of understanding in the calm expression of the man on the bed. Thoretsen scratched his head. If there was some way he could induce this stranger to utter a few words, thus furnishing a clue to go on…

He pointed his finger at the man.

"Avar?" he said, ending the word on a questioning note. "Avar?"

The spirit (god?) who had called himself Whitney must have told this one his name, Avar decided. Then why was he asking him to again identify himself? "Yes," he said, "I am Avar. I am a mighty hunter and a great fighter. What do you want of me?"

"God in Heaven," gasped Thoretsen in utter amazement.

"*Was ist?*" Rhyskind shouted, grasping the linguist's shoulder in a frenzy of curiosity. "Do you know what he is saying? Can you understand him?"

"Basque. He speaks in the language of the Basques." Thoretsen stared at his three friends in awe. "What do you make of that?"

Cabot's expression was a twisted mixture of incredulity and triumph. "Well, my friend Rhyskind, what have you to say now? Shall I quote you those authorities who have wondered why the Basques have no apparent racial affinity to any of the earth's other peoples? The Basques—whose language has nothing in common with any other known to man."

"I am confused," muttered Rhyskind, oblivious to Cabot's taunting tone.

"Shall I quote other authorities?" Cabot went on relentlessly. "Shall I remind you of the theory that *the Basques are direct descendants of Cro-Magnon man?*

"Let's sum up our evidence, Rhyskind. Before us lies a man—a man whose head is as large as the average man we see today. It is a long, narrow head, yet the cheekbones are wide. The result: a disharmonic. The eye sockets are longer from side to side but narrower from top to bottom, resulting in a rectangular-shaped eye. The forehead is high, the chin is strong. This man speaks the language of the Basques.

"There is the evidence, Rhyskind. You are a scientist—one of the leading anthropologists of the day. Were you to come upon the bones of this man in the heart of a cliff in Southern France, around Le Moustier, let us say, you would instantly proclaim them as Cro-Magnard. I defy you to say differently."

"*Ja*, I would so name them," Rhyskind admitted impatiently. "Did I not say as much only minutes ago? But this man is no bag of bones, we are not in France, and this is not two hundred centuries in the past. Ergo, he is not then a Cro-Magnon man."

"Then," snapped Cabot, "what is he?"

WHITNEY said, "Why not gather more evidence before we arrive at any definite conclusion, gentlemen? Let us permit Avar himself to testify."

"What difference will it make *what* he says?" Cabot said hotly. "Rhyskind will only repeat over and over that he alone is able to arrive at the truth."

"I—I am a man of science." sputtered the German. "Because you are willing in wild flights of fantasy to go, must I—"

Thoretsen held up a quieting hand. "Simmer down, Myles. For all I know this man may be a Cro-Magnard or the Grand Exalted Llama of San Luis Obispo. But he does speak Basque—an elementary form of Basque it is true, but one I can understand. Let me learn what he has to say for himself."

The others nodded in agreement, Cabot eagerly, Rhyskind doubtfully. The linguist absently groped for a match and lighted the pipe he had allowed to go out minutes before…

"Avar," he said, speaking slowly and haltingly, for the Basque tongue was less familiar to him than most languages at his command. "Avar, we are friends. Do you understand that we wish to be your friend?"

Avar's eyes widened slightly upon hearing words he understood come from the lips of this strange spirit. The way they were spoken sounded different but clearly recognizable. "Friend," the spirit had said. It was easy to call a man friend—even when you planned to knife him a moment later. But these spirits were old and frail; perhaps they called him friend because they were afraid of him. But were the spirits of the dead afraid of the living? Could those who had died once, die again?

He saw that his questioner was waiting, watching him intently, interest and wonder and puzzlement in his expression.

"How do I know you are friends?"

"Because we have saved your life," Thoretsen said promptly. "In your back was a bit of stone that would have killed you had we not taken it out. Would an enemy do that for you?"

Avar shrugged. "Who knows what lies in the heart of an enemy? If you are truly a friend, allow me to return to the caves of Kosad."

"'Caves? Do your people live in caves, Avar?"

Avar frowned. "Of course. That is a foolish question. Did you not live in a cave before you died?"

For a moment Thoretsen did not reply…only sat there puffing slowly on his pipe while he sought to analyze Avar's last question. It was Cabot who broke the brief silence. He put an unsteady hand on the linguist's shoulder and shook it slightly but with emphasis.

"What does he say, Emil? Who is he? Where does he come from?"

Thoretsen shook his head briefly. "This is very strange. He asked me if I had not lived in a cave—*before* I *died.*"

Myles Rhyskind gave a stentorian snort. "A madman. What else? Such a question…"

"No, Myles," Thoretsen said thoughtfully. "He is not mad—I would stake my reputation on that. He is misinformed."

He turned back to the man of the bed. "Why do you say I have died, Avar?"

Those strangely luminous eyes stared into his. "How else may a man become a spirit?"

"I am not a spirit, Avar."

"Then you are a god?"

"Nor a god. I am a man and these with me are men."

FOR almost thirty seconds Avar made no reply to this last statement, only looked up at Thoretsen from the depthless depths of those glowing, unblinking eyes. Then: "How can I believe that this is true? In the land about the caves of Kosad are no men like you. No men in my land wear strange skins like yours, nor have caves like this, nor ride on the backs of strange black monsters along paths of stone. Your words are lies, but your eyes say you are a man of truth. I do not understand."

"Where is your land, Avar?"

"I do not know. It is near, for the spear in my back would have killed me within half a sun had you not taken it out."

"Do you know how you came to this land?"

"No. I was fleeing from the warriors who wounded me. I ran into a narrow place between two mountains. A hole was there—a hole that went straight down into the darkness and it had no bottom. On the other side of the hole the trail I was following continued and I could see the sunlight and trees and reeds marking a place of water beyond. But it was hard to see those things; the air above the hole seemed thick and there was a strange smell.

"I tried to jump across the hole. It was narrow and a child could have jumped across it. But the air seemed to hold me...and I fell into the hole..."

"And then?" prompted Thoretsen eagerly.

"I do not know," Avar replied simply. "When I opened my eyes I was lying on a strange hillside. I tried to walk away but my body was as water and I fell into a stone trail, almost beneath the round feet of a black monster—a monster with men and she riding on its back. When I awoke again I was lying on this heap of strange skins and *he*..." His eyes went briefly toward Whitney. "...was sitting where you are now."

"I understand," Thoretsen said softly. "This land of yours, Avar—what did your people call it?"

A puzzled line creased the bronzed skin of Avar's forehead. "The land is land. It has no other name."

"Were there other tribes besides the one of Kosad?"

"Yes. But they are afraid of us. For our warriors are great fighters and we killed or drove away all within a distance of as many sleeps as I have fingers and toes."

"They lived in caves like your own?"

"Yes."

"And you never saw nor heard of caves like the one you are in now, nor found people like Whitney and me?"

"No."

"What was your land like, Avar? Were there animals and many trees and was the sun always hot?"

"Yes."

"What animals were there?"

"There is Kuo and Kua, his mate; there is Cita and Loka, and Boad and Adzan. There are these and many others near the caves of Kosad."

"We will talk of them later," Thoretsen said. "Now you must sleep and regain your strength. We will go away and let you rest. But perhaps you are hungry. Would you like food?"

"No." Avar smiled—a slow turning of his finely shaped lips that lighted up his tanned countenance and made it more handsome than ever. "Only a little while ago Whitney brought me cooked meat and milk."

"Good. Sleep now and when the sun comes again I will return and talk with you again."

"When will you show me the way back to my own people?"

Thoretsen's eyes went to the bowl of the pipe in his hand. "We will talk of that when you are well and strong again, Avar. A strange thing has happened, I think. That is something else we must talk about another time."

He rose to his feet, went over to the room's small fireplace and rapped his pipe against the bricks, emptying its bowl. Whitney said, "Well, out with it, Emil," in badly concealed impatience. "What have you learned?"

THORETSEN shrugged his narrow shoulders and dropped his pipe into a pocket of his jacket. "I could use some brandy, Gregg," he said, smiling slightly. "Not that I want to tell a host his business, but may I suggest drinks—in the library?"

"But—but what about Avar?" Whitney asked, puzzled. "Aren't you going to question him further?"

"Not tonight, if you don't mind. He's too valuable a property to misuse. Let him get a good night's sleep."

Whitney spread his hands. "Whatever you say, of course. Even if the rest of us could not restrain our desire for further information, we'd be helpless since you alone can speak his language." He smiled. "I have a brilliant suggestion, gentlemen; brandy, in the library."

As they filed out the door, Thoretsen, the last to leave, flicked the wall switch, plunging the guestroom into total darkness. Whitney turned a startled face to the linguist. "Is that wise, Emil? I mean, leaving the man in the dark that way? I intended posting Luke, one of my gardeners, in there with him for the rest of the night."

"Entirely unnecessary, Gregg. I'm sure of it. He's not going to run away. I think I've won his trust, if not his understanding. I'll tell you about it—in the library."

When they were seated in a ragged semi-circle facing the open French doors of the library, each holding a bell-shaped brandy snifter, Whitney said:

"You've stalled long enough, Emil. Do we get a report of what passed between you and this young Hercules I found in the hills, or do I have to go out and hire a different interpreter?"

Emil Thoretsen did not reply immediately. He tasted his brandy with slow, deliberate care, his eyes fixed on the carpet of lights beyond the French doors and far down the rolling hills to where Hollywood lay, with Los Angeles, proper, beyond that...

He said, "I'm going to say something by way of preface that will certainly have you, Professor Rhyskind, at my throat—and possibly Professor Cabot will join you there. Gregg...I don't know about your reaction. Not being a hide-bound scientist, you may be astounded and even incredulous, but I don't think you'll thirst for my blood."

"Well, *say it already!*" Rhyskind roared. "Must you babble like a sophomore? Astound us. Make us incredible. Only say it."

"Very well." Thoretsen crossed his long, slender legs and leaned back in his chair. "Putting it as succinctly as I know how, the man in that room back there was born in France or Spain...*and he was born roughly twenty thousand years ago.*"

There was the sharp brittle sound of breaking glass and all eyes swung to its source. Myles Rhyskind was looking uncomprehendingly at the shattered brandy goblet in his hand. He reached out and carefully put the shards on the edge of a smoking stand, drew a huge white handkerchief from the breast pocket of his coat and slowly began to sop spilled liquor from his trousers.

It was something of an anti-climax. By the time Rhyskind was through mopping up his spilled drink and Whitney had handed him a fresh glass, the impact of the linguist's words had lost much of its force.

Paul Austin Cabot, America's leading archeologist, was the first to echo Thoretsen's words. "You said, and I hope my ears are not playing me tricks, that this—this Avar was born twenty thousand years ago. Is that right, Emil?"

"Precisely."

"You can't mean that literally, of course. Would you mind telling us exactly what you do mean?"

Thoretsen sighed and his smile was a trifle wan. "But I do mean it literally, Cabot. Avar was born twenty thousand years ago. Yet I would put him down as being about twenty-five or twenty-six years of age."

"Of all the *verdammt* nonsense—" growled Rhyskind.

PAUL CABOT silenced him with a single, almost savage gesture. "Go on, Emil," he urged, not taking his eyes off the linguist. "You'll have to say more than that."

"I know," Thoretsen admitted. "I arrived at the startling conclusion I just gave you by talking with Avar. Here is what he told me."

Briefly the linguist recounted what had passed between the cave man and himself, giving particular emphasis to Avar's story of the mysterious abyss and the strangely visible air above it. When he finished there was a brief silence.

Cabot said, "And your theory?"

"It has been suggested," Thoretsen said slowly, "that Time is in the form of a spiral—that all matter exists simultaneously on the loops of that spiral. That all Life—from the primeval ooze of the Paleozoic to the day the sun dies—has no beginning and no end. Vivid illustrations have been used to portray that theory: a train moving along a track called Time, with the stations named as centuries, or perhaps named by geologists as periods—Cambrian, Ordovician, Silurian, Devonian, Triassic, Jurassic, Eocene and so on. When the train leaves the station called Silurian, say, and arrives at Devonian—has Silurian ceased to exist because our eyes can no longer see it? Has Chicago ceased to exist when we arrive at South Bend?

"Or let us go today by space ship to Betelgeuse in the constellation of Orion. With the superior telescopes furnished by its inhabitants we look at Earth. There is George Washington at Valley Forge. But that is impossible. Washington died almost one hundred and fifty years ago."

"No wonder the University retired you, Thoretsen," Rhyskind snorted. "Mouthing such—such foolishness. Were your textbooks written by H. G. Wells?"

The others ignored the gibe. Cabot, face flushed, eyes sparkling, said, "Then you believe that Avar, a Cro-Magnard warrior of twenty thousand years ago, stumbled upon a—a fault in the time spiral—a short cut, let us say, between two distant stations of this 'railroad line' you mentioned—is that it?"

"Exactly."

"I like it, Emil." The seedy-looking archaeologist sank back in his chair and drank a portion of his brandy. "It's simple, it's logical, and it explains everything beautifully. I congratulate you."

Rhyskind rumpled his hair with his free hand. "*Madness*," he cried. "Two men who claim to be reputable scientists accepting such balderdash. At least give the matter deeper study. We cannot arrive at such a fantastic conclusion with only two hours' investigation. Let us take weeks, months, in which to probe this wild man's case history. Let us call in other biologists, other anthropologists, I would like to have such men as Manassi and Hutchins observe this specimen. Let us see what *they* have to say about Time being a branch of the New York Central."

"I agree with you, Myles," Thoretsen said quickly. "Let others—men who are better qualified than I—study Avar and make reports. But we must wait a while. In his present—ah— state, our cave man is little more than a beast of the jungle. Not that he is dull-witted or unintelligent. Quite to the contrary."

He drummed the fingers of his right hand thoughtfully against the chair arm, his eyes fixed unseeingly on the rug between his feet. "Whitney," he said finally, "I want you to do something for me— for all of us."

"Anything," Whitney said eagerly.

"I want to—well—to borrow Avar for, say, three months."

"...Borrow?"

"Yes. I have a lodge in the mountains behind San Bernardino. I want to take Avar there—tonight, if possible. I want to spend those three months in teaching him our language, our customs, our conventions and our ethics. Not to make him the same as us and our world of today—that would be spoiling something fine, I think. But to make him able to face our so-called civilization, to fit into the modern pattern without friction.

"Think of it, gentlemen. In that room down the hall lies one of man's earliest progenitors. A human being unwarped by countless ages of what we call 'progress.' Once he can be changed externally to a point where crowds do not follow him in the street, and once he has been taught our ways sufficiently to keep from breaking society's complex laws—think what he might do in this world and for this world. Our world of today is tired and cynical and fear-ridden. It needs an unspoiled viewpoint, new horizons of hope. But perhaps man today has come to the end of viewpoints and horizons. Perhaps he must go back—back toward his beginning to find the answers to the problems that beset him. Who should be better able to lead mankind back to the clear-thinking, imaginative era of prehistory than a denizen of that era?

"Think back two thousand years, gentlemen. To another time when man was weary and cynical, when he faced a life too complex for further progress. He was burdened with spiritual and physical taboos, held mentally and physically in bondage, beaten into paying homage to false gods and falser values.

"And in the hour of his greatest need, man was given a Leader—a Leader who preached the sermon of simplicity—a Leader who restored dignity and nobility to the minds of man.

"I say that in the person of that Cro-Magnon man down the hall we have another leader—a leader who can lead the world out of its present morass and into a new era of progress toward the stars. Two thousand years ago the world was given the Son of God to extricate it; today modern man—more cynical than ever before in his history—would reject as an imposter Almighty God Himself if He came to Earth in human form.

"But give the people an object for hero-worship, a unique human who can catch their fancy, a Messiah who will give them a panacea based on something more concrete than hopes for a glorious resurrection—and you've *got* something."

THE others were staring at him in almost open incredulity mixed with alarm. Even Paul Austin Cabot, the linguist's most ardent supporter, seemed taken aback by this unexpected development.

Surprisingly it was Rhyskind who showed the least alarm. In fact an expression of satisfaction and outright approval began to dawn in his faded blue eyes.

"Superman," he rumbled. "The Man of Tomorrow from the World of Yesterday. A true Nordic—in whose veins flows blood untainted. The only living man who is not a polygenetic hybrid. What a leader he would make—with intelligent men to guide him along the right path, of course. I am beginning to see where your reasoning is leading, my good Thoretsen; and along those lines I am with you completely."

"Was Cro-Magnon man a Nordic, Rhyskind?" asked Cabot dryly.

The white-haired anthropologist glared at him. "Does it matter? The people will believe what we tell them—don't they always? We are scientists—the people in this day and age revere scientists and take their word as gospel. Let one of us pose in a white gown beside a microscope and say something about 'exhaustive laboratory tests,' and black becomes the achromatic color of highest brilliance if we so declare it. Mankind will flock to Avar's banners, 'Avar Groups' will spring up all over the world, governments will fall into the hands of such groups...until the world itself *belongs* to Avar—and the men who control him."

From between tight lips Thoretsen said, "I am not proposing we substitute the word 'Avar' for 'Hitler', Professor Rhyskind."

Angry blood poured into Rhyskind's face. "*Hitler!*" he screamed. "Don't talk to me of that madman! He chased the best scientists from Germany; he aroused the world's opposition and hatred by a senseless persecution of minorities. He was worse than a madman—he was a fool.

"But Avar will be a benign and kindly benefactor of mankind. As Thoretsen has said it: a leader who can lead the world into a new era of progress. For that is what we in this room want—and we shall be the power behind Avar."

"And what," Cabot said slowly, "of those who oppose Avar?"

"Every cause," Rhyskind retorted, "is opposed by somebody—no matter how just the cause is. We shall win them over if possible; if not, let them beware."

"I can see it now," mused Cabot, disgust strong in his face. "A dozen of the largest public relations firms putting the campaign into operation. Newspaper articles, personal appearances, radio speeches. Avar's opinions on the national debt, on raising Poland China sows, on universal military training, on the length of women's skirts, on the United Nations. Governors and senators, both state and national, running on the Avar ticket..." He stood up and dusted his palms together, looking less the underpaid bookkeeper than at any time since entering the room. "Gentlemen, I'm going home..."

"Wait a minute, Paul," Thoretsen pleaded. "Rhyskind's scheme is his own, not mine. I pictured nothing like what he has suggested. Perhaps my own ideas are not practical—in fact, I was carried away with my own—ah—eloquence. Rhyskind's words have shown us all how an idea conceived for the good of humanity can be warped into something destructive.

"But I do feel Avar should be made ready to face a world as unfamiliar to him as Mars would be to a bootblack. That's why I'm asking Whitney's permission to take him to my lodge in the San Bernardino range. If all of us agree it would be for the cave man's good, then I'm sure Whitney will agree. But if you oppose the idea, then he will be justified in refusing."

"No, Emil." Whitney was smiling at him. "I'm not at all concerned with who opposes or favors your unselfish request. My interest is in Avar—not in his possible use to our world of today, or his danger to it. What little I know of anthropology caused me to feel sure Avar was a Cro-Magnard, even before I listened to the discussion that has taken place this evening.

"To me this entire business is in the nature of an experiment—an experiment to determine whether a man of the prehistoric past can fit in with the civilization of today. And if future events prove he cannot, then I say such a failure will be an indictment of modern man; but if the world gives him the respect it would give a distinguished visitor from another planet, say, then indeed have we made true progress in becoming truly civilized.

"Take Avar with you, Emil—tonight, if you wish. Teach him our language, our customs, our laws—everything in short, but your own convictions and philosophies. For I'm sure his observations about us and our way of life will be interesting and of value only if they are not influenced by your teachings before he can express them.

"I am going to impose one condition, however. I want to be free to visit you and Avar at the lodge freely while the two of you are there. I want Avar to know me and to like me, and to realize his real home is here. Tomorrow I shall place one hundred thousand dollars to his credit at my bank. When the time comes that he wants to go into the world unencumbered with a made-to-order family (for I regard him as a member of this household), then he will be free to do so without financial worry."

THERE was a murmur of surprise and admiration from the others. Thoretsen said, "By all means, Gregg, come to the lodge with us and stay, the entire three months if you like."

Whitney shook his head. "Don't think I wouldn't like to. But I've two daughters to look after. But I'll drive up frequently and spend a lot of time observing your progress."

His eyes went to the others. "Just one thing more. I'm going to ask all of you to tell no one about Avar and the theory about his arrival in our—well—our Time. It's the kind of story newspapers would go wild over, and we'd have a hundred reporters to brush out of our hair."

The three scientists agreed promptly. This was something too good to share with the rest of the world—for the present, at least. Actually each of them was already thinking of the article or book he was going to do on Avar, when the time came.

While they were getting their hats and Thoretsen was telephoning a private ambulance service to engage a vehicle in which to transfer Avar to the mountain lodge, Paul Austin Cabot brought up an interesting point.

"You said something, Gregg, about putting money into an account for Avar. Under what name—simply 'Avar'?"

"I hadn't thought of that," Whitney admitted, troubled. He looked appealingly at his three guests. "Can any of you suggest a name?"

Rhyskind grinned wolfishly. "As long as you have this passion for anonymity as far as this so-called Cro-Magnard is concerned, why not call him John Smith?"

"With *his* appearance?" snorted Cabot. "Like calling a battleship a boat. Besides, he's used the name Avar for twenty-odd years; he wouldn't get used to another name for a long time."

Thoretsen, who had been listening to the conversation during pauses in his telephone call, replaced the receiver and rejoined the others. "Let's use a little imagination on this problem, as befits men of science. I'd suggest retaining his given name, and for a surname something to fit his history. Like—well—like 'Neolith,' He's from the Neolithic Age, you know—or close to it."

"'Avar Neolith'," said Cabot. "That's a little *too* different, I'd say. Let a news reporter hear that one and he'd be around looking for a human interest story on the humorous side."

"The Neolithic Age," said Whitney, thinking aloud. "Let's see. *Neo* is 'new'; *lith* is 'stone'... Why, of course. Newstone. Avar Newstone. Dignified and different. What do you say, gentlemen?"

"Excellent!" roared Rhyskind. "The product of an inspired mind. Let's have more brandy, that we may drink to the christening of our Herculean god-son—Avar Newstone."

CHAPTER SEVEN

ON THE last Monday in September, Sergeant Edward Korshak, of the Hollywood police, returned from his vacation. He came into the squad room promptly at four in the afternoon, ready for his eight-hour shift.

Officer Henry Gilmer was behind a desk in one corner of the sunlit room, his shapeless blob of nose buried in a racing form sheet, his stocking feet propped against an open desk drawer. There were cigar ashes along the front of his wrinkled white shirt and lint on the knees of his unpressed trousers left there from a crap game an hour earlier in one of the station's back rooms.

Korshak came over, his walk catlike, his narrow-tipped shoes soundless on the sand-colored linoleum flooring, and in one smooth-flowing motion took the form sheet from Gilmer before the latter was aware of his presence.

Gilmer's stocking-covered feet hit the floor with a thud. "Hey, what's the—Ed? Jeez, it's good to have you back. How was the vacation?"

"What vacation? I've been working—on my own time. You knew that."

Gilmer looked at the other's lean, sharp-featured face, seeing the cold lusterless black eyes and the grim thin-lipped mouth and hearing the flat metallic emotionless voice. He felt a small uncomfortable shiver move over the skin of his back. Sometimes he wondered about Sergeant Korshak...

He said plaintively, "Yeah, I know, Ed. But at least you been out in the mountains where it's cool. The heat down here's been awful, I'm tellin' you. Why, a couple days there last week the tem—"

"Okay. Skip it, will you? Let's get rolling; I've got some questions I want answers to."

Gilmer pushed protesting feet into a pair of broad-toed brogans that needed a shine and followed Korshak out of the squad room and down a ramp to the station garage. A mechanic in white coveralls brought out one of the squad cars, gave its radio communication set a brief test, and got out, leaving the door open for the two plainclothes men.

With Gilmer behind the wheel, they turned off Wilcox onto Sunset and headed west. Their duties confined them to no particular beat; they were at liberty to cruise about the streets of Hollywood ready to handle any situation calling for police investigation or action.

As they neared La Brea and Sunset, Korshak finished lighting a cigarette and said, "What did you find out about the Whitney babe, Hank?"

Gilmer shot him a troubled glance. "Not much a anything, Ed. She's seein' a lot of this Cameron monkey, but they don't do nothin' you could hang anything on 'em for." He swerved the car suddenly to avoid hitting a Buick convertible making a right-hand turn from the middle of Sunset. "Gosh, the nights I spent tailin' that Packard around. The lieutenant woulda really raised hell if he knew what I was up to. Not that it wasn't my own time and my own car, but a police officer's got no right tailin' law-abidin' cituhsons around like that, Ed."

"You want to step out of it?"

"Aw, you got no call to get sore, Ed. You know I'm on your side. But, honest now, don't you think it'd be better t give up this idea of gettin' even with Whitney and that moose a his?"

Sergeant Korshak took a long drag at his cigarette, the smoke coming out in little puffs as he said, "I don't like muscle boys, Hank—especially when they push me around and get away with it."

"Yeah, sure. But a guy like Whitney's tough to monkey with, Ed. Talk is he's worth a lot of dough—up in the millions, I hear."

Korshak's face lost none of its impassiveness. "Time he learned his money won't buy some things... Tell me about Cameron and the girl."

"Well, they been runnin' out two—three nights a week. They usually hit the spots along the Strip or a couple of the bigger places along the Boulevard. One night they went all the way down to San Diego and I was sure they was headin' for Mexico and a wedding. They might a been too, only I think she got cold feet. They stopped in front of a drive-in and had san'wiches and a argument. I pulled in as close as I could get, but not close enough to hear what they was talkin' about. Finally they pulled out and headed back to L. A. The way Cameron was drivin' I figured he was plenty mad about somethin'."

"They ever go to that gambling club of his in Westwood?"

"Not in it, far's I know." The radio receiving set came on with a stolen car report and Gilmer raised his voice to get above the sound. "He drove out there one night and parked in front, but the way she acted I guess she wouldn't go in with him. He left her in the car and went in for a few minutes, then came out and drove away."

"Any parking on dark streets or up in the hills?"

"A few times; yeah. Nothin' out a the way though, far's I could tell. A little schmoozin'—nothin' you could hang a morals rap on."

THE two men were silent for a while. The patrol car moved at moderate speed along the Strip—lined with nightclubs, antique shops and pseudo-Spanish architectural monstrosities housing Hollywood's most abused citizens—the talent agents—until it reached Beverly Hills. At this point Gilmer made a U-turn on screeching tires and started back east.

Korshak blew smoke through his nose and picked a shred of tobacco from his lower lip. He said, "What about the younger Whitney girl?"

Gilmer shook his head. "There's nothin' there, Ed. She's just a kid. Runs around steady with Perry Siddons—he was All-Conference tackle at USC here a few years back. His old man owns a steamship line, or somethin'."

Korshak nodded. "Okay. Maybe we'll take a run out Whitney's way after dark and kind of scout around. Some one of these days one of that crowd's feet are going to slip—and that's when I even thing's up...but good."

After a silence that lasted several blocks, Gilmer said, "How'd you make out up in the San Berdoo range, Ed?"

"A waste of time, mostly. This Professor Thoretsen's got that freak up there, giving him lessons out of books the way it looked to me. The place is a big log building thirty miles from the nearest town. I spent the better part of two weeks watching them through binoculars. They ate most of their meals under a tree in the yard and the way it looked through the glasses Thoretsen was teaching the freak how to eat with a knife and fork."

"Jeez," breathed Gilmer, openmouthed. "Like a baby, hah?"

"He's some baby. Among other things, Thoretsen's teaching him to drive. Well, the freak drove the professor's car into a spot where he couldn't get it turned around. Damned if he didn't get out, reach down under the front of that car *and swing the whole thing around facing the other way.* A four-door Studebaker sedan, brother."

Gilmer uttered a long low whistle. "Ed, I'm tellin' you—leave that moose alone. Any guy that could do a thing like that could wring your neck with one hand. All right, so he threw you out a windah. It din't hurt you none to speak of, did it? Let him alone; a guy like that ain't natural to begin with."

But Korshak's lips twisted into a crooked grimace. "Muscle means nothing, Hank—nothing at all. I got what it takes up here…" He tapped his forehead significantly. "…and all that freak has got is biceps. I've been in this business a long time. I've seen some of the smartest cookies on the wrong side of the law get theirs—and when they couldn't be taken legitimately, they got a frame prettier than the old masters get in a museum. If you think I can't hang one around this misfit of Whitney's—well, just watch."

Gilmer's expression did not lighten. "All I can say is, I hope it don't bounce back on you, Ed. You sure they didn't spot you watchin' them?"

"Not to know who it was; I'm sure of that. Funny thing, though; one afternoon this muscle boy was out climbing trees. Damndest thing; he ran around most of the time practically naked—just an animal skin around his middle. I watched him quite a while and it was really something to see. He'd swing up in those trees and jump from one to another—cover long distances without ever coming to the ground. Good as any monkey in the zoo—a regular Tarzan.

"Well, after a while I lost sight of him. It was getting along toward evening anyway and I had quite a ride back to town ahead of me. So I went back to the road and drove away. As I turned one of the curves up there I looked back, just in time to see the freak step into the open at exactly the same spot I had parked the car earlier. It had to be an accident, of course; he couldn't have spotted me hidden in the brush a good three miles from Thoretsen's lodge."

Gilmer shook his head briefly and blew out his breath. "I only hope you can bring it off without stickin' your neck in a sling… What's the next step, Ed?"

"The day I left up there, the owner of the general store where Thoretsen buys his supplies said the professor was planning to return to L. A. a day or two later. That means the freak will be back at the Whitney's about that time. Once he's on my home grounds I'll see if I can't figure out something to keep him amused."

THE blue convertible, its top down to let in the still-warm air of a Southern California night, swung sharply into the Whitney's crushed stone driveway, sending a shower of gravel among the neighboring bushes. At the base of the flight of gray stone steps leading to the wide porch, the car skidded to a stop as its brakes were applied too quickly.

Lauren Whitney, her ash blonde hair falling in graceful undulations to the line of her shoulders under her white coat, wrenched open the door on her side of the car the second it stopped moving. She was already in the driveway when the man at the wheel slid quickly over and caught her hand where it lay on the door's ledge.

"Look here, Lauren, I can't let it end this way. And neither can you."

She stood there, straight-backed and somehow taller than usual. "Let go of my hand." Her voice was so low-pitched he was barely able to make out the words, but they were as cold as wind across a glacier.

"Let go of my hand."

"Not until you forgive me," he pleaded. "Will you at least listen to me? Surely you owe me that much."

"I owe you nothing."

"Please don't go in for a moment."

When she made no reply, Cameron released her hand. She remained standing in the roadway, looking steadily at him, her face as expressionless as cold anger could make it.

Cameron said quietly, "You know I love you, Lauren. I love you more than anything in the world. It's my only excuse for acting the way I did tonight." He spoke very quickly, as though anxious to get the words out before the girl could turn and vanish into the house. "Won't you look at my actions in that light and accept my word that I'll never do such a—a crude thing again?"

"No. May I go in now?"

"Oh, for God's sake, Lauren. Sure I made a pass at you—I'm only human and I'm in love. What else can you expect from a man under those conditions? Be human about this, will you?"

"Your idea of being 'human' certainly isn't mine, Gene Cameron. Not if it means permitting myself to be mauled in the name of love."

His eyes narrowed and the line of his jaws hardened. "What's your idea of love—holding hands on a sun-kissed hill? Why don't you snap out of it, for God's sake. This cool, detached air of yours is nothing but a pose and we both know it."

Her thin nostrils flared. "I expected something more intelligent from a man as sophisticated as you claim to be. Good night."

"*Wait...*" So urgent was his tone that she turned back. "Let me make amends, Lauren. Go with me to the Crawford's house party tomorrow evening. Afterward we'll talk this over." His voice was pleading again. "Don't say no to me, darling."

"I'm sorry, Gene." The anger was gone from her voice now, replaced by a note of inflexible finality. "We can't drag it out any longer; it wouldn't be fair to either of us. We were attracted to each other from the first; and frankly I didn't know just how strong that attraction was on my part. I had to find out—that's why I let it go as far as it has. Now I know this much: you're wonderful company and a lot of fun and I've enjoyed being with you—that is, until our relationship started turning into something serious. When you made it necessary for me to look at it in that light I found out I did not love you. That's why there's no point in our continuing to see each other."

Cameron wet his lips nervously. "I've upset you tonight, Lauren. That's why you're talking this way. For the sake of our friendship don't end it this way. Sleep on it; tomorrow evening I'll call for you and we'll discuss the matter when we both are more relaxed. What do you say?"

She shook her head. "No, Gene. This is goodbye. There's no point in dragging the thing out."

In the faint glow from the porch light she saw anger twist his handsome face—anger and something akin to evil. It passed too quickly for her to be sure, but she was left with a chilly, repelled sensation as though she had witnessed a snake shedding its skin.

He said, "Okay, if that's your answer. Come to think about it, I'm delighted it's going to work out the way I originally planned."

BEFORE Lauren was able to comment on this cryptic retort, the Packard's motor roared into life and the car leaped into motion.

Lauren Whitney, her expression troubled, went up the wide stone steps, got out her key and unlocked the front door and entered the large reception hall.

Gregg Whitney was descending the broad staircase from the second floor. He was wearing street clothes and a hat and there was a light topcoat over one arm and an overnight bag in his hand.

"Oh, hello, Lauren," he said hastily. "I hadn't expected you home so early. I'll be away overnight."

"Is anything wrong?" she asked, surprised.

"No, no. I'm having Luke drive me up to Professor Thoretsen's lodge for the night. We're bringing Avar here tomorrow morning."

She took a deep breath and her lips tightened slightly. "Here? You mean he's going to stay with us?"

"Of course. For a while, at least." He put down the bag and began to struggle into his topcoat. "You won't recognize him, Lauren. According to Thoretsen, he's done wonders in teaching Avar our—ah—way of life. You might say he's a Cro-Magnard in name only. Speaks our language well—as long as you keep the conversation reasonably simple. I have a tailor coming out tomorrow afternoon to fit him out with a wardrobe—he's been wearing some ready-made things that don't fit him any too well. Drives a car, eats with knife and fork, knows enough mathematics to handle money. Emil says he has the most alert mind he's ever encountered in all his years as a teacher."

"All of which," Lauren said coldly, "forms a thin shell over a complete savage—a savage you know nothing about beyond the fact that you found him wandering about the hills behind

Hollywood. You've always put Joan and me off whenever we've asked you about him, Dad. All we know is that Professor Thoretsen is able to speak his native language and that the theory about him arrived at by your scholarly friends is so incredible you refuse to tell us it for fear we might accidentally let someone else in on it. Don't you think, now that you're actually bringing him into the house to live with us, that we're entitled to know exactly who he claims to be?"

Whitney said uncomfortably, "You're right, of course. The true reason I haven't told you, I guess, is that you'd think your poor old father had gone slightly daft. But—"

The sound of a car horn from the driveway in front stopped him there. "That's Luke," he said, obviously relieved at the interruption. "Darling, I've got to rush. We'll be back around noon tomorrow—then I'll tell you and Joany the truth, the whole truth and nothing but the truth—as I know it. 'Bye."

And he was gone, the door slamming behind him, and a moment later the fading sound of a car motor reached her through the open windows.

Lauren went slowly up the stairs, trailing her light coat over one shoulder, feeling a strange sense of depression she could not completely account for. Was it because of her breaking off with Gene Cameron, or because that hulking savage was about to return to the Whitney home. This last thought brought the memory of that untamed kiss the wild man had pressed against her lips and the breathlessly unexpected sensations it had aroused within her.

She shook off her thoughts with an angry movement of her head. "I must be coming down with something," she said, half aloud.

She paused outside Joan's door and rapped lightly against one of its panels. When there was no answer she opened the door a crack and looked in. No one was there and the bed was still made. Probably out with Perry, she thought and went on down the hall to her own room.

She undressed leisurely and, in an effort to escape the sense of foreboding that plagued her, took a detective novel to bed with her…

SHE AWOKE from a light doze with a start and glanced at the small clock on the nightstand. Nearly three o'clock. She was reaching for the bed-lamp button when the sound of a closing door reached her ears from down the hall.

"Must be Joan," she thought sleepily. "Late for her to be getting in, though. I'd better make sure."

She slipped from under the blankets, caught up a quilted robe, slipped her narrow, high-arched feet into a pair of bedroom mules and went softly down the hall.

A thread of light under her sister's door reassured her and she knocked softly.

"Who is it?" Joan's clear young voice.

"Lauren. May I come in?"

"Sure."

She was sitting on the foot of her bed, holding one of her silver slippers, the other still in place. She was wearing a white strapless formal gown that made her look younger than her years, and her blonde hair lay in carefully careless waves to her shoulders. There was a heightened flush apparent in her cheeks and a sparkle to her eyes that made her even lovelier than usual. She said, "Hi, Princess," with an unsteady smile and dropped her slipper to the floor.

Lauren yawned behind the thumb and forefinger of her closed hand. "I couldn't fall asleep, so I heard you come in. Have a nice time?"

"Adequate." The younger girl kicked off the second slipper and ran her hands through her wealth of hair. "Whee… I shouldn't a had that last drink. Head's going thisaway and thataway."

"Don't tell me Perry's taken to feeding you alcohol?"

"Perry had nothing to do with it. Have you understand 'nother man bought me my drinks tonight. Slick-haired gentleman with a polite leer. Boy, was Perry 'W. C. T. U.' Siddons burned up." Her giggle broke unexpectedly under an unmistakable belch.

Lauren sank down on the edge of the room's chaise lounge and took a cigarette from a box on the night table. "You shouldn't devil Perry that way, Joan," she said, reaching for the matching lighter.

"Well, he shouldn't be so stuffy. And this was all veddy, veddy correct, too. This man is a close friend of the family's, it just so happens—at least one of the family. It wasn't a casual pickup, so I don't see why Perry had to act so—so stuffy."

"Some one I know?" Lauren asked casually, putting back the lighter.

"Y'might say so." Joan blew a strand of hair from in front of her face. "Yessir, you might really say so. Man by name of—le's see now—oh, yes. Man named Cameron. Gene 'what an unexpected pleasure' Cameron. That's what he said when he spotted Perry and me at the Mocambo. "Aren't you Lauren Whitney's sister? What an unexpected pleasure.""

There was a strange sinking feeling below Lauren's ribs, followed by a sudden cold anger. She waited a long moment before she spoke—waited until she could be certain her voice would not betray her.

"Not a friend of mine, Joan. Not any more."

Her sister stared at her owlishly. "Honestly, Lauren? Why, you went off somewhere with him this afternoon while I was home. I saw you from my window."

"Our association ended tonight. I learned he's not a very nice person, Joan."

The girl on the bed waved airily in dismissal of the statement. "None of 'em are, Princess. Not even Perry Siddons. You should a heard the way he bawled me out afterwards for accepting drinks from 'that wolf.' Personally I think Gene Cameron is darned cute. Asked if he might call me some afternoon and I said yes. Lucky Perry didn't hear—or there would a been a rumpus for sure."

LAUREN WHITNEY took a long unsteady breath. "Want to take a word of advice from a woman old enough to be your sister, Blondie?" She tried to say it lightly but without much success.

Joan stared at her out of eyes that were abruptly blank of all expression. "Maybe. But I can pretty well guess what you're going to say."

"I'm sure you can. But let me say it anyway. I'd let Gene Cameron alone, Joan, if I were you. I really would. Not because he's got a bad reputation—but because he deserves the reputation he's got. I found that out."

"I like to find things out for myself, Lauren."

"Of course. Ordinarily I do too. But this is from your sister, Joan—not some idle gossip from an outside source."

"What happened between you two that makes you talk this way?"

Lauren Whitney bit her lower lip. This wasn't going to be as easy as she had hoped. "I'd rather not go into detail, if you don't mind."

"But I do mind. I mean, if you're going to expect me to avoid the man like a—a pestilence. I'm almost nineteen, you know, and I don't shock as easily as you might think."

The older girl looked down at her cigarette. She said in a curiously choked voice, "He...tried to put his hands on me. Disgustingly."

"Well, for heaven's sake, Lauren. What man doesn't? I thought he'd tried to get you to help him pull a holdup or something the way you talked."

Lauren could feel her cheeks burning. "How can you talk so lightly about a thing like that? I know a good many men, Joan Whitney, and not one of them ever attempted to do a thing like that before. Where in the world did you get such ideas? Surely not from going around with Perry Siddons!"

"Oh, him," Joan said with more force than elegance. "He's a child to begin with. I don't mean I—you know—submit to such passes. Men act that way when they're crazy about you. You just have to discourage them without telling them never to darken your door again."

Lauren took a long drag at her cigarette and let the smoke out in a thin stream. "I'm not exactly a fool, Joan. I know that the average clean-cut young man has just as much animal in him as nature intended. An intelligent girl can curb that in them without much trouble. But men like Gene Cameron are neither normal nor clean-cut. The animal in them is degraded, and through making such matters important above all else they've become adept at the art of seduction. They're older and smarter than teenage girls—

and girls past their teens for that matter. I'm going to ask you not to have anything to do with Gene Cameron, dear."

Joan Whitney met her sister's eyes, saw the angry embarrassment there and shrugged lightly. She said, "It's awfully late, Princess. I've simply got to get some sleep. Perry's coming over early tomorrow—today—to help welcome Avar home. Won't it be thrilling to have him back again?"

Lauren rose and ground her cigarette against the bottom of an ashtray, avoiding her sister's eyes. "Thrilling's hardly the word for it. Good night, Joan."

CHAPTER EIGHT

IT WAS after eleven when she awakened. For a little while she lay abed, aware of being still tired and understandably depressed. The scene with Gene Cameron still gnawed at her thoughts, made even more troublesome by the knowledge that her younger sister had found the man's attentions not unwelcome.

Ten minutes of such memories was all she could endure. She rose, took a cold shower to dispel her blue mood and slipped into a backless creation known as a "sun dress." She had just finished toast and coffee in the sun-filled breakfast room on the first floor and was lighting her first cigarette of the day when the family sedan grated on the gravel circle outside.

Luke, the gardener-chauffeur, slid into the open and swung back the Packard's rear door. Gregg Whitney emerged, followed in turn by Emil Thoretsen and a bronzed young giant who moved with the easy grace of cat.

"What have they done to him?" she thought aghast. "He looks like a—a *dock hand.*"

He was wearing a badly fitting pair of brown gabardine slacks and a checked sport coat inches short in the sleeves and much too narrow across the shoulders. A tan shirt strained at its buttons, leaving a row of unsightly gaps between them. Someone obviously new at the job had cut his thick, neatly combed black hair.

Lauren Whitney felt a wave of mingled compassion and anger at the spectacle he presented. What once had been an awe-inspiring example of perfect manhood was now reduced to a ridiculous figure who was neither a member of the civilized world nor a creature of the wild.

Why she should be so disturbed at the appearance of a man she heartily disliked did not occur to her at the moment. She left the table and hurried along the hall to the front door.

The three men were already on the porch when she came out. Her father appeared to be in high spirits. "Morning, Lauren," he said, beaming. "You remember Professor Thoretsen."

"Of course." She put out a firm, tanned hand. "How are you, Professor Thoretsen?"

"And now," Whitney said, smiling hugely with open pride, "I'd like you to meet our honored guest. This is Adam Newstone."

"'Adam'?" she repeated uncertainly. "I thought his name was Avar."

"So it was," Whitney said, nodding. "But by mutual consent it has been changed to Adam. More fitting, in a way. I'll tell you why later."

She turned her head toward the silent young man and looked into his eyes. She felt again the sense of almost physical contact at seeing the strange yellowish gray radiance blazing from those rectangular sockets.

In that moment the realization came to her that compassion and pity were necessary. He stood there, straight as an arrow, regarding her gravely and with complete lack of self-consciousness. There was a remote brooding expression to his extraordinarily handsome face—the quiet aloof dignity she had seen in lions at the zoo. She realized suddenly that the clothing he wore appeared ridiculous by comparison with the body it covered, instead of the other way 'round. Put a lion in a clown's suit, she thought, and he is no less the king of beasts.

The silence was becoming a little strained. She was aware that Professor Thoretsen and her father were staring at her. She took an unsteady breath and said, "How do you do, Mr. Newstone?"

"Hello, Miss Whitney."

She gasped involuntarily. His words appeared to rise from the depths of his cavernous chest, to ring like a muted bell, deep, filled with restrained power.

Gregg Whitney said, "We're starving, Lauren. Ask Martha to get some lunch together for us, will you?"

"Of course." What prompted her next words was something Lauren Whitney could not explain. Perhaps it was the memory of a disturbing kiss from the firm lips of this strange young man. In any case, she added, "I suppose Adam will want his meat raw?"

She saw anger come into her father's sharp eyes and a faint flush of distress touch the thin face of Professor Thoretsen, and she instantly regretted her rudeness. Only Avar—or Adam, as he now was known—seemed oblivious to the bad taste in her remark.

She said, "I'm sorry," and fled into the house.

WHILE Martha was preparing lunch, Joan Whitney and Perry Siddons returned from town and joined the group. There was a great deal of light conversation aimed openly at making Adam feel at ease, and no one touched on the subject of the cave man's past—not, that is, until Joan Whitney could no longer contain her curiosity. She said:

"How do you like California, Adam—better than your own country?"

He had been eating carefully and slowly-handling his silverware with gingerly concentration, contributing nothing to the conversation. At the younger girl's direct question, he raised his head and swung those glowing eyes toward her.

"I can not…" He groped for the right word. "…tell. All things are strange. My land has trees and hills and animals. Here are things my nose and ears and eyes can not recognize."

Gregg Whitney was seeking frantically to catch his daughter's eye in an effort to have her drop the subject. He felt it was too soon to lead Avar—Adam—into a discussion of this kind. A few weeks more, after the cave man had become accustomed to mingling with modern man, would enable him to talk about himself freely and without discomfort.

But Joan Whitney was too intent on satisfying her curiosity to heed signals to change the subject. She said, "Where is your country, Adam? How did you get up in the Hollywood hills with a spear wound in your back?"

Her father, realizing the only way to halt her flow of questions was by a verbal interruption, spoke before Adam was able to answer.

"I think," he said quietly, "we had better wait until Adam knows us better before giving him the third degree."

The cave man was frowning over his attempt to follow the conversation. He said, "Do you not want me to talk?"

There was an awkward silence. Adam looked from one to another of the strangely embarrassed faces. "Is it bad—wrong—for me to talk about myself?"

"Not wrong, Adam," Professor Thoretsen said gently. "But perhaps you would rather wait until you know our language better."

The Cro-Magnard spent almost a minute extracting the meaning from the linguist's words, while the rest of the diners waited uncomfortably.

Finally he said, "I would like to try. How can I speak as you unless I talk many times?" His gaze returned to Joan's burning cheeks. "In my country," he said, "there was much talk about a strange place where no man should go. I wanted to see what was there, so I made my way across a wide land of sand where there was no water and no food. Many suns—days?—passed before I could reach the other side and I almost died. Then I reached water and near it I found Kuo eating the flesh was left of Boad to make me strong again."

Interest was strong enough now that the listeners forgot their reluctance to question Adam. Lauren, her lips parted slightly in complete fascination, said, "Who were Kuo and Boad, Adam?"

The man of the cave smiled. It was the first time any of those present had seen him smile, other than Thoretsen, and it made him suddenly more human and less the animal as his usual air of somber reserve disappeared momentarily.

"Emil showed me—pic-tures of many animals," he said in his bell-like voice. "Among them was Kuo. You call him lion. Boad is a deer."

"You killed a lion?" Perry Siddons said, disbelief evident in his voice. "You mean they have guns in your land?"

"Guns?" Adam looked blank, his eyes going to Emil Thoretsen for help with this unfamiliar word.

"I'm afraid," the professor explained to the others, "that weapons—at least modern ones—are something I left out of Adam's lessons. I assure you, Perry, Adam has never seen any weapon more complex than a bow and arrow. A stone knife was the only weapon he carried when he entered the strange land he mentioned."

PERRY SIDDONS stared at the linguist in open scorn. "Now wait a minute. You're not going to tell us a man can kill a lion with nothing but a hunk of flint, are you?"

"Aren't you forgetting, Perry," interposed Gregg Whitney, "that Adam, here, is not a 'man' in the sense you're using the word. 'Superman' comes a great deal closer to being correct, I'd say."

Joan, her blue eyes sparkling, said, "I think it'd be better if we'd stop interrupting. Please go on Adam."

In simple words, hesitating now and then for the correct phrase—and not always finding it—Adam Newstone told of his adventures on the day he entered a new and bewildering world. When he finished there was an awed silence as the two girls and Perry Siddons stared in frank bewilderment at each other and at the Cro-Magnard.

Gregg Whitney said, "I think I know what you're thinking. Just who is Adam Newstone and what and where was this abyss he fell into. So if all of you will listen I'll try to explain what we— Professor Rhyskind, Cabot, Thoretsen and I—believe to be the truth. This is something we have told no one before—not even Adam himself—and I'm going to ask all of you to keep our theory completely confidential. Will you promise me that?"

His daughters and Perry Siddons agreed, whereupon he gave them the entire story exactly as the professors and he had pieced it together. As he talked he watched the faces of his audience, noting how incredulity gave way to outright disbelief, only to be displaced by fascinated wonder.

"And that is why," he said in conclusion, "we gave Avar the name of Adam Newstone—Adam, because he truly is the world's first man (or one of them, certainly.), and Newstone for the Age he belongs to."

"It's the most romantic thing I've ever heard in my life," declared Joan Whitney; and the expression in her eyes as she looked at the calm-faced cave lord brought a sudden rush of anger to the mind of Perry Siddons.

One of the household maids entered the dining room. "Excuse me, Miss Lauren, but you're wanted on the phone."

Lauren left the table and went slowly down the hall, her mind whirling from the theory her father had given as an explanation for Adam's arrival in California. She was aware of the nagging belief that her father and his friends were victims of some hoax, although if such a prehistoric ancestor should bridge the lap of twenty thousand years he must resemble, physically at least, the man called Adam Newstone.

She was aware that in some nebulous way her own attitude toward him was beginning to change. His act of kissing her so abruptly three months before was now easily explained as the uninhibited behavior of someone unfamiliar with modern convention. With this ready answer to his conduct, he became a figure cloaked in romance, someone to stir the imagination. His tremendous strength, perfect physical development and masculine beauty of face, plus his utter simplicity of manner and speech, combined to make him the embodiment of the perfect male...

GENE CAMERON'S voice came to her over the wire. "It's too nice a day to hate anyone, Lauren. Am I forgiven for what happened last night?"

Her hand tightened on the receiver. "I understand you ran across my sister and her fiancé last night, Gene."

"Why yes," he said readily. "Bought them a drink, in fact. Charming couple."

"I understand you asked to see her again."

"Certainly. Why not? I didn't notice an engagement ring anywhere about her."

She let her breath out slowly. "I'm going to ask you not to see her, Gene."

"I'd much rather see you, Lauren."

"We've been over that. The answer is still no." Despite her effort at control her voice began to rise. "Leave us alone Gene—all of us. I won't stand for you hanging around Joan."

His voice held just the right amount of regret. "I'm sorry you feel that way about it, Lauren. But I do reserve the right to pick my friends. Your sister is of age, I believe, so I'm sure she's at liberty to choose her friends."

"Very well, Mr. Cameron," she said coldly. "In that case I've no choice but to tell my father exactly what kind of person you are and what you're up to. I'm sure he's influential enough to do something about this."

His light laugh seemed genuine enough. "I swing a little weight myself, darling, and I can play pretty nasty too, if I have to. If you force me to play ace, you'll find it has the picture of a Queen on it. 'Bye now."

A click against her ear told her he had replaced his receiver. For a long moment she stood there staring at the instrument, then slowly returned it to its cradle.

What had he meant by "my ace...has the picture of a Queen on it?" There was a masked threat in that phrase; that was clear enough. But the mask was too perfect; she was unable to connect the remark to anything that had happened during their days and evenings together.

She was conscious of being very tired and her head was beginning to throb dully. Two aspirins and a cool shower seemed indicated. Not enough sleep last night, she told herself resolutely.

But as she went up the stairs to her room she knew that fear was beginning to lay its hold on her—fear germinated by Gene Cameron's remarks on the telephone...

AVAR, warrior of the tribe of Kosad, strolled with slow grace about the grounds of Gregg Whitney's estate. A week had passed since Emil and Whitney had returned him here from the mountain retreat where he had spent three moons learning the customs and speech of the strange beings he had been plunged among.

It had been a lonely week—broken only by long talks with Gregg Whitney, who asked over and over hundreds of questions about Avar's country and the customs of its people. Emil had left the same day they had returned from the mountains, and the two girls were around only at breakfast—if then.

He was aware of a vague regret at not seeing more of the one whose hair was like the inner surface of freshly peeled bark. Lau-ren, they called her—the one whose lips his had sought that first day when this world was new and frightening to him. She had stood there beside his couch of strange skins and looked down at him, her eyes mirroring hatred and fear and contempt—a Challenge he had met with a savage kiss—the first he had given any she.

He caught himself wishing she would look at him as that other she, the one called Joan, had—with open admiration not unmixed with awe. She was very lovely also, but she did not arouse within him the desire to crush her in his arms, to smother her upturned face with kisses. Lau-ren did that to him; she stirred within him emotions as new and disturbing as the incomprehensible world he had entered.

The odd skins Gregg Whit-ney had urged him into using as coverings for his body and feet irked him and he longed to throw them aside and let Ota's warm rays find his naked flesh. But both Whit-ney and Emil had told him over and over that men of this world must hide their bodies from the eyes of their fellow beings. From what he had seen of most of them, the reason was clear enough for such a custom—men either frail as shes or lumpy and distorted with fat like Grosar, the hippopotamus. He longed to be out of this complex world—to return to steaming jungles and grassy plains and the caves of Kosad. To stalk his food, kill with the strength and cunning that were his birthrights, devour flesh raw and bleeding and still warm with life.

But Avar was a realist. While he did not understand in the slightest the truth behind his arrival in this insane world, he knew he could never hope to return to his own land. He could best serve himself, therefore, by adopting this new way of life, by becoming indistinguishable from those around him. When he reached that level, he would take the fair-haired Lau-ren for his mate and travel to a place Emil had told him about—a place called Afri-ca—where everything was much the same as he was accustomed to. Until that time he would hide his contempt of these chattering, pale-skinned people as best he could, learning from them the things that might prove of value and disregarding the rest.

He was moving silently along a flagstone path leading to the stables, attracted by the scent of the horses and seeking them out as a welcome change from humans. As he rounded a corner of the long low building he came face to face with Lauren Whitney, who had returned a few moments before from a canter through the hills.

She smiled at him tremulously, her heart beginning to pound for no reason she could name. He inclined his head with a grave courtesy that was an inherent part of him.

She said, "Hello, Avar. Isn't it a beautiful morning?"

His glowing eyes met hers. "You call me Avar. All others call me Adam. Why do you not do the same?"

"Oh, I don't know, really." With what amounted to almost a physical effort she tore her eyes from his unblinking stare. "Avar seems to fit you better for some reason. You don't mind, do you?"

"I want you to call me Avar. It is my name." The way he said this told her subtly that it did not matter what others called him.

SHE was aware of being suddenly self-conscious of his nearness. He seemed to loom over her, to fill the horizon, leaving her tiny and alone. How silly, she thought. I have seen men bigger than he without being affected this way.

He said, "I do not understand. There is the scent of an animal about you—the same scent I smell about this house."

111

Color touched her cheeks. "What an awful thing to say, Avar. You must never tell a woman she sm—" She laughed then—a long musical laugh. "Of course. By 'house' you mean the stable, don't you? I've been riding and I suppose I do seem a little— horsey, I suppose you'd call it. Sounds like baby talk…"

She realized she was babbling like a schoolgirl and sobered quickly. "Haven't you ever ridden, Avar?"

"Ridden?" he repeated blankly. "That means to go about in an automobile? Many times. I can drive an auto-mobile."

She smiled understandingly. "I suppose that's what comes of letting a professor teach you the language. You sound a little stilted, Avar, when you say automobile. Most people call them cars.

"No," she continued. "I mean haven't you ever ridden a horse?" She saw he did not have the slightest idea of what she was talking about. "Come along with me then. I'll have Sam saddle mounts for both of us and show you what it's like."

He accompanied her into the shadowy depths of the stable, his eyes, nose and ears searching out and analyzing everything about the place while Lauren Whitney gave instructions to the groom.

While they were waiting the girl watched the cave man from the corners of her eyes. He was wearing trousers, shirt and a light green sweater—all of them to his size and part of the extensive wardrobe Gregg Whitney had ordered after two tailors had arrive that first day to take Avar's measurements. He wore clothing much more gracefully than at first—probably because his first civilized garments had been so ill fitting—but even with that they seemed faintly out of place on his magnificent frame. His hair was freshly clipped and shaped to his head—this time by an expert—and, she admitted to herself, he was the most handsome and compelling man she had ever encountered.

The groom, a wiry ex-jockey, brought out the two horses and watched with bright-eyed interest as Lauren Whitney gave instructions on mounting to the young giant.

Avar's mount was a rangy sorrel gelding, recently acquired by the Whitney estate, and still young and inexperienced enough to have a mind of its own. Lauren had instructed it to be saddled for

Avar's use only because none of the other animals seemed worthy of his use.

She was pointing out the stirrup and explaining its purpose when Avar placed a hand about the pommel and vaulted into the saddle with an effortless agility that left Lauren Whitney breathless.

Even the gelding seemed startled by the move for it reared high, its shrill whinny rising on the still air.

The groom leaped forward to calm the animal, but the reins were in Avar's fist and he brought the horse down and quiet instantly. Lauren gave a relieved gasp. "I thought you'd never ridden. Don't you know it's wicked to lie?"

He smiled down at her gravely and made no reply. She swung into the saddle of her mare and they set off, side by side, toward a bridle path among the hills.

She noticed the easy way he sat his mount, how its every movement fitted in with the motions of his perfect body. Experienced horseman could not have improved on the manner he rode and she had one more insight into the incredible muscular coordination of this man.

Perversely, she sought to make him appear to disadvantage even momentarily. She sent the mare into a trot, then a gallop, watching for some sign of awkwardness, if not actual distress, in her companion. To no avail; he rode as he walked, with an easy controlled grace that made her own riding clumsy and inept by comparison.

AN HOUR later they were deep within the hills, far from all signs of civilization. To Avar it was like being born again—how he gloried in this free untrammeled vista of wilderness. He drew great draughts of air into his lungs, his chest swelling until Lauren felt her eyes widen in awed tribute. The powerful muscles rippled along his mighty arms and across his broad back like steel cables and his head lifted to the sun causing other muscles to move under the clear skin of his neck and jaws.

At last Lauren pulled up under the wide branches of a tree and dismounted. "I need a breather," she laughed, brushing some of the dust from her jodhpurs. "And *I* was the one who was going to teach *you* how to ride."

Avar swung lightly to earth and tied the reins of both mounts to a branch. At her suggestion they sat down side by side, leaning their backs against the tree's broad bole. Lauren took cigarettes from a pocket of her light gabardine blouse and unthinkingly held them out to him. To her surprise he accepted one, took the matches from her fingers and lit, first hers then his.

"Don't tell me Emil Thoretsen taught you how to smoke?"

He shrugged, smiling a little at her expression. "I learned much from pic-tures in books and magazines at the lodge. Many of the pic-tures showed men and women doing this. I asked Emil about it. He bought cigar-ettes at the store and showed me what to do with them. I do not like them much."

Her musical laugh rang out. "You *are* an amazing person, Avar."

He said nothing, only took a deep drag at the cigarette, coughing slightly as he expelled the smoke. His arm brushed against hers by accident at that moment and she sobered instantly as her heart seemed to swell with an unfamiliar exhilaration...

"Tell me, Avar," she said suddenly, "are you happy here?"

He looked at her blankly. "Happy? What is that?"

"Why...happy. You know, satisfied—ah—at peace. Contented. Would you like to stay here?"

The glow in his eyes seemed to increase. "Here?"

His meaning was unmistakable, and she hastened to correct his impression. "I don't mean here—under this tree. I mean, here in California, with us, away from your own land."

He shook his head briefly. "Some of it is—nice. Not all. I do not like so many people and houses and automobiles. But I like you and Emil and Whit-ney and Joan and Perry. He does not like me."

She was puzzled by his last sentence. "Who? Who doesn't like you, Avar?"

"Perry."

"You must try to understand him, Avar. He thinks you—well, he is afraid—" She found herself groping for words. "Joan admires you very much because you are a—a romantic person. Because of how you came to our world, I mean. And Perry is afraid you might simply take her away from him."

"I do not want her," Avar said. "I want you."

He said those last three words without emphasis or innuendo, and Lauren did not get their full impact for several seconds. She was about to make some observation of her own when the realization of what he had said struck her with full force and she felt her jaw sag with the shock, even as her heart set up a sudden pounding.

"You—I—you…" She stopped there, searching frantically for the right words. He was looking out over the valley below, his hands resting lightly on his bent knees. How handsome he is! her mind observed. He is a savage—hardly more than an animal! her cultural training cried out. "You must not—ah—want me, Avar. You must not say that or think it."

Those flaming eyes came slowly to meet hers. "Why?"

She bit her lip, suddenly angered by the pounding of her heart, by the stirring of some newly aroused emotion deep within her. "Because it is *wrong*. Because we are different. Because I do not want you—in the way you mean."

FOR a long moment he stared deep within her eyes without speaking. Then a faint smile—so faint and so fleeting it might have been no more than a product of her imagination—touched his lips. "Your eyes are like those of Boad, the deer, when she sees a new leader has taken over the herd. I do not want you to be afraid of me, Lau-ren."

"I'm not afraid of you!" she blazed. "I'm not afraid of anyone."

He shrugged. "I am glad you are not afraid of me. But I think you fear someone. When I returned to your home with Emil and Whit-ney a few suns ago and you came out to meet us, I saw your eyes. There was fear in them then."

She looked away from him, thinking there could hardly have been anything else in her eyes after learning Gene Cameron had decided to hit back at her through Joan. She said, "You're wrong, of course. I'm afraid there's a lot left for you to learn about the people of today, Avar."

He smiled his slow, grave smile. "I am learning people never change inside themselves. They learn to talk different, to do many wonderful things, to hide their bodies under strange skins. But underneath all that the people of your world are the same as the males and she of Kosad's tribe."

She sighed. "Perhaps you are right, Avar…" She glanced at the sun's position. "Shall we go back? It's getting along toward noon."

"Of course." He rose and extended his hand, helping her to her feet.

He was freeing the horses' reins from their place about the branch, when he stopped suddenly and turned his face to the faint breeze, his nostrils quivering slightly.

Lauren, surprised by his abrupt immobility, glanced at him inquiringly. "What is it, Avar?"

"Loka."

"What?"

"Loka." His eyes were blazing in a way she had never seen before but his face was as calmly expressionless as usual. "You know him as the panther."

"Panther? You mean a *panther*—a real one?"

"Yes. There is one near us."

"Oh now, come, Avar. This is Southern California, not Africa. We don't have any panthers—unless you go to a zoo or a circus. What makes you think a thing like that?"

"Tia, the wind, brought me his scent."

"You mean you *smell* a panther?"

"Yes."

She reached out and patted one of his arms as though he were some child who had daydreamed up some ogre. "You're imagining it, Avar. Honestly there hasn't been a panther in this neck of the woods for thousands of years, probably." She reached for the saddle of her mare. "Help me up. We must be getting home."

He shrugged, smiling. "My nose has never lied to me, Lau-ren. Without it I would have died long ago under the claws and teeth of

Kua, or Cita, or Loka. That is why I say Loka is near us now. But you need not be afraid; I know him and his ways."

He swung lightly into his saddle and urged the gelding along the path in the same direction they had come. Lauren, in the act of turning the mare toward the Whitney estate, called to him.

"Not that way, Avar. We don't want to end up in Glendale or Burbank."

He drew up and looked back at her. "It would be wise to move upwind, then circle back and enter the trail from below."

"But why?"

"I have told you. Loka is abroad."

It was sheer nonsense, of course, and she knew it. He was like a child with some fantastic, but no less fixed, idea—and he must be handled like a child.

"You're not afraid of a panther, are you, Avar?"

He looked at her from unblinking eyes, without expression. "No. I respect Loka. Respect is not fear."

"Then let us go directly back to the house—even though we have to ride downwind. If the panther attacks us you will not let him get me, will you?"

THOSE burning eyes seemed to be looking into her mind, searching out the true meaning behind her words. He said, "You do not believe Loka is here." It was more statement than accusation. "You are wrong. But if you want to risk the claws and fangs of Loka, I will go with you."

She felt a pang of shame, as though a child had caught her in a lie. But her point had been won, which was the important thing.

The horses moved at a slow canter along the winding trail. Avar, ears and eyes alert, rode a half-length behind the girl's mare. There were few trees in the vicinity and the grass was hardly deep enough for an animal the size of Loka to remain concealed.

"You see?" Lauren said lightly, as they moved around the bend in a narrow defile between steep banks. "No panthers. Your nose has been playing tricks on you, Avar; blame a change in environment for that."

The Cro-Magnard said nothing. Less than a hundred yards ahead the defile ended, giving place to open ground. He would feel better when they reached that point. His sensitive nostrils could detect no further trace of Loka since the wind was at his back, but some sixth sense—the product of years among constant dangers of the jungle—warned him of imminent peril.

This was the place for it, too. The banks on either side of the pass overhung the riders' path, their edges less than six feet above Avar's head. Loka could spring down on either of them without warning.

The danger was nearly past now—open ground being less than twenty yards ahead. Avar's eyes left the edges of the banks momentarily, measuring the distance they must yet traverse.

And in that instant a tawny-brown shape streaked silently through the air directly toward Lauren Whitney's back from above.

Avar, long accustomed to think and act simultaneously, brought his open palm down on the mare's flank during the split second in which he caught the flicker of movement from overhead. As a result the horse reared suddenly under the blow, and the raking talons aimed at Lauren's shoulders struck her mount across the neck and the weight of the giant cat came down inches ahead of the saddle pommel.

The mare screamed like a woman and reared even higher, throwing both cat and girl to the ground. The former whirled up even as it fell and slashed out at its dazed and helpless prey.

Those needle-sharp talons did not reach their goal. Avar was out of his saddle before Lauren's body struck the ground—out of it and interposing a brawny shoulder and forearm between her soft flesh and the flailing claws.

Wool and linen parted and an angry rush of blood poured from three long deep furrows in the nut-brown flesh beneath.

With a growl of pain and anger more bestial than the beast's, Avar lashed out with a clenched fist, striking the animal alongside the head and knocking it, spitting and snarling, a full ten feet through the air. Before it could regain balance he leaped forward, closed steel-fingered hands about the throat and one back leg, swung the threshing body high above his head, then brought it down with all his strength across a bent knee.

Ribs and spine splintered with a horrible crackling sound, one last scream of agony was torn from the animal's throat…and Avar dropped the lifeless form into the dust of the trail.

"Avar! Avar!"

He turned, just as a flying figure raced toward him and plunged into his instinctive embrace. Soft arms slipped about his neck, a lithe form pressed close to his and blue eyes swam before him from the depths of welling tears of relief and thanksgiving—and of another emotion unmistakable and older than life itself.

Slowly Avar, the Cro-Magnard, bent his head as two trembling warm lips lifted to meet his own. Time and the world fused and disappeared, leaving a man and woman alone in a universe of their own making…

IT WAS Lauren who was the first to draw away. Her cheeks were burning, her fingers, as she lifted them to pat her hair into place in an age-old gesture, were trembling uncontrollably. But her smile was tender and filled with meaning and the light in her eyes was unmistakable still.

"Oh-h-h," she gasped. "Avar, Avar." The name on her lips was a caress. "What an incredibly wonderful person you are. No one else in the world could have saved my life."

He said nothing, watching her steadily with that somber air of reserve that was so much a part of him.

"Well, I've learned one thing anyway," she declared briskly. "From now on I'm through doubting anything you say. Your panther turned out to be a mountain lion but that's close enough for me." She shivered abruptly. "Goodness, that was close. There hasn't been a cougar in these hills for I don't know how long."

Avar said, "Our horses have run away. It seems we'll have to walk home."

She laughed almost hysterically. "It'll be the first ride with a man I've walked home from—and the man is walking *with* me. That should make headlines."

The laugh died suddenly as for the first time she noticed the blood-soaked remnants of cloth covering his left arm and shoulder.

"You're hurt, Avar…" She came close to him and gently stripped back the ripped material of sweater and shirt. "You've got to get to a doctor right away!"

"They are scratches," the cave lord said indifferently.

"Scratches or not, they need attention. Let's start back. I doubt if the horses have gone far. They've been trained to stop immediately if the rider is unseated."

They walked side by side along the winding trail, saying nothing, each intent on his or her thoughts. Avar's principal reaction to what had happened was a deep puzzlement. Judging from what he had seen in this woman's eyes and felt in the touch of her lips she loved him. Among the people of Kosad a man wasted no time in taking the woman who loved him. But he was far from the caves of his tribe and among people entirely different from any he had known before. Was this woman his, now that she had so declared herself? Could he take her from the "cave" of her father and live with her in a "cave" of his own choice? Or was there some custom he must observe before doing that?

And then sudden doubt assailed him. Perhaps Lau-ren's kisses, the light in her eyes, were the way women of this world showed their gratitude. Perhaps she did not love him at all. Had she not said only a little earlier that she did not "want" him? How could saving her from Loka's teeth and claws change her *that* much?

As for Lauren Whitney, her thoughts were a chaotic whirl of elation, happiness, doubt and outright dread. She knew as well as she knew her own name that at last she had found love—love that was complete and overwhelming and as permanent as the hills about her. But love meant marriage and marriage meant living with a man day after day for as long as either of them lived. Could she live like that with a man born twenty thousand years ago? Could they have a normal life together, make friends, associate with people of her own class and temperament? Could she introduce to them as her husband a man who possessed the instincts and outlook of a jungle beast? At a party—or a bar—a drunken insult aimed at Avar or her, would result in a broken neck with lightning-like suddenness.

And her father. What would be his reaction should she go to him and confess her love for the cave man? He liked Avar; she knew that. But did that liking go far enough to accept him cordially as a son-in-law?

HALF a mile further on they came upon the two horses grazing contentedly at the grasses bordering the trail. Avar silently helped her into the saddle and swung agilely onto the gelding. She smiled at him, her lips seeming to her strangely stiff, and said, "Thank you," in a voice so formal and polite she hardly recognized it as her own. Avar acknowledged both gestures the way he did almost anything since the day he had come back to consciousness in the Whitney guestroom: silently and distantly, with eyes that seemed to look through and beyond the people about him.

They galloped their mounts most of the way, arriving at the Whitney stables an hour later. Joan Whitney, very lovely in shorts and a light sweater and looking much less than her eighteen years, was coming down the outer steps, with Perry Siddons bulking large in gray flannels beside her. Both were carrying tennis rackets.

Joan waved to them as they turned the corner. "Hi, you two! We've been looking all over…" Her voice trailed off and her eyes grew round as she caught sight of the blood-stained shreds of sweater and shirt. "What happened to *you*, Adam?"

"It is nothing," the cave man said evasively.

Lauren Whitney gave an unlady-like snort. "*Nothing*, he says! You should have been there to see this '*nothing*.' We were riding in the hills and a mountain lion attacked me. Avar killed it with his bare hands—picked it up and broke its back across his knee the way Perry, here, would break a piece of—of egg crate!"

They stared at him open-mouthed. Joan said, "Why, my gosh, a mountain lion could *kill* people." There was a worshipping light in her eyes.

Perry Siddons, seeing that light, felt once again the stirrings of hatred for this man from the past. He said, "You sure it was a mountain lion, Lauren? There hasn't been one around these hills for years that I know of."

She turned on him. "Don't be stupid. I can tell a cougar when I see one. You'll be telling me a house cat put those rips in his arm the next thing I know."

The young man was startled by the open vehemence behind her words. "Well, no, of course not," he floundered. "I didn't mean…well, it could've been a wildcat or something like—"

Joan said with deadly calm, "You killed any wildcats with your hands lately, Perry?"

He looked appealingly from one girl to the other. "Heck, I'm not trying to run the guy down. I'll admit hardly anyone could kill even a wildcat that way." A dull anger began to show in his face. "Layoff, will you? I'll admit he could break an elephant in two if that'll make you feel any better."

In the moment of uncomfortable silence that then followed, a white-aproned maid stepped quietly out onto the wide wooden porch. "Miss Lauren," she called. "You're wanted on the telephone."

The girl turned, a slight look of relief on her face, obviously welcoming the interruption. "All right, Anna. Who is it, do you know?"

"A gentleman. A Mr. Cameron, I think he said his name was."

Joan said involuntarily, "Gene? I thought—"

Perry Siddons said, "That's the guy we met at the Mocambo last week."

Lauren said, "If you'll excuse me, please," her voice shaking a little.

Avar said nothing. He was watching Lauren Whitney's eyes, seeing the fear that rose in them, aware of her mounting panic. Then she was gone, running quickly up the steps and disappearing into the house.

"…must know him pretty well, Joan, to call him by his first name that way."

"Are you going to start that stuff again, Perry Siddons?"

"That's no answer. I'll bet you've been out with him—that's where you were those two nights when I—"

"Will you *stop* it? I'm not *married* to you, you know."

Avar left them to their bickering and went thoughtfully up the steps. There was a man named Gene Cameron and Lau-ren was afraid of him. She belonged to Avar now; her eyes and her lips had told him so only an hour before. It was not right that she should be afraid. He must put a stop to it.

CHAPTER NINE

"I MUST see you, Lauren. Something's come up that you should know about."

"You're wasting your time, Gene. There's nothing you could say that would interest me."

He said, "Look. Is there any chance of our being overheard? I mean, from an extension or something like that?"

There was an unmistakable urgency in his voice, a strained tenseness that startled her. "There are extensions, yes. But I could tell if another receiver was up. Why?"

"It's about your sister."

"Joan?" She put out a hand blindly and caught the edge of the library desk, aware of a sharp sinking feeling within her. "I don't understand. I saw her just a minute ago. There's nothing wrong with her."

"This isn't something that shows on her," Cameron said grimly. "Listen, Lauren, come over to my place in Westwood right away. I've something I'm going to have to show you whether I want to or not. I've been put in the middle on a very unpleasant kind of business and I don't like it at all. But because I think the world of you and your sister, I'm going to see it through."

It was a trick of some kind. It had to be. Joan couldn't have gotten into any unsavory scrapes such as he was hinting about. Yes, it was a trick and she would have nothing to do with him. Going to his place would be playing right into his hands.

But what if he *was* telling the truth? Joan was past eighteen, she was impetuous, stubborn, resentful of advice…

"I'll be there," she said suddenly. "But it will have to be this evening some time. I've promised father I'd go with him to a party my aunt's giving in Santa Monica this afternoon. I'll call you."

"Then you'd better make it after nine o'clock. I'll be tied up from 4:30 until nine."

She hesitated, fearful again of some trick; and in the moment of silence he said, "Unless you'd rather wait until tomorrow."

She couldn't wait that long. She had to know what was threatening Joan; there would be no rest, no peace of mind for her until then.

She said, "Around nine-thirty. I—I'll leave a note here telling where I am in case somebody wants to get in touch with me around that time."

He said dryly, "Sure. Do that. I might try to kidnap you."

She bit her lip. She had meant the words as a warning, but it was like him to let her know he understood. "Goodbye, Gene."

"'Bye."

She replaced the receiver with fingers that shook a little. Should she go straight to Joan and demand to know what she had been up to that could cause Gene Cameron to make such statements over the phone? Lauren decided against that immediately. Joan would admit nothing, if for no other reason than pride, and it would be better to know some facts before forcing the issue with the younger girl.

She turned to leave...and saw Avar standing in the open doorway watching her with steady eyes.

"You startled me," she said sternly. "You're like a big cat, Avar, the way you walk around without the slightest sound. And you really shouldn't listen when people are talking on the telephone. If we're going to make you into a man of today—"

"Is he the man you are afraid of?"

She fell back a step while the color slowly drained from her face. Not because of his words that told he had overheard her conversation, but because there was something terrible in his eyes and the set of his lips.

"What *are* you talking about, Avar? I'm not afraid of anyone."

His eyes met hers…and she was the one to look away. "That is not true," he said quietly. "I did not think you would lie to me."

"Avar, *my dear*." She crossed the room quickly and put her hands against his arms. "It isn't that I want to lie to you. It's simply something you can do nothing about. I'm not in any danger; this isn't a matter of a lion or tiger threatening me. Someone else is in trouble, I think, and it's up to me to get her out of it."

"Cameron is making this trouble?"

"I'm not sure. I don't think so." She shook her head briefly as though to clear it. "Please, Avar. I know you want to help me, but honestly this is something you mustn't mix in." Bitterness crept into her voice. "This is one of these civilized matters, probably, filled with deceit and lies too complex for a primitive, unspoiled mind to unravel."

Nothing in his calm, almost detached expression showed what he was thinking. Lauren wet her lips nervously and changed the subject.

"We must get that arm of yours fixed up. I'll get Doctor Blanchard." She went back to the telephone and put through the call…

"He'll be right over," she told Avar after replacing the receiver. "He's anxious to see you again, he says; regards you as his favorite patient. Meanwhile, I'm to wash those gashes and put a bandage over them."

IT WAS late afternoon when Avar awakened. He lay motionless for a little while, looking at the sun on the bushes and lawn outside his window and listening to the quiet sounds of an early autumn day.

His arm ached dully where Doctor Blanchard had stitched up the furrows left by Loka's claws. There was a bandage wrapped tightly about his forearm and it smelled pleasantly of medication.

He smiled to himself. How strange were the people of this world. Three tiny scratches and a wise man must come with magic waters and tools to wash them and sew them up and put a long needle into him to prevent something called "tetanus," a strange kind of beast too small to be seen but which the wise man had insisted, was more deadly than Kuo, the lion!

After a while he left the bed and dressed, taking fresh linen and one of the lightweight suits made to his order by a tailor who had spent most of one afternoon exclaiming over their measurements. He spent almost fifteen minutes forcing his hair into place the way Emil had taught him. He debated over putting on a tie, deciding against it finally because he could not become accustomed to a binding feeling about his neck.

He was ready to leave the room now, but for several minutes he stood at the open door in a listening attitude. His keen ears picked up an irregular clumping sound, which he instantly identified as the footsteps of Anna, the maid, somewhere on the floor above.

Probably no one around but the servants. He recalled hearing Lauren say that she was accompanying her father somewhere for the afternoon. Joan and Perry were undoubtedly out somewhere, since neither spent much time indoors.

He went down the hall and up the wide stairs to the second floor without encountering anybody. The upper corridor was deserted, although he could hear the sound of a vacuum sweeper behind the partially opened door of Gregg Whitney's room.

On soundless feet he approached the door to Lauren's room. It was closed but not locked. An instant later he was within, the door shut behind him.

The faint aroma that belonged to her alone seemed everywhere. It was a room furnished and decorated in keeping with the kind of woman she was. The furniture was modern, simple and excellent, dainty without being kittenish. A tailored spread of yellow monks-cloth on the full size bed matched the drapes at the room's two wide windows. The rug was a figureless rose broadloom extending to the baseboards. Restful, cool and restrained works to fit Lauren herself.

He went directly to a chest of drawers along one wall, opened the first and began an unhurried and systematic search of its contents, looking only for one thing. One by one he went through the drawers, leaving each in perfect order before going to the next. In none of them did he find the object he was seeking.

The drawers of a small desk near one window yielded a lightweight Hermes typewriter, a supply of letterheads and envelopes, rubber bands, paper clips, and a small green metal box containing stamps and sixty-eight dollars in bills. Unhesitatingly Avar slipped the money into his trouser pocket and replaced the box.

While he was closing the last drawer of the desk, he froze into statuesque immobility, head lifted in a listening attitude. The hum of the vacuum sweeper from down the hall had ceased. A door banged shut a moment later and the plodding steps of Anna sounded on the hall runner, coming in his direction.

The steps ceased outside Lauren Whitney's door, and in that instant Avar was across the room and stepping into one section of the closet where a row of dresses were hanging. Quickly and in complete silence he slid the panel door closed, plunging the recess into almost total darkness.

Feet thumped on the carpeting past the closed panel, metal clicked against metal and the vacuum sweeper began to purr again...a sound as lonely and depressing as wind across a desert.

SUDDENLY the closet door slid halfway open, leaving Avar shielded only by the row of dresses touching his body. A beefy arm, holding a formal dress on a hanger, was thrust into the opening and placed its burden with the others on the long pole inches from where Avar was crouched. A single downward glance would have revealed Avar's trousered legs.

But evidently Anna was too occupied for unnecessary glances. The door slid shut again and the hum of the sweeper went on for another five minutes. Then it ceased altogether, followed by the sound of fading footsteps and the outer door clicked shut.

Avar waited until he caught the click of another door further along the hall before he came out of hiding. His sharp eyes caught sight of a cleverly concealed door in a modern nightstand beside the bed, and a moment's experimentation enabled him to open it. Inside were an ivory telephone, an indexed pad with a white plastic cover and a small leather bound address book.

The pad came first into his powerful hands. It operated by moving a sliding metal arrow along its right edge to the selected letter of the alphabet, then by pressing a button set in the base of the pad the cover flew up under the impetus of a hidden spring.

It took several minutes for Avar to solve the mechanism's secret, but finally it opened to the letter C. While his ability to read was necessarily sketchy, having progressed little beyond the child's primer stage, he was able to make out the name he sought. Fortunately all entries were printed instead of written; script would have defeated him completely.

Cameron, Gene
ARizona 67-7700

To Avar the entry was as meaningless as Egyptian hieroglyphics to an Eskimo. He returned the pad to the drawer and picked up the address book.

Here there were many names, grouped alphabetically. Avar's experience was too limited to take advantage of short cuts however; he started with the first page and scanned every name until he reached the C's. Here again appeared the name he sought.

Cameron, Gene
5412 Selby Avenue
Westwood
ARizona 67-7700

The cave man grunted in satisfaction. These tiny markings were the key to locating Gene Cameron—just as among all the trees of the jungle, the shape of leaves of one of them would lead to edible fruit. He did not have the slightest conception of where Selby Avenue, Westwood, was; but somewhere where many people moved about the stone trails below the hills he would find a male or a she who could direct him.

The address book went into his coat pocket, he closed the night-table drawer, descended the stairs quickly and went outside.

He found Luke washing a gray-blue Buick convertible, its top down, in front of the six-car garage.

"G'd mornin', Mr. Newstone," Luke said, his voice high-pitched with palpably false heartiness. He had never forgotten the day he had helped carry this young giant, wearing nothing but a hunk of animal skin about his loins, into the Whitney home. No one had ever given him an explanation to account for the man or his strange manner of dress; only a warning by Gregg Whitney that he was not to discuss the matter with anyone. As a result Luke had built up his own explanation—that Adam Newstone was a mental case of some dangerous kind, and that the Whitney's were taking care of him only because he was distantly related to them. The young man's cat-like movements, his bulging muscles and strong white teeth, the blazing yellow-gray light in his oddly shaped eyes— all these were characteristics that marked him as different from the men Luke knew, and therein lay the danger.

"Who," said Avar, coming directly to the point, "owns this auto-mobile?"

LUKE gave him a sidelong glance and continued playing a stream from the hose against one of the car's rear wheels. "This here Buick belongs to Miss Lauren."

"Is it ready to—ride?"

The gardener-chauffeur's jaw slipped a little. "Ready to *ride?* You mean will it go? Listen, Mr. Newstone, any car I take care of is *always* ready."

"Good. I will take it." And careless of the water spraying the cement near his feet, Avar went up to the Buick and put a hand on the ledge of one door.

"Well now, just a minute, Mr. Newstone." Luke twisted the hose nozzle to cut off the water. "I don't know as you'd better. Miss Lauren's mighty fussy…"

His voice trailed off as Avar's eyes met his. "I will take it," the Cro-Magnard said again. With a lithe bound he cleared the top of the closed door and slid behind the wheel. A key was in the ignition; he turned it as Thoretsen had taught him to do and started the motor.

"What'll I tell Miss Lauren?" shouted Luke, as the car began to move.

Avar ignored the question as he would have ignored the chattering of little Sima, the monkey. He swung the convertible around in a tight circle instead of attempting to back it into position on the driveway—a maneuver that flattened a row of bushes bordering the areaway and narrowly missing Luke himself. A moment later the Buick was flashing along the private road toward the main highway.

Amid screeching tires and a shower of gravel Avar made the turn at the end of the drive, narrowly avoiding the white-haired woman in a station wagon, and roared on toward Hollywood.

There was no clear-cut line of action in his mind. He knew only that the girl he loved was afraid, and that a man named Gene Cameron was in some way a part of that fear. His life had taught him nothing of caution or deviousness in handling a problem—an obstacle must be met head on and blasted out of the way. He wasted no time devising a plan for what he would say and do when he found Cameron. That must wait until he was face to face with the man.

From scraps of conversation among the Whitney's, he knew that Westwood was a community somewhere within driving distance of their home. Whitney and Emil had taught, however, the value of asking questions and he had no doubt but that he would be able to locate Cameron's "cave."

He came down from the hills without incident, keeping the speedometer needle carefully at the point on the dial which Emil had insisted over and over must never be passed. Traffic markers were conscientiously obeyed, and his care in giving hand signals would have delighted the most particular member of the Safety Council. Although he increased the distance unnecessarily by making the wrong turn at several intersections, he finally reached the main section of Hollywood.

A filling station caught his eye and he pulled in beside the row of pumps. A young man in reasonably white coveralls came over wiping his hands on a bit of waste. His eyes widened slightly at sight of the size of the man behind the wheel.

"Yessir?"

"Gasoline," Avar said succinctly.

The youth blinked. From a literal standpoint that single word was clear, but this was Hollwywood, where anything could happen and usually did, so the attendant set about getting further details in a manner that would have been approved by the head of the corporation employing him.

"Standard or Ethyl?" he said.

THE words meant nothing to Avar, since they embodied a situation Emil Thoretsen had not, during his teachings, foreseen. The cave man, for want of a better course, shrugged to indicate indifference and said again, "Gasoline."

The lips of the attendant flattened slightly with understandable annoyance. He reached for the hose on the pump marked Standard, took a look at the Buick's sleek lines and selected the one marked Ethyl instead.

A moment later he learned that the convertible's tank could take only an additional two gallons, and his already narrowed lips became a thin line. He replaced the hose and came up to the lowered window.

"That'll be forty-eight cents, Mister," he said stonily.

Although Avar had been taught the comparative values of the different denominations in bills and coins, as well as watching his teacher pay for various purchases during those three months in the San Bernardino mountains, this was his first experience in handling such a transaction by himself. Instinctively his hand went to the inner pocket where Emil had taught him to carry the wallet Whitney had given him.

It was there. He removed and handed it to the attendant.

The youth turned, eyes suddenly round with wonder. "What's this for, Mister? You got a credit card in here?"

Avar was becoming impatient. "Take your money," he growled.

Those glowing eyes stopped cold the retort trembling on the young man's lips. He said, "Yessir," extracted a dollar bill from the wallet, taking extreme care to show it was all he was taking, clicked

131

change from the coin machine at his waist and gave it and the wallet to Avar. He would have offered to check the Buick's oil, as his job called for him to do, but the thought of extending this conversation was too much for him.

He was turning away when Avar said, "Stop."

The youth turned, suddenly aware that his legs were trembling. "Yes sir?" A quick glance around showed two of his fellow workers were within rescuing distance.

The Cro-Magnard reached into his pocket and brought out the address book he had taken from Lauren's room. While the attendant shifted uneasily from one foot to the other, Avar leafed through the pages until he found the one containing Cameron's name and address.

"Where is that?" he asked, holding out the book and indicating the entry with one finger.

By craning his neck the youth was able to make out the wording without getting too close. He said, "I don't know where Selby comes in, Mister. You'll have to ask somebody in Westwood."

"Where is Westwood?"

"Oh—Westwood." The attendant was beginning to regain his poise. "Why didn't you say so? Go on out Highland to Wilshire, then west. Take you right in there."

"Where is Highland? Where is Wilshire? Where is West?"

"Are you kid—" A glance at those eyes answered the question before it was fully asked. "Look, Mister, you're on Highland right now. Just keep on the way you were going and watch the signs. Wilshire's one of the main streets; you can't miss it. Turn right— *this* way—and go straight ahead. Westwood's got signs to tell you when you're there. Okay?"

HE WAS answered by a trail of blue exhaust smoke. He said bitterly to himself, "Jeez, the *people* you meet in this burg," and started toward the station, when another car swung into the driveway and stopped.

It was a police prowl car, its two-way radio aerial vibrating from a rear fender like an elongated buggy whip. "Hey, you!" said one of the two men in the front seat.

The young man hurried over. "Yessir?"

"That big guy in the Buick convertible who was just here—what'd he talk to you about?"

The speaker was the man next to the driver—thin-faced, hard-surfaced black eyes, a humorless mouth.

"That one, huh?" The young man nodded with satisfaction. "I coulda told you there was something screwy about him."

"Then tell it, before he gets too far away."

"Orders gas when he don't need it, for one thing. Hands me his whole wallet when I ask him for forty-eight cents. Talks like a furriner."

"He showed you something. What was it?"

"An address book. Wanted to know how to get to an address written in it."

"Yeah?" The dull black eyes developed a gleam. "What was that address?"

The attendant rubbed the back of his neck and looked at the sky as if expecting to find it written there. "Lessee now. Westwood…Selby Avenue. I think it was 5421. Or now maybe it was 5412. Y'know, the guy worried me so that I don't rightly remember."

"Was there a name to go with the address?"

"Yeah. Yeah, sure there was. Cameron. Gene Cameron. I'm sure of *that*."

The plainclothes man nodded briefly, his expression as close to showing satisfaction as it ever did. "You heard the man, Hank," he said to the driver. "Let's roll."

CHAPTER TEN

IT WAS nearly seven o'clock by the time Lauren Whitney and her father returned from Santa Monica. The girl's mind was filled with thoughts of the visit she must pay Gene Cameron in another two hours, and she jumped from the Packard and hurried toward the house.

"Miss Lauren."

It was Luke, the gardener-chauffeur. He came up to her on the porch steps, the uneasiness in his face evident in the fading light of day.

"What is it, Luke? I'm in a hurry. And while I think of it, bring my convertible around, will you? I'm going to need it."

"That's what I want to tell you about, Miss Lauren."

"What? The convertible?"

"Yes'm. You see, this here Mr. Newstone took off in it a couple hours ago and I ain't seen him or it since."

Gregg Whitney came up just in time to hear this. He said, "Took what, Luke?"

"Miss Lauren's car, Mr. Whitney. He just got in and drove away."

"How strange," Lauren said, frowning. "Didn't he say where he was going?"

"No, ma'm. He just up and took it."

"Goodness, I hope nothing's happened to him. I didn't even know he could drive. You should have stopped him, Luke."

"Stop *him*? I'd as soon try to stop a—*a lion!*"

"He's right, of course, Lauren," said Whitney absently. "I'm not too concerned. Emil taught him to drive and says he's more capable at it than most of the drivers you find out here. We'll wait a while before doing anything drastic like notifying the police."

Lauren said, "Well, I've got to run, Father. I'll call you later, to find out if he's come back. I'm not especially worried that something's happened to him; it's what might happen to somebody who, innocently or otherwise, provoked him."

"He's no fool, Lauren. I have complete faith in him." He gave her an appraising glance and a slow smile. "But I'll admit I'm a little surprised by your concern over Adam. His saving you from that cougar change your viewpoint?"

She was conscious of a sudden rush of blood staining her cheeks, for a moment words trembled on her lip—words that would have told Gregg Whitney exactly what she thought of Avar. Only the fact that Luke was standing there listening kept her silent.

She said, "Later, Dad," and rushed past him and into the house.

After a quick shower, Lauren slipped into a light wool skirt and a white blouse of heavy silk. She was fishing in her closet for a pair of shoes when she found one of her dresses had slipped from the hook and was lying on the closet floor. She brought it out and was putting it on an empty hanger when she stopped abruptly, staring at the figured material.

Clearly outlined in the light cloth was the unmistakable mark of a man's shoe.

The size of the imprint told her no ordinary foot was in that shoe. Only Perry Siddons and Avar had feet of those dimensions—at least they were the only men in the Whitney household who wore shoes that size. It was unthinkable that Perry would have hidden himself in her room. That left Avar...Avar who was unpredictable. Had he been standing there some night when she came home and got ready for bed? She felt her cheeks burn and her breathing falter. What a horrible thing to suspect him of. And yet...how else could that footprint be explained?

For the first time since she returned from the hills that same morning she regretted what had passed between her and the man from the past. How could she honor—*love*—a man capable of such a degraded act as that? A peeping Tom! Her skin seemed to crawl suddenly and she shuddered...

A GLANCE at her wristwatch broke the spell. She found the shoes she wanted, put them on, drew her hair into two braids and pinned them onto a coronet atop her head, shrugged into a white coat and hurried downstairs to the garage. Luke was nowhere in sight, but Joan's dark gray Chevrolet coupe was in its accustomed spot. She took the ignition key from the glove compartment where Joan made a practice of keeping it and started the motor. The dashboard gauge showed three quarters of a tank of fuel.

At eight-thirty she was turning into Wilshire Boulevard on her way to Westwood. As the distance between her and Gene Cameron's gambling club lessened she was aware that her nerves were tightening into near panic. What could he possibly have to tell her about Joan? A still small voice within her warned he had brought Joan's name into the conversation only to insure her coming—that actually her sister had nothing whatever to do with this meeting. Only the memory of her conversation with Joan that night her sister had come home at three in the morning kept her from being certain.

The dashboard clock showed 8:55 as she braked the coupe to a soundless halt in front of the Selby Avenue address. She was on the point of getting out, hesitated with one hand on the door lever, then settled back and lit a cigarette with fingers that shook a little.

Nine o'clock, he had said—and nine o'clock it would be before she went into that place. There were no cars along the curb on either side of the street for at least fifty feet. Down near the farthest intersection a black sedan was parked, facing her way.

It seemed to be an extra quiet street. Pedestrians, mostly couples, passed by a few times, their steps echoing hollowly in the silence. A pepper tree overhung the walk of the property next to 5412, its lacy branches casting uneasy shadows. The bushes bordering Cameron's lot prevented her from seeing the first floor windows and the entrance, while no chink of light showed at any of the windows of the upper floor.

Because she was unable to see any signs of the Packard convertible Cameron always drove, she decided he had not yet reached the club. But when nine-fifteen arrived and still no sign of him, she decided to make sure.

She ground out the cigarette—her second—in the dashboard tray, drew the folds of her coat closer about her and went quickly up the walk.

The slender gray-faced man who usually lounged there was missing—a departure from the normal that only heightened her uneasiness. The solid-looking redwood door, broken only by a closed Judas window behind three vertical thin metal bars, seemed bleak and repelling.

There was a white plastic bell button set in the doorway's edge and she put a finger briefly against it. A faint buzzing reached her ears, and almost immediately the door swung back.

It was Gene Cameron, wearing dark trousers and a sport shirt, open at the throat, a highball glass in one hand. His white teeth glistened in a wide smile of welcome.

"Hello, darling. I was beginning to think you weren't coming. Please come in."

She looked past him, suddenly aware there was no muted hum of voices and very few lights within. The white-clothed tables were unoccupied and the stools along the bar were empty.

A tiny muscle jumped in one of her cheeks. She said coldly, "I don't think I understand. Are you closed for the night?"

"Always on Monday nights, Lauren," he said readily. "I'm sorry; I thought you knew that."

"I didn't." She started to turn away. "We'll make it another night, shall we?"

"For God's sake, Lauren," he said impatiently, "don't be that way. I give you my solemn word I shall treat you with all the courtly deference I would accord my own mother. I do not make a habit of pushing my attentions upon anyone who finds them distasteful."

"I'm sorry, Gene," she said contritely. "Of course I'll come in. But really I can't stay long."

HE LED the way to the second floor, across the empty game room, its gambling paraphernalia ghost-like under white dust shields, and through the door to his private office. He switched on the lights and indicated the nearest of the two blue leather lounging chairs.

"Sit there, Lauren. What will you drink?"

"Nothing, thank you."

He lifted his eyebrows. "No? You don't mind if I freshen mine, do you?"

"Not at all."

He went over to the lightwood liquor cabinet and swung open its doors. "Believe me, Lauren, I'm not trying to drag this out especially. But as you know I love playing the host."

She made no reply. He put liquor, soda and ice into his glass with quick, practiced ease and came back to her, smiling. "A cigarette instead?"

"Please."

He took a silver case from the breast pocket of his shirt, snapped open the cover and extended it. She took one of its contents and he held a light. Then he walked lightly around behind the desk, opened its center drawer and took out a ten by twelve manila envelope.

His expression was serious, almost brooding, as he came away from the desk, dropped into the chair next to hers and laid the envelope in his lap while he drank deeply from his glass. He blew out his breath softly and put the glass on the rug beside the chair.

"Listen to me, Lauren," he said in a voice suddenly empty of all emotion. "This is the toughest, most disagreeable job I've ever had in my life. You simply have to believe that—just as you must believe it's a job that was pushed on me by someone whose identity I don't even know."

A faint breeze came in at the slightly opened French windows behind the desk and touched her cheek. Its coolness made the girl suddenly aware that perspiration was dotting her face. The tip of her tongue came out to wet lips that seemed parched.

"You're frightening me, Gene," she said simply.

"Hell, I don't want to." His voice was almost savage. "But I've got to give you this—this preface before I go any farther. I've been put in the middle—appointed as go-between—only because I know you...and your sister.

"Yesterday afternoon I received this envelope and a note from a messenger boy who did not wait for an answer. There was a typewritten note attached to the contents—a note that said, very simply— Here; I'll let you read it yourself."

He turned back the flap, reached in and took out a single sheet of white bond paper and handed it to Lauren. It read:

Cameron,

I hear you are good friends with Gregg Whitney's girls. That's why I'm going to let you handle a little matter for them. The young one's foot slipped a little one evening recently and it's going to cost her ten grand to keep the bump from showing. Have her turn the dough over to you and I'll send around to pick it up. In return she'll get the negatives. Three days is all the time she gets.

There was no signature. Lauren, fear and wonder clear in her face, handed back the note. "Negatives? What negatives?"

Cameron took a deep breath. "Of these, Lauren." He reached into the folder a second time and brought out three eight-by-ten glossy prints and handed them over, face down. The moment her hand closed about them, he rose, picked up his half empty glass and walked quickly toward the liquor cabinet.

When he turned around finally, she was sitting where he had left her. The three pictures were on the rug where they had fallen from nerveless hands. Her shoulders were drawn forward and her head bowed, giving her a strange effect of being huddled over an imaginary fire for warmth. She sat there unmoving, seeming hardly to breathe.

"Lauren..." He hurried to her and put a hand on her shoulder, feeling the tenseness of it. "Here." He bent and held the rim of his glass to her sagging lips. "Take a swig of this."

"Evil." No emotion, no inflection, a word spoken by an automaton. "Evil."

HE SHOOK the shoulder under his hand. "Stop it, will you? Don't throw a wing-ding on me, for Pete's sake." He tilted the glass and poured some of its contents between her teeth. Some of it trickled from the corner of her mouth and automatically she reached into the small bag on her lap, took out a handkerchief and wiped it away.

She looked up at him then and there was such crawling horror in her brimming eyes that he drew back involuntarily.

"It isn't true, Gene." The words came out in a hoarse whisper, as though torn from her throat. "It's some kind of trick. Photographs can be altered; I've heard of such things. It has to be that. Don't you understand? It *has* to be a trick. Joan's just a baby, Gene. She wouldn't get into a situation where filthy pictures like these could be taken of her—even innocently."

He swallowed convulsively and the distress in his face matched her own. "I'm afraid they aren't fakes, Lauren. Not these. The—details are too clear. But you know your sister, I suppose. Is there some mark or scar on her body which doesn't appear in these photos?"

"I didn't look at them that closely," she said woodenly.

"But would there be anything like that?"

"I don't know—I don't know!" Her voice began to rise. "I can't seem to *think*..."

"Okay, okay," he said soothingly. "Just sit there and breathe deeply and try to get hold of yourself. When the first shock wears off you'll be able to think clearly; then we'll find out what must be done."

He went over to the chair behind his desk, after gathering up the scattered prints from the rug. He tucked them face down under a corner of the tooled leather pad, leaned back and lit a cigarette.

A little time passed. In the silence of the room street noises, few and far apart, filtered in through the crack between the French windows, and the vines along the tiny balcony outside rustled in a slight breeze from the west.

Lauren lifted her head. Her face seemed very white, but she was composed in a frozen sort of way. She said, "When Joan was twelve she pitched off a bicycle and ran a heavy splinter from a fence into her right thigh, high up. It left a small round sunken scar about the size of a dime. Something like a dimple."

Wordlessly Gene Cameron turned over the prints and examined them, his face blank of all expression. Almost immediately he put them back. "It's there, Lauren... I'm sorry."

"You needn't be," she said composedly. "I don't know how it happened and I don't care. All I do know is that Joan has never done an evil, dirty thing in her life and she never will. I noticed her eyes were closed in each of those—those poses. She was either drugged or unconscious."

"Or asleep, Lauren," he said gently.

"I refuse to believe she was a willing party to this, Gene. But that's not important now. I'll raise that ten thousand dollars tomorrow and get it to you to buy back the negatives mentioned in the note."

"Can you raise that amount? I'd gladly loan it to you but unfor—"

"It won't be necessary to borrow it. I still have the three thousand I won at your roulette table the night I was here, plus another thousand or two in my bank account. I have jewelry I can raise the rest on. Who ever sent that note must know my finances pretty well. Ten thousand is just about every penny I can scrape up."

He said, "I won't try to kid you, Lauren. In one way and another I've come in contact with some pretty shady characters and I know how they work. Unless I'm badly mistaken—and I hope I am—you'll be asked to pay a lot more than ten thousand."

"But the letter says—"

"Sure. I, know what it says. And you'll get the three negatives when the money is paid. Then a few months will go by and you'll have put away the whole transaction as just a bad dream...and *wham!* In will come three different poses and a request for more money. You don't think whoever's responsible for this would stop after taking just three shots, do you? They may have twenty."

HER chin began to tremble. "What can I *do*, Gene? I mean, what if I should refuse to pay? They can't turn them over to any newspaper or anything where other people could see them. And there must be laws against a thing like this."

"Of course no paper would touch them. But what if your friends, the friends of your father, should find envelopes in their mail some morning and in them prints like these. Not that they wouldn't be horrified, not that you'd hear anything about it. But you'd see it in their eyes because they couldn't keep it from showing. There'd be snide remarks passed by a few of your acquaintances; it'd be something for catty women to tell others, in strictest secrecy, of course. I don't have to tell you any more; your imagination can picture the rest."

She moaned in actual physical suffering. "Isn't there some way I can lick this, Gene? I can't let Joan go through such a horrible, horrible mess."

He rose from his chair and came over and took her hands in his. "What I'm about to say may sound utterly fantastic to you but I want you to hear me out and think about it. I'm in love with you, darling, and I think you're in love with me. I made a mistake once, and you, being a sensitive girl, let it get in the way of loving me, but that doesn't mean the love isn't there. But if—"

Her expression said she couldn't believe her ears. "What has all that to do with the trouble Joan is in? Honestly, Gene, I think you'd have a better sense of timing than to bring—"

"Wait," he pleaded. "Hear what I have to say. All of what I just said leads up to this: If you will marry me, Lauren, I can put a stop to this blackmail. I carry a lot of weight around this part of the country. All the man responsible for this would have to know is that you are going to be my wife and he'd pull into a hole as far as the Whitneys are concerned. Believe me, that's the way these things work."

She looked up at him with stricken eyes. "But I don't love you, Gene."

"I think you do," he said soberly. "I only bet on sure things, dear, but I'll bet on that. Let me prove it; we'll drive to Nevada and be married tonight. Then I'll be in a position to take your troubles on my own shoulders. I guarantee no one will ever know about those photographs."

Suddenly she was very tired. She could not go on, fearing every mail delivery, afraid to face the people she knew because they might have received one of those pictures of Joan. The thought of what her father would go through if one of those things should come to his hands made her almost physically ill. Perhaps Gene would prove to be the wonderful person she had at first thought. Actually she had nothing against him except that night in the car when his hands…

She smiled wanly. "You do love me, don't you, Gene?" He nodded quickly and drew her to her feet and into his arms. She sighed and put her forehead down on his shoulder in surrender. "Then, I suppose…"

Her voice faltered, died. Abruptly the memory of Avar swept into her mind, the feel of his lips on hers tore through her like a thrilling kind of heat.

"Say it," urged Cameron, his voice vibrating. "Say you'll marry me tonight. We love each other and you'll never be sorry. It will be the one thing the blackmailer never counted on—the ace in the hole he never suspected you had. Tell me you'll leave with me, for Nevada."

SUDDENLY she twisted violently from his arms, sending him staggering back. Her eyes were blazing at him, her body tense, her hands balled into fists. *"What—did—you—say?"*

"Lauren," he gasped, completely bewildered by the complete change in her. "What's the matter with you? Why are you acting—?"

"I see it now—the whole filthy scheme. And to think you almost got away with it. I must have been blind—how *could* I have been so blind?"

His eyes narrowed. "I think you'd better tell me what you're talking about, Lauren."

"You *bet* I'll tell you! 'Ace in the hole,' you said. You like that expression, don't you? Anyone in your line of business would. Well, I'm going to tell you of another time you used it—or one very close to it. About a week ago, on the telephone. You said something then I didn't understand, something like 'Force me to play my ace and you'll find it has the picture of a Queen on it.' *Picture of a Queen!*"

The look on his face was all she needed for confirmation.

"That means there is no mysterious man in this thing, doesn't it, Gene? You wrote that note—you took those pictures yourself and the negatives you talked about are somewhere in this room. In some way you drugged Joan and took those pictures of her. Either you hand them over—all of them—this minute or I'm going to the police!"

He shrugged—and then he was smiling, a smile of contempt and a sneering kind of mock pity. "Nice going, toots. It seems you're not quite as stupid as I thought—although you did come mighty close to being taken in. Being married to you would be a legal—and much more pleasant—method of getting money out of you. Now you run right along and call the brass button boys…but don't expect to find much to back up your story with when you get back."

"Give me those pictures, those negatives, Gene." He could barely hear her. "You're not going to ruin Joan's life and kill my father—I won't let you. Give them to me!"

"Sure, sure," he said, his soothing tone a mockery. "I'll give them to you…for money. A lot of money. Fifty thousand dollars—in advance."

"I don't have that kind of money and you know it."

He seemed not to be listening. "Of course, you must understand that's only for the pictures of your baby sister." He turned and went back to his desk, opened the center drawer a second time and took out another envelope. "These," he said, tossing the folder on the desk top, "these add up to an additional fifty grand."

She was staring at the second envelope. "I don't understand."

"Look for yourself… Go ahead; there's no charge for looking."

She came forward with a kind of wooden reluctance, picked up the folder and drew back the flap with unsteady fingers. Three photographs slid, face up, onto the pad…

"Ohhh…" she leaned weakly against the desk and closed her eyes, shame and revulsion sweeping through her. "Of me. How could you? How could you?"

"It was a pleasure, my dear. I hadn't realized before that first evening you were up here how truly lovely you were. Now, of course, you know how I managed it. A friendly visit to Cameron's gambling hell, a Micky in my lady's drink timed to hit her while chatting in my private office…my trusty camera equipped with flash bulbs. You have no idea how the money rolls in."

Slowly her head came up and her eyes opened. He was standing across the desk from her, holding one of the prints and looking at it, a leer curling his lips.

And in that moment Lauren Whitney lost her last hold on reason.

With a single swift motion her hand shot out and closed about the desk set's letter opener. Back swung the brass blade, then down in a savage arc, point aimed squarely at the man's exposed throat.

Quick as she was, Gene Cameron was quicker. He jerked aside as the blade was falling, snaked out a hand and caught her wrist, then twisted sharply and the opener dropped from her nerveless fingers.

Sudden rage darkened his face. "Just who d'you think you're trying to knife, baby? If that's the way you want it—"

WITH blinding speed his open hand lashed out and struck her full across the face. Dazed, half-conscious, she stumbled back and crumpled to the floor.

Even as Lauren Whitney was falling, the room's French doors crashed apart with shattering force and a broad-shouldered man bounded catlike through the opening.

Cameron whirled. At sight of the blazing eyes and menacing figure looming above him, he cried out in sudden fear and his hand darted into the still open desk drawer, reappearing instantly with a blue steel .38 revolver.

Already two incredible powerful hands were closing about his throat. In utter panic he jerked up the gun's barrel and pressed the trigger.

A single ringing report echoed through the room and a black-rimmed hole appeared magically in one side of the giant man's suit jacket. Then the revolver flew through the air and crashed into one of the walls. Cameron's scream was cut off suddenly and his body rose vertically from the floor, suspended by those two hands about his neck.

An expressionless face, cold, implacable as though hewn from granite, swam before his bulging eyes. There was a pounding in his ears, a blood-red mist shutting off his vision. The pressure in his chest swelled into excruciating agony. He tried to cry out for mercy, to plead, to promise—but no sound would come from his tortured throat.

Lauren Whitney staggered to her feet, horror twisting her features. "No, Avar! For God's sake—stop! You'll kill him!"

Her frenzied plea fell on deaf ears. She ran to the Cro-Magnard and sought to drag those steel-thewed fingers from the throat of the dying man. She might as well have tried to blow them loose with her breath.

It came to her then that the thin shell of civilization built during the past three months had fallen from this man from the past, and he was once again an untamed denizen of a savage world—a beast-man whose mate had been attacked.

The body in those massive hands hung limp and lifeless now, and as Lauren Whitney sank sobbing to the floor, Avar lifted it high and brought its back down across the deck's edge, breaking the spine like a tiny branch.

As the crumpled clay that had been Gene Cameron slid to the floor, the madness faded from Avar's eyes, replaced by concern for the weeping woman. Gently he lifted her into his arms and stroked her hair in a comforting gesture.

"He can not harm you, Lau-ren. He is dead."

"Darling. My dearest." she moaned. "Why did you do it?"

Wonder came into his eyes. "He was bad. He deserved to die."

She motioned for him to free her and he set her lightly on her feet. She put her hands on his arms and buried her face in his chest. "You don't understand, Avar," she whispered. "They'll call it murder and lock you away like an animal. They'll put you in a steel cage with men who *are* criminals and keep you there for years and years."

"I will not let them do that," he said simply.

She shook her head angrily, trying to clear her thoughts. Cameron, she knew, had got exactly what he deserved and she wasted no pity for him. It was the thought of what would happen to the man she loved that was twisting her heart.

Perhaps it was not too late to save him. Evidently the shot had gone unnoticed, for there was no sign of alarm from outside the building. If she and Avar could only leave the building unobserved. There was always the possibility that Cameron might have told others she was coming here this night, but that was a chance she was forced to take. The nature of his business with her made it seem unlikely...

AND then with stunning force came the thought of those slimy photographs. Should any of those, or the negatives, fall into the hands of the police, she and her sister were certain to be suspected of a connection with Cameron's murder. Not that either of them would be considered as the actual killer—only a man of super-human strength could take a life that way. But once they had a glimpse of Avar—the case would be solved.

The answer, then, was to find those prints and negatives. Gently she freed herself from the cave man's embrace. "We've got to get out of here, Avar. But first we—I must find something that—uh—belongs to me."

"I will help you."

The thought of his seeing those pictures brought a quick flush to her cheeks. "No. You listen for the sound of someone coming toward this room."

Averting her eyes from the limp heap of flesh behind the desk, she started on the desk drawers. Working swiftly and with complete thoroughness, she went through them, careful to wipe away all fingerprints as she progressed. The last of the seven drawers was locked and she was unable to find the key anywhere in the desk. The thought of rifling the dead man's pockets was repugnant.

"Can you open it, Avar?"

The Cro-Magnard came over silently, placed a hand against the desk's edge and wrapped the fingers of the other about the drawer's metal handle. Muscles surged along his arm and across his back, there was a rending sound of wood and the drawer's entire face came away.

She knelt and went through its contents. Papers were all it contained—papers covered with figures relating to his "take" from the games in the next room. She pawed through them frantically but there were no negatives, no prints.

She rose to her feet, her face white with fear. They had to be here. Every nerve in her body screamed for her to quit this place before somebody came. For all she could know, a next door neighbor had heard the shot and the police were on their way.

That was something she had to risk. Somewhere in this apartment were those negatives and she was not going to leave without them. A deadly calm took hold of her, stilling the trembling of her hands and knees and slowing her pounding heart.

While Avar stood watching her like a graven image, she went over the room with minute care. She looked under the furniture, behind the cushions of the chairs and couch, in the liquor cabinet—everywhere. She tried sounding the walls, she looked behind the room's two pictures, she even examined the lining of the window drapes. Nothing. Absolutely nothing.

Then she remembered the bedroom Cameron had taken her through that first evening. She located the cleverly concealed door in the room's paneling at once and went through the opening. There was a large chest of drawers containing nothing other than underclothing, socks, handkerchiefs and the like. Hurriedly she tore the beds apart and dumped the mattresses on the floor. Nothing. A sliding panel in one wall contained a dozen suits, two topcoats and a shoe cabinet. No negatives. A pair of framed prints above the bed had nothing behind them but the wall.

Her shoulders drooped in surrender and she could feel tears of frustration forming in her eyes. She turned and went into the tiny bathroom, knowing there would be nothing hidden there but she must go through it anyway...

When she came, empty handed, into the bedroom again, she found Avar standing in the center of the room, his eyes surveying the wreckage she had left. At his unspoken question, she shrugged hopelessly. "I can't find what I'm hunting for, Avar. We'd better go before some one comes and finds us here."

"What are you looking for?"

"Negatives of some pictures." At his blank expression, she shrugged. "Squares of a paper—like material you can see through." It was the only way she could think of to describe them.

SHE turned to leave, taking a last despairing look at the room's paneled walls. Something in one of the deep grooves between two of those panels glinted in the light. Frowning, she went up to the wall at that point and peered into the crack.

A thin metal strip, notched at regular intervals, was set in the wood. Some sort of hinge, she decided, and hope leaped within her. Rapping her knuckles lightly against the adjoining panel produced a distinctly hollow note.

Almost frantically her fingers tugged at the grooves but nothing gave. She looked pleadingly at Avar, who was watching her intently, his expression puzzled.

"I'm sure this section swings out," she said. "But I can't seem to move it."

He ran his hands lightly over the polished wood, attempting to insert his fingers into the grooves. Failing at this, he drew his clenched fist and drove it with tremendous force against the panel, which parted with a rending crash and appeared to dissolve into splinters.

Lauren's amazed gasp turned to an exclamation of joy. With eager fingers she withdrew a box and tried to lift its lid. It was locked.

The key must be in one of the dead man's pockets. Like it or not, she must go through them. She was on the point of returning to the apartment living room when Avar reached out and took the strongbox from her hand.

"Is what you are looking for in this?"

"I don't know. I must open it first. I'll have to find the key."

He closed a hand over the lid and gave a single sharp tug. There was a brief sound of breaking metal and the box opened.

Her laugh was more nearly a gasp.

"There goes that manufacturer's reputation." She took the box from his hands and dug into the contents. There were three envelopes, one of them containing a thick sheaf of banknotes, the others some fifty photograph negatives. The latter she held up to the light in rapid order, finding them to be poses much like those in the pictures Cameron had shown her. Twenty proved to be shots of Joan and herself, ten of each; the others were of women also, none of which she recognized. All were equally nauseating.

So intense was her relief that she quite forgot the dead body in the other room. Quickly she tucked two envelopes into her bag. "We can go now, Avar."

They crossed the living room and she was reaching for the doorknob when a sudden thought struck her. "No; we can't go out the front way. Someone might see us. The back stairs aren't much better but we'll have to risk it."

Avar followed her back through the bedroom and down the flight of carpeted steps to the first floor. Lauren released the door catch and they stepped out into the night.

The shadow of the building made them invisible from the street, even should a passerby peer through a break in the hedge. Lauren was able to make out the top of Joan's Chevrolet at the curb. She said, "I wish I could be sure no one will see us leave."

"Wait," said Avar.

Moving with the easy grace that was one of his most striking characteristics he crossed a thin section of open ground to one of the lot's three trees. With a lithe bound he caught hold of one of its lower branches and disappeared into the foliage above.

A moment later he was back again. "The street is empty of life. Two automobiles are standing well down the square."

"Good. We can—" She stopped short as a sudden thought struck her. "But we can't leave together, Avar. You came here in my car, didn't you?"

"Yes."

"Where is it parked?" He looked at her blankly. "Parked," she repeated. "Where did you leave it?"

"On the next street crossing this one."

SHE paused, planning what to do. "All right. Walk with me to my car, then go to the one you came in. I'll pull up ahead and you follow me on the way back home. Do you understand?"

He nodded. Moving at a casual pace they crossed the lawn and stepped out onto the walk. A quick glance in both directions showed no pedestrians, although a car was turning into their street and heading in their direction.

Lauren had her keys out of her bag and was unlocking the car door. "Get in," she whispered urgently. "I'll drive you to where you left the Buick."

They were under way while the approaching car was still a block distant. Lauren turned at the first intersection and saw the familiar lines of her Buick convertible stationary at the curb.

She pulled in behind it. "Get in and start your motor, Avar. Wait until I'm half a block ahead, then follow me. Are you sure you can drive all right?"

"I drove here."

She laughed briefly. "So you did. Go ahead then. But be careful not to break any laws; if a policeman stops you and finds you have no driver's license, we *are* in trouble."

When the cave man was behind the convertible's wheel, Lauren started her car and pulled away, watching the Buick in her rearview mirror. Almost immediately she put on her brakes and motioned for him to stop. She left the coupe and went back.

"Your lights, Avar. Turn on your lights. Don't tell me you drove out here without using them."

At his blank expression she reached through the open window and turned the switch and his headlights went on. Avar smiled at her. "I do not need them. I can see well enough."

She shook her head and laughed. "When are you going to understand you're not like other people, my dear? Their eyes aren't used to jungle nights; you'd be in an accident within the first mile. Besides, it is the law.

Avar shrugged his acceptance of this edict and Lauren went back to the coupe. A moment later and both cars were marked by dwindling taillights as they moved down the street on the way to the Whitney estate.

Half a block back from where the Buick had stood, on the opposite side of the intersection, another car started up and drew away from the curb. Its single occupant swung into Selby Avenue, stopped across the street from 5412 and stepped out onto the strip of parkway between street and sidewalk. A second man appeared from behind a nearby hedge and strolled over to join the first.

"He just pulled away, Ed. The girl dropped him off; he got in the Buick and followed her. She had to remind him to switch on his lights."

Sergeant Edward Korshak rubbed his chin thoughtfully. "Okay. Now we'll go in and ask some questions about that gunshot we heard."

Gilmer's slow head shake indicated his indecision. "I don't know's we ought to, Ed. We're away off base."

"Nothing we can't explain—if we have to. Come on." Side by side they crossed the street and turned in at 5412.

CHAPTER ELEVEN

IT WAS nearly eleven by the time the two cars pulled into parking spaces in front of the Whitney home. They went up the porch steps without speaking and Lauren unlocked the front door and preceded him into the dimly lighted hall. She was shivering a little as she slipped out of her white coat.

"Guess everyone's out," she observed. "I think I need a little brandy to ward off the jitters I feel coming on. There's usually some in the library. Come on."

They entered and Lauren turned on the lights. At her suggestion Avar set fire to the logs in the fireplace and drew a pair of easy chairs to face the blaze. She came over carrying two bell-shaped glasses with a small amount of brandy in each and handed one to Avar.

"Not that *you* need it," she said, dropping into one of the chairs. "But I certainly do."

Avar was sniffing at the rim of his glass. "What is it? It has a pleasant smell."

"A French brandy of some sort. I really don't know much about such things, but Father recommends it highly." Realization came to her then. Don't tell me you've never had a drink, Avar?"

"'Drink?'" He stared at her impassively. "Water is to drink."

Her laugh was a trifle unsteady. "There's a lot of people around Hollywood who'd argue that point with you. Take a sip of it."

He put the glass to his lips and drank the inch of liquid in it at a gulp. "It is nice," he said simply.

"Spoken like a true devotee to the grape—or whatever they make it of." She sipped some of her own, feeling its warmth and that of the fire steal over her. For the first time she began to realize what the night's events added up to; up until this moment the necessity for action in getting away from Westwood and back home had occupied her mind almost completely.

She went back over the evening, seeking to think of some lead the police might pick up that would point to her. The negatives were in her possession; no chance of those tripping her up. Everything she and Avar had touched was wiped clean of fingerprints—she had been very careful of that. Many people knew she and Cameron had been seeing a lot of each other, but certainly there was nothing incriminating in that; Gene had known hundreds of men and women. The way he had died would keep the police from even considering a woman as the killer.

And even if by some miraculous means the authorities were able to learn Avar had slain Cameron—it was in self-defense. He had drawn a gun and the cave man had killed him. That gun was still lying on the floor near Cameron's broken body; surely the police could reconstruct what had happened.

The memory of the shot brought a new thought to her mind and she turned her gaze to Avar, who was sitting stiffly on the edge of his chair and staring into the fire.

"Cameron shot at you, Avar. Did the bullet miss?"

Avar looked down at the hole in his coat. There was no sign of blood, although he was aware, now that the girl had mentioned the matter, of a slight burning sensation along his ribs. "A scratch," he said quietly.

"I know about your kind of 'scratches.' They'd put most men in the hospital. Take off your coat and let me have a look at this one."

It turned out to be actually a scratch, the bullet having marked the skin along his ribs just enough to draw a trickle of blood, already coagulated. While Avar rebuttoned his shirt and got into his jacket again, Lauren drank the rest of her brandy and lighted a cigarette.

She said, "I still don't understand how you happened to show up at Gene's tonight. How did you know I was going to be there and how were you able to find out I was going to be in a spot where I would need a rescuer?"

HE REMINDED her of their conversation that afternoon after she had finished talking to Cameron on the telephone. "That's it, then," she said, when he was done. "But how'd you find his club? It isn't listed under his name in the phone book."

He smiled faintly. "I have seen Emil and Gregg use the telephone. Both would look for the information they needed in small books that they kept near their telephones. I went to your room while you were away this afternoon and found such a book there. In it were Cameron's address and telephone number."

She was eyeing him narrowly, remembering something. "You didn't happen to look in my closet for the book, did you?"

"I hid in it for a while. Anna came in while I was there and I did not want her to see me."

"And right then's when you put your big feet on one of my best dresses!" She laughed with relief. "You're utterly unpredictable, Avar—and a lot smarter about our way of life than I've been giving you credit for...

"In other words, you found out where Gene was, waited around there until I showed up, then climbed up to the balcony outside his window and did a little eavesdropping. When things got rough for me, you came in and rescued the fair damsel in distress!"

Her voice sobered abruptly. "You made one mistake, though, Avar, the hero in these melodramas never actually kills the villain; he beats him up thoroughly and walks out with the heroine. Killing brings in the police and offends the censors, who insist a killer—no matter how justified the killing—must be punished. But you haven't seen our movies or read our magazines; you couldn't know that..."

She sighed heavily and sat there staring at the glowing end of her cigarette while the minutes ticked by and the silence was broken by the snapping of flames in the fireplace.

After a while she looked at the profile of her companion as he sat there perfectly relaxed and unmoving. Most people fidgeted a great deal while not occupied: crossing and recrossing their legs, twirling a key chain, tugging at their clothing, fiddling with their fingers. But Avar could sit for hours on end, completely at ease but almost as immobile as a figure carved from stone. It was just another of the hundred little ways he differed from modern man, she realized—one of the characteristics that made her love him more than anyone else in the world...

With a sharp gesture of finality she tossed her cigarette into the fire and rose to her feet. "I'm afraid this is something too big for us to handle alone, Avar. I'm going to tell the whole story to father and we'll be governed by what he recommends. He's very wealthy, he knows and is friendly with a great many important people. If he can get to them before the police get to us he may be able to hush up the matter. That will have to be before any publicity about our part in Gene's death gets into the papers, though.

"One part of the story that mustn't be told to anyone has to do with the negatives I took from Gene's apartment. I'll tell Father, and anyone else who has to know particulars on what happened tonight, that I went to Gene's apartment and that you followed me there. He tried to—to get rough with me; you broke in and came to my aid; he drew a gun and in the struggle to prevent him from shooting you, you killed him. That's simple enough to keep us from getting tangled up, no matter how many times we have to tell it. Will you do it that way, Avar?"

"Of course." He sounded untroubled at the prospect of being questioned—actually indifferent.

"It isn't going to be easy, darling. You don't know how completely cunning and ruthless they can be."

"Kuo is cunning and ruthless, too—more so than these men can be."

"Kuo? Oh, you mean a lion." She went over to him, her face mirroring distress and exasperation, and caught his hand, drawing

155

him to his feet to face her. "You've got to understand, Avar, that this isn't something you can solve with your muscles. These are policemen; they represent millions of people. If you tried to overcome a policeman with your hands you could do it easily. But it would turn all those millions of people against you—and even you, Avar, for all your great strength and mighty muscles, would be helpless against so many. That is something you must never forget."

AS HE watched the play of expression across her lovely features and listened to the earnestness in her voice, the granite-like lines of his angular face seemed to soften. No she in all his world—or hers—was so beautiful as this one, and the strange ache, the almost painful sensation of swelling, in his left breast told him again what he had first known when their lips had met when he slew Loka, the panther.

"You are my she," he said in his own tongue. "The warmest cave shall be your home, the flesh of Boad and Adzan shall be your food."

At her uncomprehending expression he smiled his grave smile and the golden flames in his yellow-gray eyes seemed to deepen. "You belong to me now," he said. "No jungle bloom is so lovely as your face, your body is like a slender reed on the river bank, your eyes are like the skies in the dry season."

"Why, Avar, h—how poetic…" Her voice faltered, a tremulous smile touched her lips—and then she was deep in his powerful arms and his mouth was warm and firm against her own…

"Well, pardon *us!*" drawled a half-mocking voice from behind them.

With a startled gasp Lauren pulled away from Avar's encircling arms and whirled around. Standing in the library doorway was Joan Whitney, with the bulky figure of Perry Siddons looming behind her.

"Oh—hello—I—uh…" Lauren's floundering tongue gave up and her face turned fiery red.

It was Perry who restored everything to normal. He lumbered into the room and glowered at Avar. "This guy been annoying you, Lauren? Maybe a punch on the nose'll teach him his place."

"You big dope," Joan said wearily. "Can't you tell when a girl has enjoyed being kissed? Maybe you'd better punch Lauren, the way it looks to me."

Lauren had had time enough to regain her composure. She said, "I hope this teaches you to knock before you go around opening doors."

Joan laughed. "You'd better tell Adam to use his handkerchief; lipstick looks terrible on him. And—ah—were you just practicing or does this mean you've reserved him as your private property?"

"When the time comes for an announcement, you'll be the first to know, Joan. Now why don't you and Perry run along? I'm waiting for Dad to show up—unless he came in ahead of us. We just got here ourselves."

"I wouldn't know. Perry and I haven't been here since three this afternoon."

The sound of a motor reached their ears from the front of the house. Lauren said, "That must be him, now. Go ahead, you two. This is going to be a private conversation."

They went out, Joan reluctantly as though she sensed something was wrong. Lauren closed the door and hurried over to the fire. "I've got to burn these things quick," she said, opening her purse with trembling fingers and taking out the two envelopes of negatives. "I hope Father doesn't come directly—"

Heels clicked on the parquetry in the hall and she shoved the folders back into her purse. The library door swung open and Gregg Whitney came in removing his hat. He looked faintly surprised at seeing Lauren and Avar.

"Hello, you two." He sounded tired. "Emil Thoretsen just dropped me off; we attended a lecture. You look a little upset, Lauren. Anything wrong?"

She went over and took the hat from his hands and kissed him lightly on one cheek. "I'm afraid so, Dad," she said equally. "It's pretty involved, so draw up a chair and let me make you a drink to hold onto while I tell you the story."

He eyed her sharply but remained silent. He drew another chair up beside the two already facing the fire and sat down. "As long as you volunteered, make it brandy and soda… Sit down, Adam. How's your arm feeling?"

"It does not pain me."

"Good. Doc says you've the most amazing recuperative power he's ever…"

HE STOPPED there, his sharp eyes centered on the cave man's coat, his lean face set in startled lines. "That hole in your coat—there are powder burns around—"

"It's a bullet hole, Dad," interrupted Lauren, her voice curiously flat. She put a tall glass in his hand and sat down in the chair between the two men. "That ties in with the story I'm going to tell you."

He said, "Adam's in trouble." It was not a question.

"In a way. But I was the cause of it."

"What kind of trouble?"

"He killed a man."

Gregg Whitney closed his eyes and his breath rustled in his nostrils. "Tell me about it."

Speaking in short, rapid sentences, Lauren Whitney recounted the night's events, omitting only her reason for going to Gene Cameron's office and what had led to the fight she had had with the gambler. When she was finished, her father leaned back in his chair and took a long gulping drink of his brandy and soda.

He said, "I should have put my foot down a long time ago, I suppose. But what's done is done. There's an excellent chance you and Adam will never be drawn into any investigation. But of course we can't afford to risk it at all. I'd better get busy on the phone and see what kind of deal—"

The doorbell rang, and father and daughter started nervously. Whitney said grimly, "See what I mean? If we don't bring this thing out in the open, every time the phone rings or somebody comes to the door we'll die a hundred deaths."

The bell rang again, sounding impatient in the stillness. Whitney said, "I'll get it," put his glass on an end table and went into the hall.

Voices, too low pitched for Lauren to make out the words, reached into the library. But she gasped a little as Avar rose swiftly to his feet and faced the doorway, his giant body crouching slightly, a low growl rumbling deep within his throat.

"What is it, Avar?" she said sharply. He seemed not to have heard her. His head swung from side to side in a gesture indescribably menacing, like a lion preparing to charge. She left her chair and went swiftly to him, placing a hand on one of his arms. Beneath the material of his coat she could feel taut muscles like steel rods.

"Please, Avar," she whispered, "don't do anything we'll all be sorry for."

Footsteps echoed in the hall, then Gregg Whitney entered the library, two men close behind him. At sight of the latter Lauren's heart sank like a plummeting stone. They were the same two police officers who had come to question Avar over a month before.

"Sergeant Korshak and Officer Gilmer," Whitney said, his voice pitched a shade higher than usual. "It seems they want to ask you and Mr. Newstone some questions, Lauren."

Only Korshak came all the way into the room. Gilmer remained in the shadows near the door, his squat figure seeming to bulk larger than usual. His hands hung at his sides and in one of them something glittered in the unsteady light from the fireplace.

Korshak said, "Let's sit down, if you don't mind. This may take a little time." His narrow face seemed sharper than ever, his thin lips bore the ghost of a smile that might have been triumphant, and there was a glint to his usually lusterless black eyes.

With Lauren, Gregg Whitney and Avar back in their chairs, the sergeant swung the one offered him around until he was facing the others, his back to the fire so that its light would reveal their expressions and leave his shadowed. His movements were slow and deliberate; he was enjoying this. He said, "Do you mind if I smoke?" to no one in particular.

Whitney said, "Go right ahead," without any warmth in his tone.

Korshak took his time getting a cigarette burning. Let them stew a little, let them worry over what they were going to say. This was going to be one of the highlights in his career and he was savoring every moment of it.

HE LET smoke seep from his nostrils and tossed the match into the fireplace. He said crisply, "There's a matter I think you can throw a little light on. You don't have to answer any questions, of course, but I'd appreciate your cooperation."

"Anything within reason, naturally," Whitney said quietly.

"Thanks...Miss Whitney, have you been home all evening?"

Her eyes met his calmly. "I'd like to know what you're getting at Sergeant Korshak. If I'm going to do any cooperating it'll have to work two ways."

"That seems reasonable enough," Korshak agreed pleasantly. His eyes shifted to Gregg Whitney. "You told me while we were in the hall, Mr. Whitney, that you'd just returned home a few minutes before I arrived. Mind telling me where you were?"

"Not at all. I attended a lecture at the University of Southern California with Professor Emil Thoretsen."

"Um. Did you drive there and back?"

"I didn't; no. Professor Thoretsen picked me up in his car around 7:45 and brought me home no more than ten minutes ago."

Korshak crossed his legs and leaned back. "I believe you have another daughter, Mr. Whitney. Is she home now?"

"I really don't know. I can find out, if you—"

Lauren said steadily, "She and Perry came in just ahead of you. They went to the Bennett's early this afternoon. Joan told me earlier they were going to have dinner there."

"Did they drive?" Korshak asked.

"I suppose so. I wasn't here when they left. Perry's roadster wasn't in the driveway then, so I suppose they used it. Is all this important?"

Korshak looked at her levelly. "It could be. Sometimes I take the long way around, Miss Whitney, but the scenery makes it worth while… You say you weren't at home when your sister left. Mind telling me where you were?"

"Certainly not. Father and I were in Santa Monica all afternoon, at the home of a relative. Would you like her name and address?"

He ignored the edge to her voice. "That won't be necessary, Miss. I'm prepared to believe what you tell me. I've been in this business long enough to know who will and who won't tell me the truth."

"Thank you." Her tone added, "*for nothing.*"

Korshak leaned forward and deposited ash from his cigarette into a chrome ash-stand. He did it slowly, lingeringly; he was enjoying himself. "You said, Miss Whitney, that you were in Santa Monica 'all afternoon.' You came home after that?"

"Yes."

"In whose car."

"In our own car."

"What kind of car?"

She frowned, puzzled by what lay behind the question. "…A Packard sedan. This year's model. Would you like the license number?"

The biting sarcasm in the last remark failed to dent his imperturbability. "What time did you get home from Santa Monica?"

"Around seven o'clock."

"Did you go out again?"

Lauren's lips tightened into a straight line. "I think this has gone far enough, Sergeant. At least until you give us some idea where all this is leading."

HIS SMILE had no humor in it. "There are two cars parked outside your front door. One is a Buick convertible, the other a gray Chevy coupe. Both engines are still warm. Were you out in one of them tonight?"

"…Yes."

"I see. Which car were you driving?"

"The Chevrolet."

"Why?"

She wet her lips, then silently scolded herself for showing even that amount of emotion. "Why not, Sergeant?"

He said heavily, "The registration on the Chevy's steering wheel shows it belongs to your sister. The one on the Buick says that one's yours. How come you didn't use your own car?"

Her blue eyes snapped at him. "Am I charged with stealing my sister's car, Sergeant Korshak?"

His tone sharpened abruptly. "Let's stick to the subject. Did you use the Chevy because your own car was in some one else's possession?"

"Perhaps. If so, it was with my permission."

"Who was using it, Miss Whitney?"

Her jaw set. "No. If you want any further information from me, Sergeant, you'll have to give some first. What's behind this official call? It is official, I suppose."

"You bet it's official, Miss Whitney. And when the time comes for me to give information, you'll get it. Now this may be something you can clear up here and now. If you want to go along with me, well and good; if not we'll go down to the Wilcox Avenue station and do it right. It's strictly up to you."

"You're not scaring me a bit, Sergeant."

"Well now, Miss Whitney, I don't waste time scaring people." The drawling way he said it was so unlike his previous crisp manner of speech that she was startled. And then it came to her: he was playing this scene out at length for the sadistic feeling of satisfaction it was giving him. He knew the answers to most of the questions even before he asked them. She noticed now that not once since he had taken the chair facing them had he so much as glanced at the immobile figure of Avar. She recalled how the Cro-Magnon man had thrown this police officer through a window that day over a month ago and how her father had balked his efforts to have Avar taken to the station. Hatred was behind this calm, polite interview; hatred for the cave man and for her father.

How much did he know? She was thinking quickly now, looking ahead, mapping a campaign. In case it came to where a charge of murder was placed against Avar—and—her. An attorney would want to know just how much the police and the District Attorney knew. Perhaps this was her chance to find out. Korshak, in his desire to torture his prey, might end up telling everything he knew…

She said, "I've nothing to hide, Sergeant. You wanted to know who I *loaned* the Buick to? I loaned it to Mr. Newstone, here. I believe you met him a few weeks ago."

The muscles in Korshak's lower jaw twitched slightly but nothing showed in his expression. He did not turn his eyes to the young giant seated a few feet from him. "Uh-huh. We met. Where'd he take the Buick?"

"Why don't you ask Mr. Newstone that?"

"Don't you know where he went?"

"I doubt if I have the right to speak for him, Sergeant Korshak," she said sweetly.

Very slowly the police officer turned his head and met the blazing eyes of the rock-faced cave man. "You understand English, Mr. Newstone?" The words came from between set teeth.

"Yes." The single word rang in the silence like the note of a muted bell.

"Picked it up pretty fast, didn't you?"

AVAR did not reply. There was a sort of contemptuous indifference in his steady gaze: a lion regarding a jackal.

Twin spots of color burned in Korshak's cheeks. "Okay. What time was it when you borrowed this young lady's car?"

"Ota was deep in the sky."

"Huh? What kind of double talk is that?"

"He means," Whitney said quietly, "that it was along toward sundown."

"Oh. Indian talk, huh? You can do better than that, mister. What time was it on the clock?"

Avar shrugged and said nothing.

"Where did you go?"

In the silence that followed, Officer Gilmer, near the library door, shifted his feet and cleared his throat.

Whitney said coldly, "You're dragging this thing out beyond the limits of patience, Sergeant. Specifically what are you getting at?"

Korshak's jaw hardened. "Murder, Mr. Whitney!"

"Oh? Whose murder?"

"A man named Gene Cameron—a two-bit blackmailer and gambler."

"I see. Are you intimating that my daughter and my guest are involved in his death?"

"'Intimating' isn't strong enough, Mr. Whitney. I'm saying they're responsible for it!"

As a bombshell it was pretty much of a dud. Lauren's gasp was almost inaudible, while neither Whitney nor Avar so much as blinked. Whitney said, "That's a pretty serious charge, Sergeant. I trust you're prepared to back it up."

"I'll leave that to you. Both your daughter and Newstone were seen entering Cameron's place in Westwood. The time of death has been set as being between nine and ten-thirty this evening. Your daughter entered the front door at nine-eighteen. Cameron himself let her in. Newstone entered through a second floor window at 10:02. At 10:26 both Miss Whitney and Newstone left by a side entrance, taking great care to keep from being observed. Both entered a gray Chevrolet coupe, license number 333V610, and Miss Whitney drove to Senaca Street, a block away, where Newstone left the coupe and entered a gray-blue Buick convertible, license number 9A742. He drove several yards when Miss Whitney stopped him and told him he had forgotten to turn on his headlights. The two cars then drove away—and are now parked outside your door. You have heard these two people admit they were using those cars this evening."

He paused to take a deep drag on his cigarette before tossing it into the fireplace. No one said anything. Lauren and her father were staring fixedly at Korshak, while Avar, apparently bored by the lengthy conversation, seemed half-asleep.

Whitney said, "You seem to have all this down to a fine point, Sergeant. I'm a little surprised that your picture is so complete. It sounds as though a trained observer had been holding a stop watch on the alleged movements of my daughter and Mr. Newstone."

Korshak permitted himself a grim smile. "That's exactly what it adds up to, Mr. Whitney. Luck enters into it, of course; we don't often have a case all nicely wrapped up and laid in our laps. But I'm not going into that right now; it'll all come out at the trial…

"Here's where I'd like to talk about the killing. When Officer Gilmer and I entered Cameron's place, we found him dead in his apartment on the second floor. He wasn't pretty to see. His back was broken, there were marks of fingers so deep in his throat that the skin was broken. His head had been battered in with a desk lamp standard until there was hardly any face left. It was—"

"That's a lie!" Lauren was on her feet, trembling with indignation. "The only mark on him was where Avar—" She stopped suddenly, realizing what her words were doing.

"Go on, Miss Whitney," Korshak urged mockingly.

"I don't think so," Whitney cut in decisively. "I suppose you're determined to make an arrest, Sergeant?"

"Two arrests," Korshak corrected blandly.

WHITNEY bit his lip. "That's up to you, of course." His eyes swung to Lauren and he smiled encouragingly. "Don't worry, Princess. I'll start things moving before you reach police headquarters. We'll have both of you out of there in no time."

Korshak was smiling almost openly—a smile of complete triumph and satisfaction. "I wouldn't bet on that, Mr. Whitney. You put the fix in once and got away with it. This time it's murder and not even *you* can fix that."

Lauren, her face very pale, stepped between Korshak and her father. "It was not murder. It was self-defense. Gene Cameron was trying to manhandle me and Avar—Mr. Newstone—came to my aid. Gene—"

"Lauren… Stop it." Whitney's voice was hoarse. "Don't tell him a thing; this isn't the time for it."

"I won't stop it!" she cried wildly. "Avar was trying to help me. When he came to my—my rescue Cameron drew a gun and shot him. Look at the coat he's wearing! Go ahead, look at it—all of you! You'll find a bullet hole in it and a wound in his side. In trying to get the gun away from Gene, Avar killed him in self-defense."

Korshak was shaking his head. "It's a nice try, Miss Whitney, but it won't do. When a man is trying to take a gun away from an enemy he doesn't choke him to death, break his back, and pound his face to pulp with a chair. Believe me; I know."

"He didn't hit him with a chair!" she cried hysterically. "He didn't hit him with *anything!* You're lying and you know it! Why do you tell such horrible lies?"

Aroused by the angry sobs tearing from the girl's throat, Avar came lithely to his feet and started slowly toward the sergeant, his arms half raised, his purpose plain to see in his expression.

Korshak fell back a step, his hand slipping beneath the left lapel of his dark blue coat. "Keep your pet under control, Whitney," he warned, "or I'll plug him where he stands."

Whitney was standing now. He pushed in front of Avar, seizing him by the arms. "No, Avar." He spoke quietly, a soothing note in his voice. "That will only make matters worse."

The cave man stopped his advance reluctantly and Korshak's hand came from under his coat, empty. "That's better," he said. "I'm sorry, Miss Whitney, but I'll have to take you and Mr. Newstone in. Would you like to get some things together?"

The words, by themselves, sounded friendly, even solicitous. But there was an undertone of self-satisfaction, which the girl was quick to recognize. Her head came up proudly and her lips twisted into an open sneer.

"So this is your revenge, Sergeant Korshak—this is your way at hitting back at Avar for throwing you through that window, and at my father for keeping him out of your hands that day. You've been waiting for a chance to get him!

"And when you saw him drive away this afternoon alone, you followed him. That's how you are able to give the time we arrived and left Gene's club. You waited outside while we were in there—you waited until we left before you went in to learn what had happened. It was you who beat Gene's dead body with a lamp—*if* he was beaten. What about the gun on the floor? I suppose you didn't find a gun lying near Gene's body."

The glitter in Korshak's eyes was stronger now and his nostrils were flaring under the lash of her words. He said, "This isn't going to earn you anything but more trouble, Miss Whitney. Police don't do things like you're suggesting."

"What about that gun?"

"When the time comes for—"

"What about that gun?"

HE PURSED his lips and shook his head slowly from side to side. "There wasn't any gun in that apartment, Miss Whitney."

"That *proves* it." Her voice rang out with a kind of savage satisfaction. "This is what you call a 'frame', isn't it, Sergeant? You think you've got us where you want us, don't you? You think you're going to put Avar in the gas chamber, eh? Well, let me tell you some—"

"That *all* you're going to tell me, sister!" Korshak's lower jaw came out like the prow of a ship. "I suppose I'm the guy who wrecked Cameron's apartment hunting for something, too? I suppose I'm the guy who cracked a wall panel in his bedroom and tore the top of a metal box with my hands?"

Her stricken expression was all he needed. Whitney was staring round-eyed at his daughter and deep down in them was a flicker of doubt.

"That's what's going to bust your 'self-defense' story apart, lady." Korshak went on, his caution ripped apart by his anger. "You and your he-man boy friend went there to get something. You had him kill Cameron when he wouldn't turn over what you were after. Then you turned the place upside down looking for it. What was it you were after, Miss Whitney—love letters?"

She opened her mouth to speak, to deny the accusation...but the words wouldn't come.

"Maybe you found 'em, huh?" Korshak said, hammering at her, "Maybe you didn't have a chance to get rid of them. You say you came home just a few minutes ahead of your father. Maybe those letters are still in your bag—*the one right there on that desk!*"

Instinctively she turned to get it. But Korshak, moving with surprising speed, was ahead of her. He backed away from her frantically clutching hands, his fingers fumbling at the clasp.

It was then that Avar acted.

A single giant stride brought him beside the policeman, his bronzed hand shot out and tore the white leather bag from Korshak's futile grasp.

The sergeant, his small white teeth exposed in a snarl of complete hatred, backed away, his shifting eyes catching a glimpse of Gilmer moving up and seeking to line the sights of his gun on the cave man.

"Okay, brother," Korshak grunted. "You asked for it." His right shoulder dipped suddenly as his hand darted for the gun under his coat.

But the brain and muscles that so often had outwitted and outmatched such crafty and fearsome jungle denizens as Kuo, the lion, and Loka, the panther, were not to be so easily overcome. With a single lithe movement Avar was upon the sergeant. His free hand knocked the gun flying even as it appeared, then darted down and closed in the folds of the man's coat. With a single sweeping motion he lifted Korshak completely from the floor and hurled him headlong into Gilmer.

There was the dull thud of body against body and the two men went down in a tangle of arms and legs. In that same instant Avar wheeled, Lauren's bag still clutched in one hand, and raced toward the library's French windows.

"Avar!"

The Cro-Magnard paused in mid-stride and half turned in the direction of the cry. Lauren Whitney ran to him and threw herself into his arms.

"Don't go without me, dearest," she panted. "Take me with you."

She could feel the tenseness go out of his arms, and he smiled into her eyes. It was a smile tinged with sadness and regret.

"No, Lau-ren. Your world hates and fears me—and hates you because of me. That is why I must go alone."

He put her gently aside and turned back to the windows.

Tears rolled from the eyes of the stricken girl. "But where will you go? What can you *do?*"

He looked back over his shoulder at her, and his smile was undimmed.

"Who knows?" he said, and then he was gone into the blackness outside, just as a gun barked from somewhere behind Lauren.

CHAPTER TWELVE

AS AVAR, warrior of the tribe of Kosad, felt the firm earth beneath his feet, the thin veneer of civilization that so carefully had been molded to his unresisting body during the previous month dropped from his shoulders.

No longer was he bound to observe the stupid and incomprehensible customs of a strange race. He was free to do as he pleased; and although the hands of an entire world were turned against him, he was accustomed to facing heavy odds and the prospect left him indifferent.

Despite the heavy darkness, his eyes, veterans of countless jungle nights, instantly caught the outlines of a row of thick bushes to his left and he dived behind them a second ahead of Korshak's appearance at the open window.

Avar lay there watching him, noticing the gun in his hand. Despite his contempt for the people of this world, he had the greatest respect for many of the strange things they possessed. Guns were among them; Emil had taught him how to shoot during those three weeks in the hills, and he knew the power for death they carried. He wished he could have taken a gun with him.

For a full minute Korshak remained in the opening less than twenty feet from where Avar lay. He peered this way and that into the darkness, but his eyes were not the eyes of Avar, and so at last he turned back into the room.

The instant he had disappeared, Avar rose to his feet and ran lightly away from the house. After a few yards the stables loomed ahead of him; these he skirted cautiously, aware that Luke might be with the horses, then plunged on into the night.

A little while later he was passing the row of poplars marking the eastern boundary of the Whitney estate. The ground dropped almost vertically here into the deep narrow valley called Needle Canyon.

For a few moments he stood there on the lip of the valley, debating his next move. Instinct urged flight into the hills, as far as possible from modern man and his works. But his native cunning and the knowledge he had acquired of the people of this world gave him pause. Men like Korshak would expect him to flee into open country and attempt to put as much distance between him and his pursuers as possible. The entire countryside for miles around would be alerted; farmers would be cautioned to shoot him down on sight; bands of armed men would roam the hills and prairies in search of him.

Not that they would find him. He had little doubt but that he could outwit an enemy whose nose was hardly more than an ornament, whose eyes were barely worthy of the name, and whose ears were attuned only to violent noises. Avar would be able to filter through the lines of his hunters with ease.

But that would mean he must forever be on the run, and eventually they would get him. Were any of them able to catch sight of him away from cover, their guns, like great long arms, would reach out to pull him down. Every foray against some outlying farmhouse in search of food would mean the risk of a bullet in his back.

He thought of the things Emil had taught him about the humans of this world. And as he went over the odds and ends of information his active mind had retained, the certainty came that his best means of shaking off pursuit would be to lose himself among those humans, to go where they were in large numbers, to become one man among thousands. Certainly he was not so different physically that it could not succeed.

The sheer foolhardiness of such a plan intrigued him and made that its chief virtue. Yes, he would go down among those men of today, he would become one of the hunters instead of the hunted.

BELOW him, to the south, was a vast carpet of twinkling lights spread as far as eye could see. Those millions of glowing embers marked the dwelling places of many people—a great sea of humanity into which he could submerge himself and find safety.

A slight smile touched his strong lips as he turned and began to work his way south down the hillside toward Hollywood.

"Can't see him, Hank." Korshak came away from the window and went to the phone on the desk, completely ignoring Gregg Whitney and his daughter. One side of his coat was ripped almost to the sleeve and the knot of his blue-fingered gray necktie had slid into the vicinity of his right ear. While he was dialing, Gilmer lumbered heavily up to the desk, gun in hand, and stood there glaring at the Whitneys.

"Who is this?" Korshak said into the mouthpiece. "This is Korshak, Steve. I found out who knocked off that Cameron guy in Westwood, but he made a break for it and got away into the hills. If my guess means anything he headed north the minute he broke away—they better throw a cordon around the... Oh, sure. Needle Canyon. Tell 'em whole vicinity. The more unsettled the country the better for a guy like him... Yeah, I know quite a bit about the guy. Had my eye on him more'n a month now because of another matter. Name's Adam, or Avar, Newstone. A-V-A-R. Like two words: New and Stone... Yeah; that's right. He's a good six-feet four, around two-twenty I'd say, built like a cross between one of those Greek gods and Man Mountain Dean. Muscles like you never saw in your life... Not when he got away but he might pick up a gun someplace. Tell the boys they better shoot on sight or he'll make hash out of 'em with his bare hands, *and I'm not foolin'!* Black hair, kind of yellow-gray eyes with a fire in each of them, good-looking in the face but kind of wide across the cheekbones, shoulders a mile wide. Wearing a lightweight gray two piece suit, light blue sport shirt open at the throat and no tie, black socks with a white clock and a pair of black loafers; no hat... Yeah, sure he's on foot... No doubt about it, Steve; he's the guy who killed Cameron. Broke his back and choked him and beat his head in with a lamp base. He's dynamite, I tell you. ...this phone?

Hillside 6-69974. 3815 Needle Canyon Drive. Gregg Whitney… Okay… Yeah… Yeah… Okay, Steve."

He put back the receiver, flexed the fingers of his right hand a time or two, then looked up at Gregg Whitney. "Looks as if I'm going to have to stick around a while, Mr. Whitney. There'll be some phone calls I'll have to take and some officers up here pretty soon to look for your guest. That all right with you?"

"It appears I have little choice," Whitney said grimly. "I do think that 'shoot on sight' order of yours was uncalled for and I intend to say so to the right people."

Korshak's lip curled. "Go as far as you like, mister. You heard how he killed Cameron; you saw what he did to Gilmer and me. I'll back anything you can say with that—and not a police commissioner in the State would fail to back me up."

A voice behind them said, "What's happening? Did I hear a shot, Mr. Whitney?"

It was Perry Siddons, wearing a light cotton robe over blue and white pajamas. He came into the room, blinked at the disheveled attire of the two policemen and at Lauren's stricken expression.

Lauren said brokenly, "They're after Avar, Perry."

He frowned at the circle of faces. "What for?"

"He—he defended me against a man…and killed him. They're trying to claim it was m—*murder.*" Her chin began to tremble uncontrollably. "They're going to kill him, Perry—shoot him down in cold blood."

Suddenly she whirled and put her head down against her father's chest and began to cry in great tearing sobs that shook her entire body.

WHITNEY patted her shoulder clumsily. "Don't, Princess. They'll never get close enough to kill him; you know that. He's a better and smarter man than all the policemen in Los Angeles County."

Korshak grunted with grim amusement. "I've heard a lot of people make cracks like that in my time, Mr. Whitney. Those that didn't end up behind bars are propping up tombstones."

Whitney glared at him. "When I want a remark from you, Sergeant, I'll ask for it. You're legal rights go just so far; don't overstep them."

The color heightened in Korshak's cheeks but he said nothing. Gilmer cleared his throat and sidled up to his partner. "Whadda we do now, Ed?"

"Not much we can do until some of the boys show up. Unless you'd like to go out looking for him."

"The moose?" Alarm flooded his round heavy face. "Not without I got ten guys with guns with me."

The telephone shrilled and Korshak scooped up the receiver. "Hello... Yeah, yeah... Nice going, Steve. Say it might be a good idea to phone a lot of the residents around here and tip 'em off on what... Good... Okay, fella..."

There was a thin-lipped, crooked smile creasing his cheeks as he replaced the instrument. When he spoke he appeared to be addressing Gilmer, but the others in the room knew he was speaking for their benefit.

"It won't be long now, Hank. The Highway boys have been tipped off and are already covering the entire district...and six carloads of our boys are on their way here right now!"

A line of gnarled eucalyptus trees marked the northern edge of a paved, two-lane road and Avar crouched under the drooping branches of one of them, his eyes and ears seeking the sound of an approaching car. But the only sounds to reach him were the skirl of tree frogs and the distant cry of a coyote, the first he had ever heard.

As he knelt there he realized he was still clutching Lauren's purse. He cleared a small circle of ground, opened the bag and dumped out its contents. The two envelopes of negatives went into the side pocket of his jacket, to be destroyed at a more convenient time. A thin sheaf of currency, held together by a gold plated clip caught his eye and he put it together with the money he had taken from Lauren's room earlier that day into his wallet. Money was the most important thing in this world, he had learned; without it his chances of escape were materially lessened.

The rest of the heap was the usual hodge-podge found in any woman's bag. An unopened package of cigarettes and a tiny gold lighter went into his pocket. A cigarette between the lips would help to make him indistinguishable from the men of this world— another member of a numberless fraternity. What better way of achieving anonymity than by taking on all the visible attributes of the people around him?

The purse and the remainder of its contents he left on the ground and, the stretch of roadway was deserted, he came into the open, trotted across the ribbon of asphalt and on into the rolling hills beyond.

As he drew nearer the northern outskirts of Hollywood he was forced more and more often to take the circuitous route to avoid the increasing number of homes covering the lower slopes of the hills. The land now was divided by streets, and the blocks contained fewer empty lots.

Finally he was forced to follow one of the streets continuously. It led apparently straight into Hollywood, the heart of which appeared to be no more than half a mile ahead of him. Houses lined both sides of the street, their white stucco walls and tile roofs gleaming among shadows from the trees.

Cars passed him occasionally, moving in either direction, and twice he passed pedestrians who seemed to make a point of not looking at him. A few times he caught the sounds of laughter, of music, of gay voices through open windows along the way.

HE REACHED Hollywood Boulevard, the district's principal thoroughfare, and stood at the intersection for a moment, blinking in the glare of neon's. An illuminated clock dial in a jewelry store window told him it lacked only a few minutes of being midnight. A movie theater half a block down the boulevard had just finished the feature and the audience was spilling out into the sidewalk.

Avar turned right then and sauntered slowly along the wide, lighted street. He allowed his shoulders to droop slightly and his step to drag, seeking to take on a protective coloring by aping the gait and posture of the average man of this world.

But no amount of camouflage could adequately conceal the nobility of carriage and the arresting handsomeness of his face and figure. Three different young women, two of them with escorts, stared at him in open admiration as he went by; while the third went deliberately out of her way to get in front of him. As he stepped aside to avoid running head on into her, she smiled frankly up at him, inviting a verbal lead. Avar passed her by as though she did not exist.

Two blocks further on he caught sight of a blinking sign on the roof of a four-story white building across the street—a sign that spelled out the word: HOTEL. He stopped abruptly. Emil had told him about hotels. People without homes could sleep in them in exchange for pieces of money. There were usually public places in them where a man could get food, also in exchange for pieces of money. While he could, if necessary, go several suns without food and many hours without sleep he knew the wisdom of getting both when the chance presented itself. Tonight those hunting him would be beating the hills. While they were doing that, he would eat and sleep against the time when they might be hunting him here in the place of many caves.

At the next intersection he turned left and started across the street, forgetting the significance of the glowing red traffic light.

Car brakes squealed suddenly and only his uncanny agility kept him from being run down. A voice yelled unintelligible from the car's interior as it passed him.

Avar retreated to the curb to wait until the signal changed. Another car pulled to a stop in front of him and he saw two men, in blue uniforms, looking out at him. The one at the open window nearest to him said.

"What's the idea, fella? Don't they have traffic lights where yuh come from?"

The tone of that growling voice lifted the hair on Avar's neck and his shoulders rose slightly in instinctive preparation for attack.

"What's a matter, big boy—can't you talk? I ast yuh a question."

Avar beat down an impulse to reach out and drag the owner of that nerve-jarring voice from his seat. But an inherent cunning warned him such a move on his part would be fatal.

The driver said, "Skip it, Joe; yuh got the poor guy scared to death."

The first officer said, "I know, but these out-a-towners come out here and get theirselves run over and then yell about how punk a system we got. Okay, fella; go ahead. The next time, though, yuh get a ticket, see?"

The light was green now, and Avar crossed over, aware the officers were watching him. Deliberately he turned left and walked away from the hotel that had been his goal. Half a block later he looked back. The patrol car was nowhere in sight.

He retraced his steps to the hotel entrance. Beyond a low ceilinged lobby containing chairs and a couch or two and lighted by table lamps was a semicircular desk brightly lighted, with a key and mail-rack behind it. A middle-aged man with a round face bisected with dark-rimmed glasses was seated behind the desk reading a paper.

Avar was on the point of passing through the open door when the scent of food reached his sensitive nostrils. With it was carried the familiar stale grease odor which had made eating something of a task ever since the day he had awakened in the Hollywood hills.

But hunger was strong in him and he turned from the hotel entrance and followed the scent to a combination bar and grill a few doors farther to the west.

HE PUSHED open one of the two glass-paneled doors and went into a long narrow room. A gleaming white counter ran almost the fun length, a line of stools, dotted at intervals with diners, in front of it. Against the opposite wall were small tables for two; and halfway down was an arched opening leading to the bar.

Avar sat down on the stool nearest the door. A small dark waitress in a blue uniform drifted wearily over and put a glass of water and a menu in front of him.

When the cave man made no move toward picking either of them up the girl looked at him for the first time and her eyes widened perceptibly in involuntary tribute to his handsome face and splendid figure.

"What's yours, mister?"

Avar felt he was on safe ground. He knew the names of several kinds of foods, any of which he should be able to buy here.

"Steak," he said decisively and finally. This should close the conversation; she would go somewhere and get a piece of meat, put it in front of him with the necessary tools for eating, then leave him to feed in the manner he had so laboriously learned.

The girl's forehead developed a wrinkle. "Tenderloin, porterhouse, sirloin or Swiss?"

For a brief moment he hated her for thus complicating matters. It appeared there were more than one kind of steak—something Emil had never pointed out. The one with the shortest name stuck in his mind and he said, "Swiss," hoping the word would terminate the conversation.

"Well, medium or rare?" Some of the impersonal inflection was gone from her voice and she was staring at him curiously.

He was being given another choice, he realized. All this specialization was wearing his patience thin.

"Rare."

"Yessir."

TO his relief she went away. He sipped from the water glass and, rather awkwardly, tore open the package of cigarettes and lit one. He sat there, very straight in the back puffing amateurishly on the cigarette and staring fixedly at a display of pies behind a glass-doored cabinet across from him.

One of the diners left his stool, tucking a newspaper under his arm, and sauntered past Avar's suddenly tense back. He paused at the cash register and one of the waitresses came over, took money from the man and rang up the sale. The customer returned to where he had been sitting, slipped a coin under the edge of his plate and went back to the door and out.

Once more Avar allowed his muscles to relax. He sat there silently, allowing his senses to soak in the atmosphere. Halfway down the room beyond the archway leading to the bar, a jukebox was blaring out one of the day's popular songs, the noise jarring at Avar's keen ears. Like most jungle denizens loud noises confused and angered him, but he realized there was nothing he could do about this one.

His steak came, flanked by soggy French fried potatoes and a nauseous mess of cold slaw. With slow care he buttered a piece of bread, as he had been taught, and began to eat.

"Coffee?"

He looked up, the corner of his upper lip lifting in an unconscious snarl. The waitress was back, staring at him with frank interest.

"Yes." It seemed the simplest way to get rid of her.

THE jukebox ceased its racket while she was putting the cup beside his plate. The sudden quiet gave a small radio near the cashier's station a chance to be heard.

"...cupant of the second car died en route to the hospital," said a crisp-voiced announcer. "He was, Michael Miller, 8216 Estes Boulevard, Pasadena... The murder of Eugene Cameron, thirty-two-year-old proprietor of a Westwood night spot, whose body was found in his office a few hours ago, is near a solution, police claim."

Avar very carefully put down his knife and fork and glanced about him with slow care. No one in the restaurant appeared to be paying any attention to the newscast.

"Cameron appeared to have met death at the hands of a man of incredible strength who was motivated by insane rage. His body was a mass of bruises, police say, his back was broken and he had been brutally choked. Although the name of the suspected killer was not revealed, he is described as being in his mid-twenties, well over six feet tall, well-built, black-haired and exceptionally handsome. He is believed to have fled into the hills north of Hollywood, and all residents of that area have been warned. One of the largest manhunts in Southern California's history is said to be taking shape... Two unidentified youths held up a Pico Boulevard filling station late this afternoon and escaped..."

Very deliberately Avar picked up his knife and fork and went back to his steak, while the radio voice droned on. It appeared his ruse in doubling back had succeeded. They were hunting him exactly where he had suspected they would. With the time thus gained he must find a place to hole up where he could never be found...

He finished his steak, drained his coffee cup and picked up the check as he had seen two of the other customers do ahead of him. He gave it and a bill to the waitress behind the cash register, accepted his change and put another bill under the edge of his plate as he had seen the others do. True, the others had placed coins there instead of bills, but there was none in the change the girl had given him. A bill, he had learned, was worth several coins, so he was fairly sure his waitress would be satisfied and not attract attention to him by asking for more.

He was outside before the girl came over to clear away the counter, so he did not hear her awestruck remark to the girl at the cash register.

"Well, for—! Katie, looka here. That guy eats a dollar steak and gives me a five-buck tip. How d'ya like a thing like that?"

"You musta give him your phone number, Gracie," said a cab driver three stools down, smirking at her.

"Mebbe I would of—if he'd asked me!" she said. "A real high class gentleman that didn't try to get fresh, like some I seen. D'ja see the eyes on him, Katie? Like they had *fire* in 'em."

CHAPTER THIRTEEN

THE desk clerk of the Brevort Arms looked up from his paper suddenly aware that he was not alone. A man was standing across the ledge from him—a tall, young man with wide shoulders under the folds of a gray suit and the most direct eyes the clerk ever had seen in Hollywood.

He dropped the newspaper and jumped to his feet. "Sorry, sir, I didn't hear you come in. Was there something you wanted?"

"A bed," said the young man simply.

"A—you mean a room?"

"Yes."

A little prickle of uneasiness moved along the clerk's spine. The direct, unwavering scrutiny of those strangely glowing eyes, the man's monosyllabic way of speaking, the way his long muscular arms hung loosely at his sides—all these marked the stranger as different in a disquieting way.

A table model radio on the shelf behind the clerk had been droning the muted strains of a dance orchestra into the quiet lobby. The music stopped now and a man said ponderously, "Ladies and gentlemen, our national anthem…"

The clerk reached back and twisted the dial, shutting off the first strains. "Going off the air for the night," he explained, for no other reason than an inner compulsion to talk as a relief to the strain of looking into the young man's eyes. "Now you want a room. Ah—let you have a nice single-with-bath on the third floor for three-fifty a day. No weekly or monthly rates, of course; you know what the hotel sit—"

"I will take it," Avar said curtly.

"Ah—yes, of course. Glad to have you with us, Mr….uh." He put a small white card, ruled off into lines and printed directions in front of Avar and drew over the desk pen. "If you'll register…"

Avar said, "What is this for?"

The clerk's hands fluttered nervously. "Why—why—ah. Register, sir. Rule, you know…all guests must register. On the white card, sir."

Avar was in too deep to retreat. There was so much Emil had neglected to teach him. He said, "This is the first time I have stayed at a hotel. What does 'register' mean?"

The clerk designated the ruled lines with a wavering forefinger. "Just put your name and address on these lines, as directed."

His eyes goggled as the young giant took hold of the pen awkwardly and began to write with the slow care of a student in the third year of grammar school.

Finishing, Avar pushed card and pen back to the clerk and stood there impassively, waiting.

"Ah—uh—Mr. Newstone. Glad to have you as a guest. How long are you planning on being with us?"

"I do not know."

"I—uh—see. Now a rule of the hotel, Mr. Newstone—you understand I don't make the rules; that's up to the management—"

The cave man was growing weary of the fat man's babble. "Where is my bed?" he growled.

"Oh, right away, Mr. Newstone. It's late, I know, and I'm sure you're tired. But the rule is, if a guest has no—ah—luggage the room must be put on a day-to-day basis, payment in—uh—advance."

The word "payment" struck a responsive chord in the Cro-Magnard's mind. The man obviously wanted money for his bed—just as everyone in this world wanted money for everything.

His hand slid into the inner pocket of his jacket and, as the clerk turned noticeably pale, came out again holding his wallet. "How much money?" he said quietly.

"Well—uh—now you understand, Mr. New—"

"How much money?"

"Now—uh—you wish the single-with-bath that I men—"

Avar's free hand shot out and closed about the clerk's lapel. "How much money?"

The man hung there trembling. "Three-fifty, sir." The words came out with machine-gun rapidity.

AVAR released him so suddenly he nearly fell and drew out most of the currency in his wallet. "Take your money," he growled.

"Ah—yes, sir." The clerk plucked a five-dollar bill from the collection and made out a receipt with unsteady fingers about the desk pen. He took the necessary change from a drawer under the counter and handed it and the receipt to the waiting cave man. Then his hand came down on the button of a desk bell, sending a single clanging note through the lobby.

The sound galvanized Avar into instant action. The sweep of one hand sent the bell flying, the other darted out, caught the amazed clerk by the shoulder and lifted him completely across the counter and held him there, his feet three inches off the floor.

"Why did you do that?" Avar demanded in a terrible voice.

"Ah…ah…ah…"

Those steel fingers bit into the flesh beneath them. *Why?*

"The b—b—bell boy," stammered the clerk. "I—I had to send—he'll show you to—"

A faint sound at his back brought Avar around in a flash, still clutching the petrified clerk. A slender young man in a maroon uniform was standing there, his ordinarily age-weary eyes threatening to pop from his head. "What do *you* want?" Avar snarled.

The bellboy fell back a step. "Mr. Hamilton rang, sir…"

Everything was clear to Avar now. He put the clerk down. "I did not understand," he said simply.

The man seemed too dazed to speak; in fact he was barely able to stand. Avar, with a sudden flash of insight, took out his wallet again, extracted the first bill his fingers encountered and handed it to Hamilton.

Blindly the clerk's fingers closed about the bill and he turned and scurried behind the desk. Hurriedly he snatched a key from the rack and tossed it to the boy.

"Show the—ah—gentleman to 317," he said, some of his dignity seeping back.

"Yessir. This way, sir." The bellboy's eyes had ceased to protrude but they were still round with wonder.

When the elevator door had closed, shutting off the boy and the hotel's latest guest, Mr. Hamilton sank into his chair and closed his eyes. For several minutes he sat there, spasmodic tremors shaking him. The sound of the elevator door opening brought him out of his chair in sudden panic.

It was the bellboy. He came over to the desk and said, "jeez, Mr. Hamilton, what a beaut *that* one is. I thought for a minute there he was gonna tear yuh head off. What's a matter with him?"

Mr. Hamilton became aware of the bill in his hand and he brought it up slowly and looked at the figure in one corner. It was a ten-dollar bill.

"Ah—eccentric, William. A trifle eccentric."

"Eccentric, hell! That guy's *nuts!* Did you see the eyes on him?"

Mr. Hamilton fluttered his hand in a gesture of dismissal. "We don't speak of our guests that way, William. You go along now, and forget this—ah—this incident."

The bellboy withdrew, shaking his head, and Mr. Hamilton returned to his paper. Absently he flicked on the radio and turned the dial until the softened beat of a dance band filtered through. He was in the act of turning to the "Help Wanted" columns, when the music from the radio faded out and an announcer said:

"You have been listening to the music of Lee Colton and his orchestra. And now for a five minute roundup of the latest headlines: Police report that the killer of Eugene Cameron, well-to-do nightclub owner, is still at large although police, county and State officers are scouring the hills north of Hollywood in search of him. He is described as…"

The oily-smooth voice chanted on—and Mr. Hamilton, night clerk at the Brevort Arms, found himself hanging onto every word. Finally he put up an unsteady hand and clicked off the set, then in a bemused way he reached for the house phone beside him.

"Lilian," he whispered into the mouthpiece, "get me the police station right away."

GREGG WHITNEY fumbled with the cigarette he was holding and shook his head wearily. He seemed to have aged years in the last few hours: there was an unnatural pallor to his cheeks, fresh lines cut faint furrows in the skin of his forehead and his hands were trembling.

"Father, you've got to do *something!* You can't let them shoot him down without an opportunity to—to defend himself."

"I don't know what to do, Lauren," he admitted resignedly. "You heard me call Larry Abbott and I told you what he said. When a police commissioner says his hands are tied, that he can't give orders to take Adam alive in view of what he's supposed to have done to Cameron—then I don't know what else can be done. Our only hope is that Adam permits himself to be taken alive; that he gets a chance to surrender before some nervous officer can shoot him in the back."

He looked around the library at the others waiting in the dimly lighted room. Emil Thoretsen was sitting in a lounge chair near the fireplace, the flickering flames highlighting the troubled expression on his thin face. Joan Whitney sat huddled in one corner of the sofa, her tear-filled blue eyes shifting from Perry Siddons, slumped in a chair and studying his hands, to Lauren, who was ceaselessly pacing the floor.

"Like an *animal*," Lauren burst out, more to herself than anyone else. "Like they were hunting a mad dog that had bitten some child!"

"Well gosh, Lauren," Perry said slowly. "In a way he *is* an animal. Sure; I know he's big and handsome and—and majestic. But according to the Prof here he's from a world where you had to be an animal to live."

She whirled on him. "How *dare* you say such a thing. How *dare* you! He has more decency, more honesty—"

"Easy, Princess," Gregg Whitney said softly.

"...more understanding than any other man in the world! He was good, Perry Siddons—*good!* Do you know what it is to be good—to be truly human and unspoiled? No, you don't—and neither does any other 'civilized' man or woman."

"Civilized!" She spat out the word in revulsion. "If Avar is an animal, then I say we could all stand to be shoved back twenty thousand years and start over again. Maybe the next time we wouldn't sell our natural heritages for the glitter and comforts of what we call civilization."

Emil Thoretsen crossed his legs and leaned back. "Relax, Lauren. You're only saying what has been said before—said many times and much better by some pretty wise men. What you're overlooking is that this isn't Avar's fault or modern man's. The fact remains that he is a Cro-Magnard: born twenty thousand years ago and plunged into a machine far too complex for him to survive. That we are able to survive it is not because of what we are ourselves. We are the present end products of countless generations of forbears who traveled for us the road between prehistory and today. As a result we have had built up in us a protective armor which enables us to survive the rigors of our era. Avar made that twenty-thousand-year jump in the twinkling of an eye. Consequently he does not have—he *could* not have—our resistance, our tolerance for life in this age. His body is open to the invasion of much of the sickness and disease we have become immune to, his mind is no less pregnable to countless neuroses which time and evolution have enabled us more or less avoid.

"He may come through this mess unscathed. If so, he will go on trial for killing Cameron. Whether the killing was justified or not is a matter a jury will decide. But can you imagine him in the courtroom? Can you see him sitting there day after day while attorneys wrangle and spectators stare? Will he remain sullenly quiescent, like a caged tiger, indifferent to the taunts and questions of the State, which wants him sent to the gas chamber?

"Can you see the newspapers during the trial? Can you picture what they will do to him? The highly colored and inaccurate stories of his background, the picturesque sobriquets they will nail to him? The Ape Man. The Astral Assassin. The Terror out of Time."

HE SIGHED heavily. "And you, Lauren. You and your father and your sister. Yes, and me, I suppose. Do you know what the papers and the tongues of people will do to us for defending and explaining him to others? How we'll be lambasted for swallowing such an "impossible" theory that Avar is a man born twenty thousand years ago?"

Lauren was glaring at him. "I don't care! I love him."

"Certainly you love him. Do you think we're blind? I love him too—and so does your father and your sister and anyone who had the chance to know him. But that mustn't blind us to what and who Avar is—and to what his fate in our world may be. Personally I regard it as having been a privilege to have known him and to have learned that the first man on Earth—the first *true* man—was as the Bible says: in the image and likeness of God."

The room was very quiet when he finished speaking. Lauren stood there staring at him until, very slowly, the tenseness went out of her face leaving it defenseless and without hope. Slowly she turned away.

Gregg Whitney said, "It's after one o'clock. I think we ought to—"

The phone on his desk rang—a sudden shrill sound that caused everyone in the room to start. Hastily Whitney scooped up the receiver, conscious that all eyes were fastened on him—waiting.

"Hello," he said, his voice steady.

"Mr. Whitney?" It was the sharp decisive voice of Sergeant Korshak; Whitney recognized it immediately.

"Yes; this is Whitney."

"Just wanted to tell you, we found our man."

"Ya mean you—you've captured him?"

No one in the library seemed to be breathing.

"A matter of minutes, Mr. Whitney." There was an unmistakably gloating note in his tone. "We found him holed up in a Hollywood hotel and we've thrown a cordon around the place that a gopher couldn't get through. Show you how stupid the big guy is…he registered under his own name!"

"I'm afraid he doesn't have a criminal's cunning, Sergeant."

"Yeah. Well, I'll let you know where you can claim the body."

"You're determined to kill him on sight?"

"Well now, Mr. Whitney, you know the kind of nut he is." The appeal-to-reason note in his tone was open mockery. "A homicidal maniac like that—we can't take any chances of having one of our men killed."

Anger was rising in Whitney—an anger he knew was utterly futile. "Isn't this a little unusual, Korshak, keeping an ordinary citizen informed on the progress of a police case?"

The ghost of a chuckle came over the wire. "I don't think I have to draw you a picture, mister. Next time a friend of yours takes a poke at a cop, don't go putting in the fix. Cops don't like it."

"Is that all you have to tell me, Sergeant?"

"Sure; that's it. We're going in now. I'll keep you posted."

The receiver clicked in Whitney's ear.

AVAR awakened from a sound, untroubled sleep. Awakened as a jungle denizen always awakens—instantly and completely. He lay unmoving, his ears, keen beyond the understanding of modern man, listening for a repetition of whatever sound had penetrated his subconscious and aroused him.

The room was in complete darkness. A thin thread of light from the corridor marked the lower edge of the door. An almost inaudible gurgling whisper was water in the bathroom pipes.

There. The sound of carpet piling rustling under the pressure of a foot. Only an animal's ears could have caught the movement, but Avar's ears were as the ears of the most wary of animals. Some one was coming down the corridor toward his door—someone moving with the utmost stealth, pausing between each cautious step. Only a hunted creature is approached thus; and Avar was being hunted by an entire world.

He slipped quietly from the bed and, moving to the door on soundless feet, pressed an ear to the planks. Other whispers of sound were audible now: there were four men in that corridor, two approaching from either end of it.

Silently he returned to the bed, slipped his feet into his shoes, put on his coat and moved to the window. With slow care he drew up the Venetian blind and raised the window.

This side of the hotel was in deep shadow, the quarter moon's rays reaching only the other side of the building. Two cars were parked in the side street below their lights burning, a radio aerial rising from a rear fender of each. There was no one visible along the street but Avar caught the glow of a red ember in the front seat of one car as somebody dragged on a cigarette.

Coolly Avar analyzed his position, it was a twenty-foot drop to the sidewalk below—not too great for him under normal circumstances. But there was hard rock at the end of the drop, instead of springy jungle turf, and enemies a few feet away— enemies who would cut him down instantly with their guns.

He leaned on the jutting sill, risking the chance of being observed from below, and looked in both directions at the expanse of wall broken only by the protruding sills of other windows. The nearest on either side of him was too far away for him to reach.

Behind him the knob of the corridor door slowly turned, the wood creaked faintly as pressure was applied, then ceased as the would-be intruder realized it was locked.

Suddenly the almost oppressive silence was shattered as a heavy fist pounded against Avar's door. A thick voice shouted, "Okay, buddy; open up in there! This is the police!"

For all their effect on Avar the voice and the fist might not have been there. Unhurriedly he glanced up along the hotel's outer wall. Directly above him was the stone ledge of another window perhaps ten feet away.

"C'mon, unlock this door or we kick it in!"

Other doors along the corridor began to open and there was a babble of voices, over-ridden by other voices, heavy and authoritative. "'S'all right, 's'all right, folks, stay in your rooms and keep your doors closed and nobody gets hurt!"

A heavy shoulder crashed against the door behind Avar, shaking the wall.

With the window pushed all the way up, Avar stepped onto the six-inch ledge and stood there, his body completely outside the room. Carefully he bent his legs in a slight crouch, his muscles coiling like steel springs, his arms lifted high above his head, the fingers on each hand bent and ready.

Again a ponderous shoulder crashed against the door and it flew open with a crash, a bulky body half tumbling into the darkened room.

And in that same instant Avar shot upward in a cat-like leap; his clawing fingers closed about the stone ledge above him, and with the effortless ease of a trained gymnast he drew himself into a standing position on the narrow outcropping of stone.

The window was closed and beyond it the blind was drawn. Avar applied pressure on the bottom half of the window and it slid up. Quickly but in perfect silence he drew aside the blind and stepped into the blackness of the room.

Sounds of angry voices came up to him through the floor and somebody yelled something at the men in the street below his former window.

"You're nuts, Blake! He never come down here—a drop like that'd a killed him!"

"No other way he could'a gone! Door was locked from the inside! If you guys down there let him get away—"

The sound of slow, even breathing came from the bed a few feet from where Avar was standing. His nose verified what his keen eyes suspected from the size of the small mound under the blanket: a young woman lay sleeping there.

HE CROSSED to the door like a wind-blown shadow and put an ear close to the jamb. The hall outside was empty of life, although he realized it would not remain so for long judging from the racket his pursuers were raising below.

His fingers found the lock's knob and released the bolt. He drew open the door just enough to permit him to slip through and was stepping into the lighted corridor when he heard the creaking of bedsprings and a voice, shrill with alarm, cried, "Who's there?"

The closing door chopped off the volume of her scream. He turned right and fled silently along the long ribbon of maroon carpeting, past a succession of doors bearing numbers behind small glass pane's.

He could still hear the woman screaming in the room he had left, and sounds of people awakening and leaving their beds came to him from beyond some of those doors along his path.

A door opened suddenly a few feet ahead of him and a large man in voluminous green pajamas put his head out. At sight of Avar, his eyes widened and he stepped into the center of the corridor with the clear intention of blocking the other's progress.

"Hey, you! What's go—"

Avar bent while still running and slammed his shoulder into the man's belly. There was a whoosh of exploding breath, the man literally flew back through the open door, and Avar, his stride unbroken, raced on.

Other doors opened, all of them in his wake, and other voices, heavy and shrill, set up a jumbled cacophony that beat against his sensitive ears. The elevator door, far behind him, clanged open and policemen began to pour into the corridor.

"There he goes!"

"Stop, you, or we shoot!"

"Get out of the way, for cry—"

Avar, running now at full speed, rounded an angle of the hall and found a short stretch of empty corridor ahead. At its end was a door bearing a sign reading: JANITOR—Keep Out.

Arriving, he found no avenue of escape unless he forced his way into one of the rooms. He had only seconds to act, he knew; at any moment his pursuers would come pounding into view.

He tried the door marked JANITOR and it opened readily. Within was a shallow closet containing brooms, a mop, a bucket with ringer attached and a pair of brown coveralls on a nail.

Nothing he could use there. He was about to try forcing the nearest guestroom door when he caught a glimpse of a small trap door in the ceiling of the hall almost directly overhead.

Sight and action were simultaneous, as it must always be among the jungle bred. Jerking open the closet door, he drew himself up to its top, one foot against the wall to hold it steady, flipped aside the catch and shoved back the cover. An agile leap enabled him to close both hands about the opening's edge, just as two uniformed officers rounded the bend and came lumbering toward him.

A hoarse shout was followed by the echoing report of a revolver and the plaster wall behind Avar's swaying figure developed a hole. Before a second shot could sound, Avar had drawn himself onto the building's flat roof and replaced the cover.

Strange motionless objects loomed about him, ghostly in the faint light of the quarter moon. The Cro-Magnard, a grim smile playing about the corners of his mouth, raced past them, heading for the edge of the roof. He knew this last maneuver had gained him valuable time—not enough to be figured in more than minutes, true, but he did not require more than minutes.

A waist-high ledge marked the hotel roof's edge. Below him some twelve feet across a ten-foot gap was a second building, its black-coated roof covered with a thin layer of sand.

IT WAS but the work of an instant for muscles accustomed to tree-top travel to hurl him across that gap and down to the roof below. He landed with legs and arms outstretched to cushion the shock, regained his feet instantly and hurried on.

By the time the first of his pursuers appeared at the edge of the hotel roof, he was three buildings away. They caught sight of him as he dodged among elevator shafts and a volley of revolver fire sent several bullets whining and ricocheting about him.

But none touched him, however, nor did any of his hunters attempt to leap the gap between hotel and the adjoining roof in an effort to follow him.

When the cave man reached the rim of the last building in the block he peered down two stories to the street below. No more than fifteen feet to his left a telephone pole pointed skyward, its base set in the sidewalk and out perhaps a dozen feet from the building itself.

Parked at the curb was a police car, its rear wheels even with the pole. A thin stream of smoke from the exhaust told him the motor was running and he could make out the outlines of a bent forearm resting on the window ledge next to the driver's seat.

In that instant a plan leapt full-formed into Avar's mind and his smile broadened. Not for an instant doubting the gravity of his situation, he was nevertheless enjoying himself completely for the first time since awakening on that strange hillside over a moon before.

Climbing to the top of the building's protective wall, he launched himself in a cat-like leap into space. There was a brief sensation of flying, then his arms and legs encircled the pole, gripped there—and held.

Once more he looked down. The slight sound as he caught hold of the pole had evidently gone unheard by whoever was in the police car.

Avar went down that pole like a falling stone, yet he came to rest against the pavement as softly as a drifting leaf. His quick eyes darted along the street, searching for a sign that he had been observed. But this was a side street, and at one o'clock in the morning it was as deserted of life as a mountaintop.

Crouching low he began a stealthy advance toward the car door beside the driver. Kuo, the lion, stalking the wariest of prey, could not have moved with greater care.

"...and here was this dame, dressed to kill, waltzin' down Highland. Mike said, 'Take a load a that, Harry!' and I said, 'Hell I can spot 'em a mile. She's had a couple of bit parts and thinks she's Hedy LaMarr!' But Mike..."

A bronzed hand came up and wrapped itself gently about the door handle. Muscles seemed to ripple along a broad back and down into the arm behind that hand...

And then several things happened almost simultaneously.

With a single wrench Avar tore open the squad car door and launched himself at the two men in the front seat. A lashing fist caught the first squarely behind the ear, knocking him into instant and complete unconsciousness. Before the second officer could do more than start a reflex movement for his gun, Avar closed a giant hand on the moving wrist and swung his fist a second time.

The battle was over before it started.

Avar stepped into the street, reached into the car and dragged the two unresisting bodies onto the pavement. He had just finished this and was on the point of sliding behind the wheel when a siren wailed around the corner of Hollywood Boulevard and a prowl car, its red warning light moving from side to side, turned in behind him. A gleaming white shaft of light bathed the two huddled forms on the pavement as Avar's foot came down on the gas pedal. He heard a shouted command, drowned out by the roaring motor, a gun cracked twice, metal went *spanggg* under a bullet's impact—then he was around a corner and the speedometer flicked past the sixty mark.

CHAPTER FOURTEEN

A SIREN, wailing like a lost soul, started up behind him. A glance into the rear vision mirror showed Avar that the pursuing police car was less than half a block back and coming up fast. He caught a glimpse of a figure leaning from one of its windows and pointing a hand in his direction; a second later fire seemed to spurt from that hand and the report of a gun reached his ears.

He crouched low over the wheel and let his foot sink forcibly against the gas pedal. The car seemed to leap ahead like a wounded thing and the distance between him and his hunters ceased to narrow.

A warning sign ahead marked an intersecting through street. Without slackening speed, Avar shot past the crossing, saw at the last moment the street he had been traveling did not continue, and swung sharply south, his tires screaming a shrill protest.

There was traffic here—not much, but enough cars to make driving at such speed hazardous to a driver who had never seen a car until slightly more than a month before. But the siren's wail behind him served to clear his path and the way lay open before him.

Wind whipping in at the open windows ruffled his mane of black hair and cooled his sweat-dampened face. He was conscious of that spirit-soaring exultation common to all drivers when, for the first time, they find themselves cutting down the miles at great speed. Objects on either side seemed to blur as he shot past. He realized he was smiling with a kind of grim satisfaction, the song of the powerful motor was a soothing roar, the tangle of lights moving and dipping and swerving about him was almost mesmeric.

Gradually the foot on the gas came nearer the floor, and as gradually he began to draw away from the squad behind him. Confidence began to surge within him. If nothing rose in his path he would outdistance his enemies and get cleanly away.

And then, away off to his left, he heard a second siren. At first he thought it an echo of the one now almost three blocks behind; but the sound grew steadily louder until he was aware that another police car was flashing his way with the intention of intercepting him.

He spun the wheel to the right at the next intersection. White letters on a black signpost told him he was now on Fourth Street and leaving Highland Boulevard. Fourth Street proved to be fairly wide, lightly traveled and free of parked cars.

Another main thoroughfare loomed ahead, and even as he caught sight of the warning markers, a third siren went off less than half a black to his right. He shot out into its path at the intersection, swung the wheel left, felt the tires slide sickeningly, then grip and carry him ahead at breathless speed. There were three pursuing police squads behind him now, almost side by side on the wide street, their unsteady red warning lights and screaming sirens sweeping all traffic to the curbs like giant brooms.

His jaw stubbornly set, Avar began a series of wild turns and maneuvers designated to throw off his enemies. In and out the narrow streets he wove amid the screech of complaining tires and the creaking of straining metal.

But to the veteran drivers of those police cars this was an old story. While they, in spite of their experience—or perhaps because of it—did not attempt to make turns at Avar's reckless pace, they avoided many of the time wasting mistakes he made—and little by little the distance between grew less.

Avar saw this was true after a few minutes and he sought to rectify his error. At the next intersection he swung south again and shoved the gas pedal down as far as it would go in an attempt to outdistance the other cars.

A block or two later the Cro-Magnon knew he could go no farther—at least on wheels. Now the sound of sirens was everywhere about him, the nearest within three blocks. He could not understand, knowing nothing of two-way radios, how his pursuers were able to hem him in so rapidly and unerringly. But hem him in they had and he must try other means to throw them off his trail.

The beginnings of a small park, surrounded by a high hedge of bushes and dotted with trees, appeared at the next corner. Instantly Avar slammed on the brakes, prevented from going through the windshield only by his grip on the wheel, and leaped from the car. A few giant strides brought him to those bushes and through them fifteen seconds before the first squad arrived on the scene.

AVAR stopped within the sheltering foliage and turned to learn if his hunters would pass by the abandoned car. But the squeal of brakes dashed that hope, and a police car ground to a stop inches behind it. Two uniformed officers, guns ready in their hands came cautiously up from the rear, called out something he could not hear, then flashed their pocket torches into the machine.

A second squad, siren shrilling, came down the street from the opposite direction and shuddered to a stop. The first two officers hurried to it and engaged in a brief colloquy with the newcomers. While this was going on, a third squad arrived and pulled up across from the second. A shouted conversation took place.

"What happened, boys?"

"Abandoned the car, Sarge. He's around here on foot somewheres."

"Bet he's in Hancock Park."

"Could be. Hope he falls into one of them tar pits."

"Get in touch with the other squads, Glenn; tell 'em to throw a ring around the park. It's our best bet."

"Right, Sarge."

"All right; three-four you other guys get in there and see if you can flush him."

"Yeah—but—"

"Get on the ball. The minute you see him and know for sure it's the guy we want—let him have it!"

"What if he comes out with his hands up?"

"He won't. Some kind of a nut—kill-crazy. Muscles like a elephant. Broke this Cameron in two like you'd bust a matchstick. Come on—get movin'."

Three of the officers, guns drawn, crossed the street and moved toward the row of bushes about the park.

The cave man turned and melted into the shadows behind him. After a few feet the grove of trees ended at the edge of open, uneven ground. There was an unfamiliar stench about the place and Avar's sensitive nostrils wrinkled in protest.

He skirted the line of trees to his left, moving as only the jungle-trained can move: silently as a cat. He was not especially concerned as to his chances for escape from his present position;

not even a hundred of this world's warriors could prevent him from slipping through their lines under cover of darkness.

Already the sound of heavy feet trampling among leaves and twigs reached his sensitive ears. He moved silently away from their proximity, flitting shadow-like among the trees.

He caught sight of a low hillock perhaps thirty yards into the open ground, its base overgrown with bushes and small trees. His ears told him the searchers had not yet passed through the belt of trees behind him; and so he broke for the hill, running very fast, his body bent until his head was hardly higher than his knees. At any instant he expected a shout to rise from among the trees behind him, but none came and a few seconds later he was prone among the hillock's bushes.

Crawling, his moving body passed among those bushes without sending the slightest quiver along their stems, he circled the mound without incident and peered out into the open ground beyond.

Less than a dozen feet from him was the immense figure of a great white cat, large as a lion, facing in the opposite direction. So unexpected was its presence that Avar recoiled sharply, confused. But even as he shrank back his eyes told him this was only the likeness of a giant cat—an image formed from stone. It was like no animal Avar had ever seen. Kua, the lioness although smaller, resembled it except for two giant tusks curving down outside the lower lip from among its upper teeth. Kua had no such fangs.

From where Avar lay he could see other images of animals scattered about the cleared ground and moving among them were the dull shapes of men, each carrying a small object that sent out a white lance of shining light.

FOR the first time Avar began to question his ability to slip through the circle of enemy warriors. Should he be impaled on one of those spears of light he would be instantly identified and the long arms these men called guns would reach out to pull him down.

There were many of them, at least a score within range of his eyes, and slowly but surely they were narrowing the noose-like circle about him. Already he could hear feet on the opposite side of the low hill.

A small clump of three bushes hardly higher than his knees caught his eyes at the base of the low pedestal supporting the giant cat. If he could reach the shelter of those bushes the hunters at his back might pass him by. Let them turn their backs to him for even a moment and he could double back and regain the rim of trees at the park's edge.

He was rising preparatory to making an attempt to reach those bushes, when his hand brushed against one of the pockets of his jacket. At the touch of a bulky object within he came to a startled halt.

The envelopes he had taken from Lau-ren's purse. Those strange things she had called "negatives" and which she had feared someone would find. What if his dash for freedom should fail and those bits of transparent paper come into the hands of these men?

He must stay hidden until those things were utterly destroyed. How could he do so, quickly? Fire was the best answer—but he had no fire...

But he did. The metal fire-maker he had taken from Lauren's purse—the fire-maker used to burn cigarettes.

With swift, sure motions of his hands he tore open the envelopes and made a small heap of the negatives on the ground in front of him. Quickly he brought out the lighter and set his thumb to the tiny that operated it.

Suddenly the full implication of what such an act might mean hit him. The glow of those burning negatives in this darkness would instantly be spotted by any number of enemies and a rain of bullets would follow to cut him down. Could he risk almost certain death to protect a she from this alien world—a she whose existence he had not dreamed of much longer than a moon before?

And in that moment the memory of warm lips against his own came to him. He saw those blue eyes shining into his, heard a soft voice repeating his name over and over. Once more he felt those sweetly curved arms slip about his neck, felt a vibrant young body pressed against his own...

With a sudden, almost convulsive, motion his thumb came down. There was a brittle click, a spark—and a wavering flame appeared in the cave man's cupped hands. Instantly he touched the flame to the heap of film and a puff of fire shot up.

"There!" a thick voice called. "In those bushes!"

The lighter was already falling from Avar's fingers. With the lightning speed of a lion's charge, he was on his feet and dashing for the shelter of the stone cat. A flurry of shots sounded only feet behind him but the unexpectedness of his appearance and the speed with which he moved, together with the almost complete lack of light, kept him from being hit. He circled the stone image of the long-toothed cat...and four shafts of light struck him full in the face.

He twisted aside with incredible agility and started to run. There was a sharp burst of staccato sound, something seemed to strike many swift silent blows against his chest, and he was knocked back against the cold stone of the huge cat.

His hands came up and pressed against the folds of his coat there and his knees swayed, buckled and gave way. A low growl rumbled deep in his torn chest and he felt a warm flood of blood fill his mouth and wash past his lips. The rays of light against his face seemed to dim, to flicker, then go out...

And very slowly life left him.

THE END

If you've enjoyed this book, you will not want to miss these terrific titles…

ARMCHAIR SCI-FI & HORROR DOUBLE NOVELS, $12.95 each

D-51 **A GOD NAMED SMITH** by Henry Slesar
WORLDS OF THE IMPERIUM by Keith Laumer

D-52 **CRAIG'S BOOK** by Don Wilcox
EDGE OF THE KNIFE by H. Beam Piper

D-53 **THE SHINING CITY** by Rena M. Vale
THE RED PLANET by Russ Winterbotham

D-54 **THE MAN WHO LIVED TWICE** by Rog Phillips
VALLEY OF THE CROEN by Lee Tarbell

D-55 **OPERATION DISASTER** by Milton Lesser
LAND OF THE DAMNED by Berkeley Livingston

D-56 **CAPTIVE OF THE CENTAURIANESS** by Poul Anderson
A PRINCESS OF MARS by Edgar Rice Burroughs

D-57 **THE NON-STATISTICAL MAN** by Raymond F. Jones
MISSION FROM MARS by Rick Conroy

D-58 **INTRUDERS FROM THE STARS** by Ross Rocklynne
FLIGHT OF THE STARLING by Chester S. Geier

D-59 **COSMIC SABOTEUR** by Frank M. Robinson
LOOK TO THE STARS by Willard Hawkins

D-60 **THE MOON IS HELL!** by John W. Campbell, Jr.
THE GREEN WORLD by Hal Clement

ARMCHAIR SCIENCE FICTION CLASSICS, $12.95 each

C-16 **THE SHAVER MYSTERY, Book Three**
by Richard S. Shaver

C-17 **THE PLANET STRAPPERS**
by Raymond Z. Gallun

C-18 **THE FOURTH "R"**
by George O. Smith

ARMCHAIR SCIENCE FICTION & HORROR GEMS SERIES, $12.95 each

G-5 **SCIENCE FICTION GEMS, Vol. Three**
C. M. Kornbluth and others

G-6 **HORROR GEMS, Vol. Three**
August Derleth and others

If you've enjoyed this book, you will not want to miss these terrific titles...

ARMCHAIR SCI-FI & HORROR DOUBLE NOVELS, $12.95 each

D-61 **THE MAN WHO STOPPED AT NOTHING** by Paul W. Fairman
TEN FROM INFINITY by Ivar Jorgensen

D-62 **WORLDS WITHIN** by Rog Phillips
THE SLAVE by C.M. Kornbluth

D-63 **SECRET OF THE BLACK PLANET** by Milton Lesser
THE OUTCASTS OF SOLAR III by Emmett McDowell

D-64 **WEB OF THE WORLDS** by Harry Harrison and Katherine MacLean
RULE GOLDEN by Damon Knight

D-65 **TEN TO THE STARS** by Raymond Z. Gallun
THE CONQUERORS by David H. Keller, M. D.

D-66 **THE HORDE FROM INFINITY** by Dwight V. Swain
THE DAY THE EARTH FROZE by Gerald Hatch

D-67 **THE WAR OF THE WORLDS** by H. G. Wells
THE TIME MACHINE by H. G. Wells

D-68 **STARCOMBERS** by Edmond Hamilton
THE YEAR WHEN STARDUST FELL by Raymond F. Jones

D-69 **HOCUS-POCUS UNIVERSE** by Jack Williamson
QUEEN OF THE PANTHER WORLD by Berkeley Livingston

D-70 **BATTERING RAMS OF SPACE** by Don Wilcox
DOOMSDAY WING by George H. Smith

ARMCHAIR SCIENCE FICTION & FANTASY CLASSICS, $12.95 each

C-19 **EMPIRE OF JEGGA**
by David V. Reed

C-20 **THE TOMORROW PEOPLE**
by Judith Merril

C-21 **THE MAN FROM YESTERDAY**
by Howard Browne as by Lee Francis

C-22 **THE TIME TRADERS**
by Andre Norton

C-23 **ISLANDS OF SPACE**
by John W. Campbell

C-24 **THE GALAXY PRIMES**
by E. E. "Doc" Smith